Ballytreeny Boy

Paul Kaye Jones

Copyright © 2022 Paul Kaye Jones

All rights reserved.

ISBN: 979-8-7964-7400-6

All rights reserved. No part of this book may be reproduced in any form or by any electronic or mechanical means, including information storage and retrieval systems, without written permission from the author, except in the case of a reviewer, who may quote brief passages embodied in critical articles or in a review. Trademarked names appear throughout this book. Rather than use a trademark symbol with every occurrence of a trademarked name, names are used in an editorial fashion, with no intention of infringement of the respective owner's trademark. The information in this book is distributed on an "as is" basis, without warranty. Although every precaution has been taken in the preparation of this work, neither the author nor the publisher shall have any liability to any person or entity with respect to any loss or damage caused or alleged to be caused directly or indirectly by the information contained in this book.
This is a work of fiction. Names, characters, places, and incidents either are the product of the author's imagination or are used fictitiously, and any resemblance to actual persons, living or dead, events, or locales is entirely coincidental.

DEDICATIONS

TO MY LATE WIFE MARILYN, WHO ENRICHED MY LIFE AND HELPED ME FOLLOW MY DREAMS. I MISS YOU EVERY DAY.

TO MY GREAT FRIEND AND GOLFING BUDDY JOHN WITHOUT WHOM THIS NOVEL WOULD NEVER HAVE BEEN WRITTEN.

TO MY LONG-SUFFERING FRIEND CAROL WHO READ EACH DAY'S SCRIBBLINGS WITH PATIENCE, PROVIDING VITAL READER FEEDBACK AND CONSTANT ENCOURAGEMENT.

Contents

ACKNOWLEDGMENTS i

1. GIRLS, GOLF, MCGRUNDY, MISCHIEF AND HEARTBREAK . 1

2. FARMING, FUMES, WOOLLEN TRUNKS AND MORE GOLF 66

3. UNEXPLODED BOMBS, SCHOOL, SNOWBALLS, GHOSTS & GRAMDMA 106

4. CHRISTMAS, TRAWLERS, NEAR DEATH, CRAZY COWS & A FREE SPIRIT 142

5. FOOTBALL, RECLINING REFS, TRAGEDY, BIKES, CRAMP & CAROLINE 179

6. OFF TO SEE THE WORLD, SEA-SICKNESS, A FAMOUS FOUR, NIAGARA FALLS & FIREWORK FOLLY 213

7. CHRISTMAS, CAROLINE, BIG BROTHER STUFF & SANDY ISLAND.. 279

8. DUNCAN, MOUNTAINS, SANDCASTLES & VEGAS 345

ACKNOWLEDGMENTS

THERE HAS BEEN A SMALL ARMY OF FAITHFUL LOCAL READERS WHO HAVE GIVEN FEEDBACK ON THE VARIOUS INCARNATIONS OF THIS BOOK AND TO THEM I AM INDEBTED. THANK YOU FOR BEING HONEST AND FRANK ABOUT YOUR FIRST IMPRESSIONS OF BALLYTREENY BOY AND MY OTHER NOVELS.

COVER PICTURES BY KIND PERMISSION OF PHOTOGRAPHER JOHN MELLOWS

1. GIRLS, GOLF, MCGRUNDY, MISCHIEF AND HEARTBREAK

In telling this story, I've revisited parts of my life that I haven't thought of in years. One memory leading to another and then a cascade effect, careering from the deepest depths, engulfing my present with multitudinous reminiscences. Some of the above were bitter, but the vast majority were joyous celebrations of a wonderful youth.

For those of you who were born in recent times, the way of life may well seem deprived by today's standards, but it was far from that! The young of each generation have a way of creating their own inner world, full of imagination and wonder. It was no different for me! I made mistakes and learned from them (hopefully). I met wise and unwise people, in equal measure, along the way and assimilated their knowledge, or lack of it into my expanding life experience.

Some of the multitude of memories will, I suspect, remind you of your own childhood and transition to adulthood, as growing up is universal, hopefully triggering recollections of sunny days and long-lost friends.

This is not a detective story with dead bodies littering the floor, rather the diary of a young Irish lad dipping his toes in the well of promise and finding the ocean.

My little piece of rural Ireland was a wonderland to me and I would often walk the short distance from our house to the beach, where my gaze over the water from Ballytreeny always left me restlessly dreaming of the world beyond. Seeing in my childhood fantasy, places infinitely different from the little fishing village of my youth.

I threw pebbles into the water and wondered if the ripples from Ireland would eventually arrive in Liverpool, the great city languishing, enticingly, across the choppy but inviting sea.

Looking back, I can see clearly how I learned to love the water at an early age, enthralled by the power of the waves and the promise held in distant horizons.

The pastoral way of life in my birthplace during the 1940's would be looked on now as laughable, with its pony and traps outnumbering by far the odd motor vehicle, but to me as a young boy, it was a wonderous playground where we would run, laugh and sing at the tops of our voices.

I gaze out of my window as I am writing this and parked in the drive, I see a big shiny car, invitingly poised to take me anywhere I would like to go and in great comfort.

It wasn't always like this for me in my childhood, of course! Everything was transported by horse and cart. Bread, milk, coal, it was all delivered to us and that was normal. I had no concept of busy cities with their furious pace of life, it never entered my head. Why should it? Toilets inside? Electricity? We had neither, so we didn't miss it!

We had little but we had everything! I lived about two hundred yards from the beach and I was free as a bird to wander with my friends along the shoreline and then up past the golf course, catching glimpses of a game I would come to love, but not for a few years yet.

I was the first born and for a short while was the centre of attention, but that soon changed as another and then another sibling appeared on a regular basis.

With the family expanding rapidly, we quickly outgrew the tiny house I was born in and I was reluctantly torn from that miniature haven as we moved to another house, further from the beach. It was larger but still having only basic services.

Those first few years have a rosy glow about them. Maybe I have supressed the bad times, but looking back I remember being loved, safe and free to roam wherever my ever-growing limbs would take me. In that respect I was always bigger, taller than my friends, so much so that people always thought I was older and therefore I received the blame for most of the tom foolery we got up to! Believe me, there was a lot of it! As quickly as my legs grew, I guess my sense of mischief grew faster.

There was always work to do, of course. As the eldest I was expected to help my father tend our large, somewhat overgrown garden, in a bold attempt to grow our own vegetables. I was a big lad for my age and working on the soil came naturally to me, putting on muscle and instilling a work ethic that has stayed with me.

I was not to know, at this age, how such an early grounding in horticulture would make such an impact on my life. Even now, when I can afford a gardener, I still tend to the lawns and the flowered borders adorning our house, although with advancing years it is admittedly much harder. My wife keeps a constant eye on my wellbeing and interrupts me regularly, reminding me I am not as young as I used to be! Maybe that too will resonate with you readers!

Back to my story! Inside the house we had neither electricity nor running water, except for holes in the roof! Our main water supply for washing was provide by natural precipitation and collected in two rather large water barrels. Water for drinking and cooking, however, was drawn from a well that was across two bumpy, oftentimes muddy, fields and it was my job to fetch all we required. It was thirsty work and I think I drank a lot of it just carrying it from the well. Of course, if it didn't rain for a while, I had to refill the rain barrels as well. That didn't happen often where we lived, as anyone from Ireland will tell you!

In the new house, we did have more bedrooms, but we were still overcrowded. Because I didn't have my own bedroom, there was no sanctuary that I could escape to when I was caught breaking the rules or getting up to things, boys got up to. Being boys, we fought a lot! I usually won being older and bigger, but it also meant I had the occasional thick ear for making my brothers cry! I am sure the girls would have rebelled as well but the world was a different place then.

I've neglected to tell you my name so far, as it didn't seem very relevant to my story but for the sake of the record, it is Niall O'Sullivan. I should have told you right at the start but as I already knew it, it didn't occur to me to pass the knowledge on to you.

This writing business is a bit more complex than I thought, so please excuse me, if I comment on things I missed. You are not of course reading the original draft, complete with multiple corrections and crossing out of passages I deemed boring, but even at this late stage I find myself remembering random events.

Let me skip forward to the age of twelve. I could never have had any concept of the life I was going to lead and to be fair, I was more interested in Erin, a girl who lived in the village, than picturing the winding path I was to follow.

She was a beautiful, redheaded angel that I was besotted

with, but for some reason or other she looked at me with a disdain that bewildered me.

Surely, I was a catch? I was taller and stronger than anyone in my class. I could run faster and swore with the best and I had a reasonable singing voice that could shatter a window from ten paces, or so my mother said! So why didn't Erin see me as a catch? I had no idea. She didn't even bother to stick her tongue out at me like some of her friends, or giggle when I walked by on my way to school.

It was a lost cause, but that didn't stop me gazing at her at every opportunity, trying unsuccessfully to catch her eye, only succeeding in receiving a swift clip around the ear from the teacher I was inadvertently ignoring.

Yes, life could be confusing and painful but it was still exhilarating and running down the beach, against the wind, with my mates in tow, I was king of the shoreline and I would temporarily forget Erin.

That shoreline was our playground! The road formed a border with the sea and as soon as we were across, we were free! If the tide was in, we stayed on the safe side of the wall and let the spray from the crashing waves, shower us with salty water. If the tide was out, we ran like devils, yelling at the tops of our voices, usually kicking a football or a can, if that was all that was available.

Those whose childhood was spent entirely on grass will not fully understand the impact of sand on the leg muscles. Keeping a firm grip was essential but almost impossible when travelling at warp speed!

I know you grass lovers will say that you got muddy, but we got sand into places where sand should not be allowed to go! And we didn't have showers in those days, unless it rained on the way home.

We didn't wear shoes and socks, so between the toes was a nightmare! No matter how many times you washed your feet, there was always some residual sand tucked away, waiting for you to go to bed.

Believe me, once sand is in the bed, especially one you share with your brother, it will lead to a restless night and a subsequent argument.

Shopping was another of my daily tasks, running to the butchers or the general store where everything was piled up in sacks and propped against the wall. Most of all I remember the smell.

There was a moment when I first stepped in off the street, when that glorious mixture of aromas would hit my young nose, sending it into overdrive. No perfume in the world could ever contend with the smell of the general store and I would stand there for a moment, transfixed by this

Aladdin's cave of precious items. No gold or silver but practically everything else in the world, I was sure.

Our local shopkeeper was always smartly dressed in a shirt and tie plus a long brown apron, made of some magical durable cloth that spilt items seemed to run straight off. In the early days, I used to think how tall he was, but as I grew rapidly, he went the opposite way! By twelve I was almost as tall as him and he fondly remarked on it each time I entered the shop.

How different to the anonymous shopping experiences of today, where we hardly take notice of the person taking things off a conveyor and sliding it towards us. Our humble retailer would religiously pack each item, making sure all the heavy objects were on the bottom and breakables at the top, something most have no concept of these days.

Mum would give me the ration book, yes, they still existed and I would guard it with my life. If I lost it, I was aware that I could never go home again!

Another life lesson I was unaware I was learning, responsibility, whilst protecting my family's precious food source.

It wasn't all work of course, football, mostly on the aforementioned beach, was a way of life, where we kicked the ball and frequently each other. Even somehow managing to get the ball to go between the improvised goal posts that were usually our jackets. Everyone was welcome to join in, good or bad, although which side you ended up on was frequently open to heated debate.

If you have never headed a ball, plastered in wet sand, you have never lived. Many a 'bonce' ended up with rash like abrasions in various forehead positions. Kneecaps were prone to finding sharp objects embedded in the sand and let me tell you, once sand gets into a cut it is absolute torture.

To be fair, most of us didn't notice any injuries until after we had stopped playing, then we would winge about it all the way home. Not that I got much sympathy when I arrived there!

My mother used to say, "Serves you right for running round like hooligans!" My brothers would take any chance to fetch me a blow to my injured area, at any opportunity and then run away. I would limp after them, threatening murder, until my mother berated us and I was sent to my room!

What about my sisters, you ask? Well, they, whilst more civilised than my brothers, would side with my mother, learning their trade, chiding me on my oafishness, although I suspect they envied my rebel persona.

One day, the tide in and no one else around, I set off to wander near the golf course, where I found an abandoned golf club nestling in some bushes, probably tossed there by some frustrated golfer who had shanked another ball out of play (Those who don't play golf may need to Google that last phrase). I swished that old club for hours, knocking pebbles along the beach, snapping the wooden shaft several times and having to heat the head of the club to burn out the broken part of the shaft and then pare down the remaining shaft to fit in. As you can imagine the shaft got shorter and shorter but that didn't perturb me in the least.

I eventually found a few 'lost' balls and spent hours knocking them up and down the beach, until the tide came in and I reluctantly gave in for the day.

Inevitably I ended up more frequently at the Golf Club, where I pestered them until they gave me a job as a caddy, carrying a golf bag around 18 holes, for five hours, in all kinds of weather and for a pittance. The money although derisible was welcomed by my mother and with the family growing, became extremely helpful. I made my mind up that I would be a member one day and I would pay my caddy a decent amount.

Members came from miles around and were generally made up of wealthy farmers, solicitors and bankers.

Most of them had to be told which end of the club to hold and my fellow caddies and I took great pleasure in giving them nicknames. "Thunderguts" was so fat he could hardly see the ball and had to take regular 'refreshment' breaks, the smell that emanated from his backside stunk like a rat had crawled up there and died. If he miss-hit the ball, I was blamed and sworn at for not lining him up! I ask you, what an arsehole.

I was a child and I could play better than him with my eyes shut. However, it did teach me to keep an even temper and to understand that although a person has money and position, it does not make them worthy of my respect. I found out that must be earned.

There was one member "The Colonel" who was strict with the caddies but never spoke down to us, rather, he asked for our local knowledge. He walked with a limp, that we imagined came from heroics at the front, in the war and it made him a man to be looked up to.

One day after we finished his round, I was carrying his clubs to the clubhouse in order to clean them, when I noticed a woman and a young girl greeting him. The hair was unmistakeable, the red curls that cascaded down her back, it had to be Erin.

I approached this object of my affection with gusto, intending to use my best smile to win her over. She turned on my touch, only for me to be stunned that it wasn't Erin. I was dumbstruck! She smiled at me and said "Hello!", just as her father spotted me. "Ah, this is my caddie, Niall. Do you two know each other?"

I didn't know whether to laugh or cry, I must have blushed, it was either fight or flight and I did neither. Standing there, I might as well have been stark naked, I felt so exposed. Mrs "Colonel" broke the ice by shaking my hand, she was a beauty as well, with her red hair in a bun, partially covered by a stylish hat. I found my voice and croaked "Sorry, I thought you were someone else".

"Did you think I was my cousin Erin? People are always doing that".

Struggling to continue my conversation I muttered "Yes … ah … Erin … my class", I knew I was blushing then.

"I'm Clodagh", she offered.

"I'm Niall".

"I know! My father introduced you".

"Oh yes", … Another awkward pause

"I think you should take those clubs and clean them Niall", the Colonel said, smiling, as he rescued me from my living hell.

"Yes sir", I gratefully replied as I hurried away, oblivious to what the family were saying about their close encounter with an idiot, as I thought myself.

"God she was beautiful", I felt. Out of my league but at that age anything was possible and I could not stop myself wondering if I would ever see her again. I wouldn't have to wait long.

I cleaned those clubs with a diligence that sprang from me with anticipation I had never known before, they positively sparkled, looking almost like new.

"When you've finished, could you show me how to play golf?" The voice came from the ether like an angel on high.

I looked up to see Clodagh, arms crossed and looking quite serious.

"Ah … yes. I could but … have you asked your father?"

"Not yet, but he won't say no".

Standing up I realised I towered over her. She was delicate and petite, with a grace I had never seen before. Deep green eyes and a perfect pale complexion completed the vision.

I was totally hooked and she knew it. If she had said "Bring me the moon", I would have run off in search of rope.

My life changed that day. There would be many more pivotal moments in my life to follow but this was the first and therefore monumental to a young boy.

Maybe I imagined the tension between us, but it still felt real to me. I struggled with the emotions surging through my brain, as I noticed, once more, those gorgeous green orbs, suggesting a depth I was totally unaware of in other girls including Erin.

The spell was broken as her parents called for her to join them once again. She smiled, the like of which I have rarely seen since, full of promise and mutual attraction.

Before she left, we hurriedly arranged to meet at the golf club, after school in two days. She told me she attended a local private girl's school St Agatha's and her mother would take her there in their car. THEY HAD A CAR!

Some days, she walked over to the Golf Club to see her father, where her mother would pick them up later. It was on one of those days that we were to meet!

I don't recall much about the days in between, apart from anticipation almost overwhelming me at times.

I arrived at the Golf Club having run all the way from school, only to sit there for an eternity, kicking my heels and wondering why time was going so slow. "Was she still coming?" "Did I get the wrong day?" "What time is it?"

Endless thoughts collided in my head and exploded with the power of nuclear bombs, causing me to sweat to the point where I thought about going home to change.

Then she was there! But she wasn't alone! Her mother was beside her as they approached.

"Hello Niall. It's good of you to teach Clodagh. Her father loves the silly game and he says you are very good".

It was her mother, breaking the ice again. I'm sure she could see I was nervous and did her best to put me at ease. Was she early to pick them up or just checking me out? I had no idea!

"My pleasure!", I said, trying to be as grownup as I could. "Let me carry those", I offered, taking the golf clubs from Clodagh.

That first lesson was forever burnt into my mind, spending time with this vision and even briefly touching her hand during the lesson. She was very quick to follow my instructions and surprised me with her dexterity and it was clear she would quickly become a very good player. It was her smile that registered the most, her eyes sparkling and dancing with a light I had never seen before.

I was in love for the first time, hook line and sinker, head over heels, all the old clichés and all of them true.

The line of her body as she swung the club was truly magnificent, sleek as a gazelle. I didn't recognise the effect she was having on me. All I knew was, I liked it. I mean, I REALLY liked it! I just wanted to be near to her, to hear her laugh, see her smile. I was besotted!

It never occurred to me that she may not feel the same way I did! I was new at this game and didn't understand that, just because I felt something, the other person may not necessarily reciprocate.

We all live in hope, whether we realise it or not!

That afternoon went so quickly I was shocked when her mother approached, with the colonel not far behind.

"How is she doing, Niall?", she queried.

"Very well! She's a natural."

"That's my girl!" chipped in the colonel, as he wandered up. "Well done my dear!"

Clodagh chatted to her parents as I packed away her clubs.

"Niall! How would you like to play a round of golf with the three of us next Saturday?" asked the colonel.

I was speechless! Me ... play on the actual golf course ... on a Saturday ... with Clodagh! My reply must have sounded apprehensive, but the colonel soon put me at ease. "We can play against the ladies! What do you think, Niall?"

"I'd love to sir! It would be an honour!"

"Meet us here around 9.00am. I'll book a tee time. OK?"

"Yes sir!"

With that they trooped off, the colonel with his arm around Clodagh, his other arm carrying her golf bag. I was waiting for her to turn around as she walked away, but alas I was not rewarded with a wave. Perhaps she couldn't turn with her father's arm around her. Who knows?

I watched them turn the corner into the small carpark at the rear of the clubhouse and finally out of sight. I wanted to do a jig! I wanted to shout out loudly! "I'm playing golf at the golf club on Saturday!", but of course, I couldn't, so I internalised my joy and ran all the way home.

Breathless and exhilarated I leaned against the wall outside our house, not believing my luck! Should I tell my family? I thought about it and decided not to say anything until I was going out of the door on Saturday! I wanted to see the look of surprise on their faces when I said, "I'm off to play golf at the golf club!" Oh, the perceived joy of it all.

My world was suddenly different, brighter, full of promise and anticipation, but it was still anchored in daily routines that brought me quickly back down to earth.

One of my family jobs was to walk the local railway line and pick up any stray coal that had fallen from the steam engines that rattled and puffed their noisy way along the coast, as they climbed up towards Dublin. We were not too far from the line and lucky enough to have a steep incline, where the old engines used to puff and pant, plus a wicked twist in the track that used to make them violently lurch from side to side, spilling coal out of the tender that rocked in sympathy with it.

Filling a sack was tedious and time consuming, to say nothing about dangerous, as I had to keep an ear open for any approaching train, lest I get squished in the procedure.

It also had a habit of making me filthy in the process, but the resultant load I carried home to my mother helped keep the oven going.

Can you imagine children being encouraged to do that sort of thing these days? We never thought it was unusual or demeaning! It was survival! To be fair, if we didn't pick up the surplus coal and by 'we' I mean our community, not just me, it would eventually have become a hazard to the smooth running of the line. So, you could call what we did, a public service! Well, it's what I like to think we provided!

Small but necessary tasks, like picking up coal for the fire or collecting horse manure for the garden vegetables, were vital in keeping the family warm and fed. That week I worked doubly hard to finish all my tasks, so that I could have Saturday to myself.

That morning I was up with the lark, whistling and singing, much to the surprise of my sisters. My brothers as usual took little notice of anything I did, unless it directly affected them!

I saw the girls talking to my mother, all of them half whispering, a secret conversation that most obviously was all about me!

They knew something was afoot, but it was driving them crazy that they did not know what it was. Their imaginations were running riot as they speculated on what I was up to. I was loving it!

Their mutterings became stage whispers they knew I could hear, but I still refused to acknowledge any of them. It eventually caused them to confront me, as a posse! The questions came thick and fast, but I ignored each and every one of them, even though they came very close to the right ones to ask.

Eventually it came time to leave, but just as I was about to walk out the door, I turned and said, nonchalantly, "I'm off to play a fourball at the golf club! See you later!"

The effect was so precious, I wish I could have bottled it! Their mouths hung open in amazement! An image I kept with me as I walked up the road, whistling! I said nothing about going to meet a beautiful girl, something they had suggested several times.

I met the colonel and his wife on the veranda of the club, they were having morning tea, as I expected every posh person to do. There was no sign of Clodagh and my heart sank! It must have been visible, her mother immediately picking up on my disappointment.

"Clodagh is inside, changing … for the third time!" she laughed, turning to her husband, who seemed oblivious to the connotation.

Almost immediately Clodagh appeared, looking wonderful. I must have seemed suitably astounded, because she giggled when she saw the stunned look I gave her.

They invited me to sit down for tea with them and I duly did so, even though I had no idea what I was doing. It was one of the most awkward moments I have ever endured, but I survived it and was stronger for it. Another life lesson; to never be afraid to broaden my horizon! It seems strange now to think of my self-conscious boyhood persona, knowing how, since then I have dined in the most prestigious places in the world, with some very famous and some extremely infamous people, without a scintilla of embarrassment.

Thankfully, my companions were lovely people who had no desire to embarrass me, even though they knew I was from humble beginnings.

The talk turned to school and I had them all laughing with tales of my escapades at school! You will hear more of that in a while, so I won't give anything away, except to say, I had a colourful education.

Clodagh was quiet, allowing me to take centre stage, serenely confident in her own skin, not needing to prove herself as I was trying desperately to.

Morning tea over, we collected our golf clubs, my measly set looking completely out of place amongst their pristine equipment. They had purchased theirs from the best shop around and I … well … I 'found' a lot of mine! Let me explain! As you know I caddied for various people at the club and invariably they were dreadful players. This type always blames the club when they hit a duff shot! If they hit consecutive bad shots with a club, they have been known to hurl them into the bushes. I was usually dispatched into the undergrowth to retrieve said abandoned club. If I was out of sight, I would find the club and then stash it where I could retrieve it later. Well, they had thrown it away and I had found it! A touch immoral? Who cared! It was mine now and I would treat it properly! If I was questioned when I returned empty handed, I would say, "You are well rid of that club, sir!

You need one that is fit for a person of your ability!" They would usually agree with me and write off the loss as well deserved! With the resultant growth of my set of clubs. If I 'acquired' a club I already had one of, I would barter an exchange with one of my fellow caddies, who somehow, unexpectedly 'found' a club I needed. What a bunch of young rogues we were! We thought we were like Robin Hood, taking from the rich and giving to the poor. Which was us!

That round of golf fades in my memory, but the sense of occasion does not! Did I play well? I would like to think so! Did we beat the ladies? I have no idea and honestly, I would gladly have 'thrown' the match, if it meant pleasing Clodagh.

If there was a happier boy on the planet that day, I salute him, because it was probably the zenith of his life.

Walking home to that tiny, crowded house, where my noisy siblings chased each other incessantly, I was suddenly aware that the world outside was much bigger than Ballytreeny and I wanted to see it, experience it and afford my own golf club membership.

Thoughts of Clodagh followed me deep into the night, restless, sleep deprived hours when I could not shake the image of her from my insomniac's brain. How could I go on without her? It was one bemused boy who finally fell into the depths of slumber, still thinking of what was to come, or rather, what I hoped would! Now that was a scenario that was never going to happen! But of course, I wasn't to know that at the time.

Our family was expanding as a unit and playing my part became both necessary and second nature. As the eldest, I was expected to earn from an early age.

Picking potatoes was an annual summer event, back breaking and relentless work paying the princely sum of £2. 8s for a 6-day week, but I was a big strong lad and I felt immense pride in handing over the money to my mother.

There were a few different jobs when picking potatoes and we rotated them to avoid boredom and ease back pain. Picking up the potatoes directly from the ground and placing them into boxes was tough on the back, even for fit young things like me! What it was like for the older folk, I can only speculate, but it must have been hard.

Some people had no option but to take on this type of work on a temporary basis, just to earn a few pounds to see them through the year.

When the potatoes had been transferred to sacks, they were transported back to the sorting shed, where they were placed on a rickety old contraption that sifted out the smaller ones that would be used for the next years seed potatoes. The remaining potatoes were then bagged up for storage. As there was no electricity, the sorting machine was powered by a large wheel that was manually revolved. Funnily enough, although this was also hard work, I found it ok, getting into a rhythm, singing a song or two to keep me in time! My muscles got a good work out and the farmer knew the wheel would turn at a constant rate.

It was grubby work handling the potatoes, fresh from the soil and I was filthy by the end of the day.

One poignant afternoon, not long after we had started our summer break from school and about a month after the Saturday golf match, I was sitting by the side of the road, outside the potato field, with a few other mucky urchins, when a posh car came into sight. Of course, all the others said, "Caw! What a beauty!", as the car came ever closer.

As it passed by, imagine my horror when I realised it was Clodagh and her mother! With eyes on the road, Mrs 'Colonel' didn't see me, but Clodagh did! The shock on her face was immediate, her head turning, fixed on me, as they passed.

"Please don't stop to offer me a lift!", I prayed and for once my prayers were answered, the car continuing its journey, probably to the golf club.

It wasn't often I felt ashamed of who I was, but that day I

felt small and poor. There was no resolve in me to improve my status, just a resignation to my plight. Maybe this was part of what spurred me on in later life! One thing I never forgot was that feeling of desolation and no matter how successful I became, I never felt aggrandised around people with less than me.

I was sure that I would never spend time with Clodagh again after that day. The look on her face said it all! My evenings were subsequently spent moping around the house, listless and downhearted.

Mum noticed my melancholy state and as she always gave me a small amount back from my potato earnings, she suggested I go out and cheer myself up. So, that evening I went off to the local cinema, clean and tidy for a change, resolving to be full of life and even joking with my friends.

I thought I was seeing double, there outside the cinema were a crowd of girls dressed in their finery, right in the centre were two beautiful redheads, Erin and Clodagh, looking like twins. Heads together, deep in conversation about what ever girls talk about, I know they both saw me, but they completely ignored me, doing their best to avoid my eyes.

To say I was devastated would be understating my feelings, more like, pierced with a spear through my heart. My mates were all around so I did my best pretending and it must have been worth an Oscar, because no-one said anything, not even in fun. Sitting through that film was excruciating, I wanted to run as far away as possible, screaming into the night, like a hysterical hyena.

My world was shattered, my life over, I wouldn't live through the experience, but of course I did. I have never forgotten that time nor the temptresses that scorned me, it left a scar that never completely healed and I vowed to stay away from girls for ever, again of course that was never going to happen.

Standing outside the cinema with the lads, after the film, we discussed all the Hollywood stars and which ones we liked, in shall we say, animated conversation. To rub the hurt in even more, Erin and Clodagh walked right past us, no more than two metres away, without giving me a glance. Plus, they were arm in arm with a couple of older boys!

My devastation was complete! I returned home and went to bed without talking to my mother, or anyone else in the house. I will admit a few tears dampened my pillow that night. All part of growing up I suppose but why did it have to be so hard!

My attitude was becoming more rebellious and school became a nightmare for me.

I was always in trouble, for one reason or another, usually ending up in detention with the rest of the reprobates I called friends. It was on one of these terms of imprisonment that I had what I thought was a marvellous idea, our teacher, old McGrundy, had a cane, hanging on the wall, that I had the pleasure of shaking hands with on several occasions. McGrundy would take frequent leave of us to visit the staff room for a cup of tea or something stronger.

During one of these absences, we derived a plan to sabotage said weapon of mass destruction. While Tommy watched for McGrundy's return, we (by we of course I mean me) took a razor blade, something every boy had for sharpening pencils and proceeded to nick the cane in several places. The shout came from Tommy and I hurriedly put the cane back in its position of threat. Stifling a laugh was the order of the day, but knowing smiles were exchanged for the rest of our sentence.

Now, dear reader you may think that would be the end of the tale but you would be wrong, very wrong. I told you there was a rebel streak in me since the cinema incident and it showed up the following day.

It was raining hard all night and the lane into the school was littered with muddy puddles that pupils avoided at all costs, all except one idiot, namely me. Did you guess that already? My boots were covered in mud and I made exaggerated stamps as I made my way theatrically to my desk. The boys thought it hilarious whilst the girls simply ignored me as usual.

McGrundy came into the classroom, in his normal foul mood, hung over probably, discontented with his lot more than likely, facing a classroom full of horrible smelly children. It must have been demoralising and on top of that he eyed the muddy footprints. Like a deer stalker his head went down as he attempted to follow the trail of his prey, I swear his nose was twitching as if attempting to catch a whiff of the perpetrators blood, namely mine. He stopped at my desk, eyes gazing down at the space where my feet should be but being the genius, I thought I was, I had shifted my boots out of his sight. Boys were muttering words like "You'll be sorry" and giggling whilst the girls were silently shifting in their seats.

"Stand up boy!", bellowed McGrundy. "Step out from behind that desk!"

My valour was quickly vanishing but my overall plan was working.

McGrundy saw the mud on my boots and grabbed me by the ear. It wasn't the first time this had happened as I had large ears but being dragged to the front of the class by a protuberance is not to be recommended as a mode of transport. Still, my plan was working. Did I say that before?

You've probably guessed by now that the cane was duly taken from its prominent display position and the command was given, "Hold your hand out boy!"

Smiling inside, but feigning terror, I held out my hand, not a small hand, but as I was a big lad, an oversize one. The whoosh of the cane descending from the cosmos onto its target area was followed by an enormous gasp from the audience viewing it with trepidation, as the cane shattered into a multitude of parts and flew in every direction.

The roar from the crowd that followed the gasp was like music to my ear, even though it was still throbbing!

McGrundy was beside himself with rage, he knew his trusty cane had been tampered with but to give him his due he never raised his hand to me, just sort of snarled, a twitch developing in his right eye and his nicotine soiled teeth grinding together in an ominous forecast of my future.

"Stand there boy!", he ordered as he left the room.

"You're in for it now!", someone shouted.

"Run while you can, you idiot!", said another.

Suddenly it went deathly silent. I felt sweat running down my legs, at least I hoped that's what it was. McGrundy was standing in the doorway with an expression like a rhinoceros on heat. I swear steam was coming out of his ears and the twitch had doubled in speed. There was that swoosh again and then again. A new cane, virgin and bloodless was waiting to be initiated, keen to produce maximum pain on a poor boy's skin.

"Hand out!", came the final order. No last meal, no last request, no visit from the local priest.

Then the trilogy started, swoosh, pain, "Ohh!" Uttered not by me but by the onlookers. This pantomime repeated until I felt like fainting, it was if the rest of the world had ceased to exist and the pain of the universe had descended on my hand.

Not so smart after all was I? Or was I? The pain eventually subsided after a year or two, but my fame on pulling off such an audacious prank is still legend at the school. Or so I'm told!

I wonder now If I could have done better at academic studies? Although I would not consider myself to be a mathematical genius, I have had to conquer the subject on my way to having a successful life.

As I became older, recognising that I needed to improve my education, I worked hard to do so. What a pity someone could not have got through to me when I was a child! All that corporal punishment I received! Did it do me any good? I don't think so, because it added to a rage of injustice that roared in me until I was well into my twenties. There must have been a way to curb my excesses without resorting to brutality! I don't know what action could have been taken and funnily enough I understand the frustration of my teachers and their lashing out at me.

It is too late now of course, but if any teachers read this book, I hope my pain resonates with them and helps some other wayward child to receive the correct help.

As you have come to realise, school was never a favourite place for me, but there was somewhere I really loved. It was the cinema. The wonderful lives that people led in those films filled me with envy and made my itchy feet long to leave my Irish home, to wander like a cowboy across the wide-open plains of America, free and happy, gun on hip and girl in my arms.

One memorable evening my friend Joe and I set off for the flicks, as we called them, with a pipe we had found. There was no way we could afford tobacco so we obtained, what we thought was a brilliant substitute. Peat! OK so the smarter ones amongst you are saying, "What idiots!", but remember we were just boys experimenting and who was to say peat tasted any different to tobacco? We also had a miniature whisky bottle that served as a repository for the diesel fuel we had acquired.

Plonked in our usual third row seats in the flea pit, I stuffed the peat into the pipe. So far so good! It looked quite a professional job if I say so myself. We were proud of our efforts and sat there for a few minutes just gazing at it, which is where we should have stopped. Looking back, I realise we should not have poured a copious amount of diesel onto the peat, but it seemed a stroke of genius, to assist the notoriously slow to burn peat with lashings of a highly combustible fuel. I put the pipe in my mouth and immediately took it out again to cough uncontrollably, choked by the overpowering diesel fumes. Even people in the row behind started coughing and soon there was a chorus of coughing, meeting with cat calls to shut up that just added to the general pandemonium. Just as the cacophony climaxed, I took a deep breath and put the pipe back in my mouth, Joe struck a match and held it up to the pipe. There was an almighty flash, I lost my eyebrows and a layer of skin.

I swear, from the smell that someone in the row behind had shit themselves, several ladies screamed, the cinema staff arrived with a fire extinguisher at the ready. The accursed pipe was safely stowed away in my pocket but of course the peat then decided to go from smoulder to burn and ignited the pocket of my jacket. The extinguisher was put into action and I received a full blast of the whitish-brown foam, a mixture of water, liquorice root and sodium bicarbonate, smack into my body. The force knocked me into Joe and as I fell back, the twat on foam duty kept spraying, hitting not only me but half of the row in front and half of the row behind. It was a bit Charlie Chaplin, so I was told by onlookers sometime later and much mirth was shared by all those not directly affected by the splash area.

The peat, you might think was doused and well out but peat doesn't work like that, once lit it is a bastard to put out and my jacket continued to alternate between, "It's out" and "It's burning again". The smell of the diesel, the foam, my poor burning jacket and the smell of the kid who shit himself combined to create a perfect storm and the flea pit rapidly emptied except for me and my foamy assailant. I was unceremoniously ejected from the cinema and told I was barred for life. A sentence that was commuted a few months later only to be reinstated after the next debacle.

To add insult to injury, as I was being manhandled out of the cinema, I was horrified to see Erin and Clodagh sitting a few rows back, laughing uncontrollably, whilst the two boys sat with them shouted profanities. So, I say to any younger reader, please do not be so stupid as to light peat with diesel whilst sitting in a confined space or any other space come to that and do not under any circumstance try to smoke it.

As a footnote, can you imagine the excuse I made to my mother about how my best jacket had a massive burn hole in it and stank of peat and diesel? If you can think of a good excuse, could you please contact me and let me know what it is, because I still like to believe my mother is patiently waiting for a credible answer and not the absolute rubbish, I told her.

Punishment in our house usually manifested itself as a list of horrid jobs to do. My job list from hell, after the cinema fracas, contained one of my favourite (not) pass times, collecting seaweed to spread on the garden as a fertiliser.

The farmers from Rush would send horses and carts out to Gullin Island at low tide to gather seaweed and they would dump it on the roadside before going back for more. There would be huge banks of the obnoxious stuff at the side of the road for weeks, then tractors and trailers would come down from Rush to take it back for spreading on the land.

In those days there was not a lot of traffic, so the banks of seaweed did not pose a problem and the locals helped themselves to as much as they needed.

I would have to gather it in a handcart and push it all the way back to our house over a mile away, being kept off school to get it. Waiting until no one was around, I would fill the handcart from the piles left by the roadside and my mother would send a sick note to my teacher.

My friends knew what I had been up to by the smell of the

seaweed that clung to my body like leeches, refusing to let go even after a good scrubbing in cold water, a shower of course was a luxury we hadn't even heard of.

I always hoped collection day would be on a Friday, meaning I wouldn't have to go to school the next day.

Of course, it invariably worked against me, contriving to be any weekday but Friday! Meaning I would have to go to school to endure them calling me 'Stinky!', 'Pongo!' or the like, especially my so-called mates who would sit there with fingers holding noses, having fake coughing fits!

No wonder I am obsessive now about my cleanliness! Not to mention a particular hatred of seaweed, to which I have long attached the smell of humiliation.

Looking back, I remember the laughter but there were times of extreme sadness as well. My mind has driven some memories into dark recesses where the light of day rarely goes, only jumping into conscious thought on rare moments of fragmented recall.

One such recollection is of a couple of urchins named Pat and Alfie. They were an incorrigible couple of lads even by my standards and my father often warned me not to have anything to do with them. Usually in trouble with the local police, rarely in school, up to no good even on a good day, they were notorious in the area and by all accounts destined to be wasters and layabouts for the rest of their lives.

I found them to be funny, without guile and very friendly! An assessment I still stand by. They were from a very poor family and that's coming from someone with a standard of living where the bar was set so low it was impossible to limbo under, but they were genuine good kids, just the product of their environment.

One hot day during the holidays, I was doing my usual, hitting golf balls up and down the beach, when I noticed some activity in the distance that looked interesting, so I tucked my golf club and balls out of sight and went to investigate.

It was Pat and Alfie, staring out to sea, looking towards Gullin Island. I asked them what was happening and they told me they were waiting for the tide to turn, so they could walk the three quarters of a mile out to the island. It was a stroll that took about fifteen minutes, or less if you ran, pretending to be on horseback, which was our usual mode of running.

They were after buried treasure, something we boys thought about a lot, having dug up numerous places along the shorefront looking for gold and silver.

It was common knowledge that pirates once lived on the

island and that they had buried their treasure there, until they had time to recover it. By common knowledge I mean, invented by the fertile imagination of a group of boys, spoon fed on pirate films at the cinema.

There could be no persuading us that the treasure was non-existent, as far as we were concerned it was the gospel truth, signed in blood and tattooed on the chest of a drunken sailor.

Having led a number of these swag hunting expeditions in the past I could quite understand the boys' enthusiasm for exploring Gullin Island.

There had been an ancient feud between the owner of the island and the locals on the mainland, to such an extent that a wall had been constructed on the island to block access to it. The wall had been partly torn down during the dispute sometime in the dim and distant past and it didn't take a lot of wit to imagine the wall having been built to protect the treasure buried somewhere on the island.

Pat and Alfie tried their best to persuade me to join up with their merry band and help storm the wall and search every nook and cranny until the treasure was found, certainly before it got dark, but for once in my short life I heeded my father's words. I had already been in a heap of trouble that week and was on a last warning, so I made up a feeble excuse and left them there to wait for the tide to turn.

To be honest I immediately forgot about the lads as I rescued my club and restarted my imaginary game up and down the beach, until it was time to go home for tea.

Late that evening dad was called away from the house, we heard him go, after talking in subdued tones to a neighbour. Watching him walk away from the house into the darkness was intriguing, this didn't happen very often. Mother was tight lipped on the subject and we reluctantly went to bed without the mystery being resolved.

There is no way for me to retrace the moments scorched into my life story that unfolded the next day, without a dreadful sorrow threatening to engulf me and once again take me back to that long distant time.

My mother sat me down at the table and talked in a very soft voice about a tragedy that had happened the night before. It appears that Pat and Alfie had followed their dream to Gullin Island but didn't leave until it was almost dark.

In the twilight they must have misjudged the progress of the tide, which was notoriously fast flooding. It had drowned grown men and horses in the past. Both boys were found that morning washed up on the beach.

I was inconsolable. I had never had an intimate knowledge of death and the finality of it all was too much for me to bear. Mum hugged me and I remember crying like a baby, refusing to believe it was true. I was sure that if I went back to the shore that Pat and Alfie would still be there looking out to sea, waiting for the tide to turn.

In my dreams, I can still see the boys, young and free, full of hopes and dreams, totally unaware of the dreadful fate awaiting them and I am consumed by grief. Such a tragedy creates unseen scars that manifest as guilt, for surviving when they perished or not reminding them of the speed of the tide.

I carry it to this day, even as I attempt to type this passage with tears blocking out my computer screen.

As a footnote, the treasure is now seen as having a curse on it, that is summarily added to, generation by generation. Few personally remember Pat and Alfie but they are now part of legend and I suppose a sort of immortality was granted to them.

That summer ended badly and wasn't improved by the arrival of the new school term.

Mr McGrundy was even snappier, finally telling my father it was a waste of time for me to attend school. I took him at his word by attending as little as possible.

My only incentive to show my face was the occasional glimpse of Erin, having given up on ever seeing Clodagh again. She seemed somehow different after the cinema incident, returning my eye contact every now and then, something that was new and exciting.

I hung around to speak to her after school but she was always with her friends. Now, I am by nature a persistent bloke but this was getting to be a bit tedious. It seemed I would be old before I ever got her on her own, maybe twenty or so and I was not going to wait that long. So, I devised a plan, ill thought out as usual and destined for disaster but as usual I jumped in feet first.

I wrote her a note on paper I was supposed to use for homework, my best penmanship flowing over the pages like a spider and a snake in conflict. Time has erased the exact wording of my missive from memory, but suffice it to say it was written by a naïve boy of thirteen and I leave the rest to your imagination, after all, who amongst us has not written that note at some time or other?

Getting the message to her proved the hardest part of the exercise, shielded as she was from the likes of me by her harridans. Somehow a moment arrived, completely out of the blue and spurred me into action. There was a fire drill, usually done once a term, to assuage the school governors and as such we marched out of the class in single file.

Unbeknown to me my shoelace was untied and I tripped over, only to be told, "Do your shoelace up boy!", by grumpy McGrundy.

By the time my shoelace was retied I was alone in the classroom. Seizing my chance, I took my billet-doux and hurriedly placed it inside her notebook, just in time to hear old grumpy shout, "Come on boy before you burn to death".

I left the classroom at the gallop, pleased with myself at having breached the personal security wall encamped around my would-be girlfriend.

As luck would have it, the fire drill took longer than anticipated and we returned to our classroom just in time for the end of school bell to sound.

I watched discreetly as Erin picked up her book and walked out of class. Following a respectable distance behind I was overjoyed that the note was now delivered and all I had to do was wait for her to read it when she did her homework. I sometimes think someone looks down on boys like me and laughs to themselves, "Let's give him a hard time".

Walking down the corridor, some idiot decided to attempt to slalom through the crowd, bumping into Erin and sending her book flying and my outpouring of undying love subsequently doing a double somersault before unceremoniously unfolding and falling at the feet of corporal horrible harridan.

I knew I was undone even before she started laughing. A wicked grin seemed to take hold of her face and turn it into a witch's cackle wagon. Her mouth moved, in slow motion, or so it seemed, first towards Erin and then towards me.

The whole school must have heard, well at least those in our immediate proximity. I was now the idiot who wrote the love letter and my blushing didn't help the situation. The floor didn't open up, my exit was blocked, thank goodness I was head and shoulders taller than most and could just gaze over their mealy mouths.

Embarrassment was the name of the day and I was so that person, wishing I had never put pen to paper or even learnt to write. Yes, that was it, blame it all on being taught to write. Why couldn't we have stopped at reading and bypassed writing.

The scene was becoming more and more like a bad nightmare and when we finally spilled out into the school yard I was drenched in sweat and my feet were yearning to take me as fast as they could, as soon as they could, as far as they could. I would have gone but out from the crowd came Erin and smiled at me.

There is no way to really describe the feeling, it made me gasp for breath, my heart doing its best to explode, my limbs beginning to shake like a puppet on a twisted string. She smiled again and thanked me for the note.

I can't remember her exact words as my ears didn't seem to function either. I tried to speak but had lost all control of my tongue.

She smiled again, I think recognising genuine panic and then, softly and unexpectedly she touched my hand.

SHE TOUCHED MY HAND. I was in heaven, I'm sure. SHE TOUCHED MY HAND. The unspoken words rolling round my head and the physical contact bombarded my mind as I watched her and her entourage walking away, leaving me a quivering mess. Oh, to be able to relive that precious moment of unbridled sensuality, that innocent touch, that seminal second in a boy's brain where it almost exploded. I will never forget that brief but beautiful awareness, not for as long as I live. The first step on the long and winding road to adulthood had happened and it could never unhappen, never be taken away.

Although my lessons on love were on the up, (Considering where they were, things hadn't moved far!), my education at school still suffered!

You've probably gathered by now that I hated my time at the Brain Torture Unit, apart from meeting up with friends and getting into mischief. Its therefore no surprise that I longed to escape from my personal parochial prison.

At the time, in Ireland, the legal age for leaving school was

14 and I prayed for the day to arrive as soon as possible. It was evident to all that I was not suited to academic work, nor it to me and the sooner I left the better.

I was a big lad for 13 and could pass for much older and I often walked down to the harbour where the trawlers came in, pestering them for a job. They seemed interested in taking me on until they learnt I was still at school.

One of the skippers, a man named John Williams, took me to one side and said he would employ me as soon as I left school. You can imagine my excitement, leaving that Torture House to go to sea on a trawler, every schoolboy's dream, well, mine anyway.

Could the world get any better? A girlfriend of sorts, a job, a life on the sea, the very sea I had looked out over my whole life, what could possibly go wrong?

I am not sure which is the hardest, relationships or fighting the mighty waves on a tiny trawler, miles from land? At least I understood the waves and their motions!

My sea days were much closer than I thought, but in immediate need of attention was my 'relationship' with Erin.

The episode with the note had gone viral, or what passed for viral in those days, namely the grapevine! If you are too young to know what the grapevine was in this context, then ask your grandparents!

My brothers, all younger than me, did not dare to tease me about the situation but my sisters were a different bunch entirely. They teased me mercilessly, giving me notes, supposedly written by Erin, covered in kisses and silly rhymes.

My blushing was now mandatory in our house and the yells would ring out, "He's blushing again!" My sisters would scream as I chased them but they knew I would never lay a hand on them.

Getting to speak to Erin at school was next to impossible, she was always surrounded by wandering witches and approaching her was against the question in those circumstances, so imagine my delight when I saw her standing on her own just outside the school. She smiled at me as I walked over to her, which was a good sign. "Want me to carry your books?", I offered gallantly. She handed me the books and we set off leisurely towards her house, not saying much but that was ok, we were together for the first time and it was exhilarating.

I remember the feelings but not much about the few words we exchanged. The air was different somehow! The joy of being alive was running rampant through my brain and I remember thinking how beautiful she was.

Just before we reached the corner of her road, she stopped and asked for her books back and said thank you. It was a message to me not to walk her to her door. I wondered why but knew better than to ask and as I walked away, I turned to see her watching me.

She gave a wave and disappeared around the corner. My heart did a high five in my chest and I had to take a deep breath before I started on my way home, my heavy hobnail boots ringing out on the cobblestones. Did this mean I had a girlfriend? What happened now? How do I find out? All questions I would find answers to in time, but at that moment it was all brand new.

Despite the infernal footwear weighing my legs down, I felt I was walking on air! Her face was still emblazoned on my retina and it's a wonder I didn't trip over a matchstick, as I practically waltzed down the street. I imagined kissing her, holding her and ... and ... I was confused about what happened after that. She was suddenly my whole world. I couldn't stop my heart from doing back flips, that notification of love's inoculation!

It suddenly started to pour with rain, but I was oblivious to it! Nothing could dampen my mood! I was king of the world. I had a girlfriend! Soaked through, I dripped into the kitchen via the back door, only for my mother to scold me for ruining her clean floor, throwing a towel at me and telling me to take my boots off!

That evening was spent in blissful contemplation of things to come. I made plans in my head that were constantly being revised and as I had no-one as a sounding board, I got more and more confused. Oh, the joy of youth! I lay on my bed, juggling scenarios, mostly based around films I had seen. Unrealistic? Maybe! But the important thing was I felt happier than I had for a long time! For ever, probably! At least, that is what I told myself.

The next morning, I was feeling very jaunty and full of myself so I persuaded my brother Seamus to pool his money with mine and we bought a packet of five Woodbine cigarettes. How proud and how grown up we felt with this prestigious package in our possession.

When we arrived at school, I found a suitable hiding place in a hole, high in the playground wall and safely stashed the prized item for later use. Being caught with cigarettes at school was frowned upon and my hands didn't need any more punishment.

During the break Seamus and I retrieved the ciggies as we called them and found a sheltered spot, out of sight of prowling teachers and lit one each. I was warrior chief of the world, having tired of being King, listing a girlfriend and a Woodbine smouldering in my hand as all the trappings I needed for this exalted position.

We had learnt to hold the ciggies with the lit end in

towards the palm of our hands, making it easier to conceal from prying eyes. This method we had adopted after watching a large quantity of war films, where they held their smokes in such a way it would not be visible to an enemy sniper.

Mind you it could be painful if you forgot where you were holding it, as I did a few times in my youth and the burn marks were red and sore for days after. The other problem was young oiks asking for a drag on my ciggie. I told them politely to 'F' off but the occasional one wouldn't take no for an answer and matters could get out of hand.

Dermot Donaghy was a persistent nuisance and would not shut up about having a drag, so I gave him a right good shove with my unencumbered left hand, whilst finishing my ciggie with the other. He was not pleased at having my big mitts connect painfully with his sternum so he started to come for me and impulsively, I stubbed the ciggie out on his forehead. I know now that was a stupid thing to do, but at the time and in the heat of the moment it was an inspiration. He screamed blue murder and clutched his head as if it had a bullet hole in it. Bloody snipers everywhere!

To be fair he didn't cry, but he wagged his free hand in my face and challenged me to meet him after school, which I of course accepted.

If that wasn't bad enough, grumpy McGrundy pushed his way through the surrounding throng and pulled Dermot's hand away from the affected area.

"Who did this?", he demanded to know.

Dermot to his credit said nothing, but all eyes pointed to me.

"Oh, good god! Will you never learn boy?" he growled, looking me straight in the face. "Headmaster's office! Now!"

He grabbed me by my ear although being taller than him, he had trouble finding it and with the other hand towed Dermot along.

The humiliation of being paraded through the school like a bullock to the slaughter, was made even worse as we passed Erin and her friends. She had a look of shock that I tried desperately not to connect with but too late, the eyes said it all.

"Stay there!", was the furious command given to me and Dermot, as we arrived outside the dreaded Headmaster's office as he knocked and entered, closing the door slowly behind him, a backward glance threatening us with more wrath if we moved from that spot.

People talk about fight or flight as the major responses in

times of crisis but as neither option was available, due to my feet having cemented themselves to the concrete floor! The next best thing was, think of a good excuse, but unfortunately my mind, for once, was blank.

My tortuous squirming was put to an end by the door opening, shall we say, rapidly and a bent finger beckoning us to enter the gladiatorial arena beyond.

Dermot and I entered the inner sanctum, as it was affectionately known, with the mental torture level at 10. Terrified would not be a good enough description, shitting ourselves probably more anatomically correct.

"Show me boy!", was the command to Dermot before he had come completely into the room. Having forgotten totally about the minor burn on his bony forehead, he stood there completely flummoxed, wondering quite what it was he had to show the headmaster.

"Your head!" Then much louder! "Your head! Boy!" was the signal needed by his rabbit like stare, to regain partial control, lifting his arm and holding his floppy hair away from his forehead.

The headmaster advanced so quickly to see the offending burn mark that Dermot stepped back even faster, falling over a small waste bin behind him and with great agility did a perfect backward arse dive straight into the aforesaid bin. He squealed like a small pig being chased with a pitchfork, his legs flailing around like a dervish and accurately catching grumpy McGrundy right between the legs, which in turn caused the teacher to spasmodically bend in two, smashing his head straight into the headmaster's nose.

Would you have laughed at that point? Well, it might have been spontaneous but once out, there was nothing to be gained by attempting to put it back. So, I had a good laugh. I admit it. Not proud of it mind, but an altogether logical reaction to the pantomime that had just played out in front of me.

I did my best to extricate poor Dermot from the almost flattened bin, but he was wedged good and proper. Old grumpy was still nursing his balls and bent double, whilst the headmaster was desperately trying to staunch the flow of blood from his now wider than normal nose. Not forgetting of course, the broken pince nez glasses that were partially embedded in his left cheek!

There has been many a time over the years I have recounted this tale of escalating mayhem and I suspect, time has embellished it, but it remains one of the funniest things I have ever seen, probably will ever see, in my lifetime.

Punishment of course came in a large dose, later in the day, but the least said about that the better for those squeamish at heart. Let's just say thank goodness we can't remember pain, just the effect of it.

It may have been worse because of a chance remark I made on the spur of the moment!

The headmaster, sleeves rolled up, cane swishing like a racehorse's tail, came right up to me and said, "Do you have anything to say, boy!"

"I think a bee stung him, sir!", was the only thing I could think of.

I swear the headmaster's eyes rolled right back into his head, only the whites of his eyes were visible! If I was not hallucinating at the time, smoke came out of his ears!

What was a little strange, was the half smile that momentarily flickered on Mc Grumpy's face, on hearing my retort! He may have thought it funny or he may have been relishing the escalation of my punishment, but I prefer to think it was the former.

After that, the pain descended on my poor suffering hand. Blow after blow erupted on my flesh, blood flicking over my partially clean shirt. The head never did reply to my implausible excuse, unless the muttering he punctuated each drawing back of his arm with was an attempt at a language he had temporarily forgotten.

Like all bad and good times, it came to an end. I stood there defiant as ever. How I didn't go back there years later, when I was fully grown and beat the shit out of him, I'm not too sure.

Did I forgive him? No, I bloody didn't! The man was a sadist! I guess I consigned those memories to a place I rarely approached. If they had been stored somewhere I regularly visited, I might be in prison now, serving a life sentence instead of sitting in the garden with a cold Guinness!

If it had stopped there it might have ended with the one punishment, but the challenge to a fight with Dermot was still very much on the cards and even though my hands were raw, there was no way I was backing down.

Oh, incidentally, I neglected to tell you that I had to disclose the whereabouts of the stashed ciggies. After my brother and I took our two Woodbines from the packet, I hid the remainder high in the wall again. Our precious status symbol and rebellion fuel was torn up in front of me and consigned to a bin. I have to say that I did not at any time implicate my brother, he never entered the conversation and was spared any retribution.

I say this as a prelude to what took place when I arrived home, a scenario you will learn more about in a short while.

On to matters more glorious.

Dermot fully recovered from his trauma with the now defunct bin but still with a mark, smack in the middle of his forehead, he was waiting for me down the road, as I left school.

Ok, I was quite a lot taller than my foe but he was as solid as an Irish Front Row and could kick like a mule. I have already mentioned the hobnailed boots we all wore and in situations like this they could become lethal weapons. There were no rules in school fights apart from last standing wins!

I could see the baying public, crowded around Dermot, egging him on for revenge! I walked up to him, pushing through the wide circle of onlookers calling for blood and was about to take my battle stance when he caught me by surprise, landing a hefty boot to my shin that made me hop on one leg and yelp, because to be honest, it bloody hurt.

He promptly took another kick this time to my only standing leg. Now, if it was possible to lift both legs off the ground and hug them, I would have done, but as gravity would have dropped me to the ground in a heap, it was an option I couldn't take. So, I put both feet in touch with terra firma and swung my best right hook and caught him, still laughing, fully on his jaw. He flew backwards, as if he were Superman reversing, knocking over several younger lads who had ventured to the front of the crowd, to get a good view.

Somehow, he stayed on his feet and came flying back at me launching himself at my lower extremities, sinking his teeth into my arm and tearing my shirt collar with his outstretched arm, whilst pinching my calf with his lower arm.

I grabbed him by the hair, yanking out a fairly large chunk which had the desired effect of stopping his all-out attack.

I was a good boxer and gave him the old one two and as he staggered backwards, I hit him full in the chest, taking away his breath and causing him to collapse on the floor.

The fight was over. It seemed like an eternity, but in fact it could only have been seconds. I held out my hand to him and helped him to his feet, there was no malice there and he accepted I had beaten him fair and square, both walking away nursing cuts, bruises and torn bloody clothes. We remain friends to this day.

There was no way to disguise my pitiful state, so I wandered off home, hoping I would not see Erin or any of her so-called friends.

Walking in through the doorway I knew something was afoot, the house was uncharacteristically quiet, the smell of food cooking in the kitchen but my mother nowhere in sight. It didn't last long, my father on hearing my entry loomed large and it would be a few years yet before I overtook him in height and width. He stood there, belt in hand, I thought there was no way he could have heard about the fight yet and I was right.

It appears that my loving brother, that I so willingly protected by leaving him out of ciggie-gate, had told my father about my smoking at school, saying, I forced him to smoke a ciggie against his will. A lie that took me a long time to forgive.

Again, I see no benefit in putting my punishment in writing suffice it to say, without fear of repeating myself, it bloody hurt. It seemed I was punished three times that day but it escalated to four when I was sent to bed without any dinner.

Life was tough enough those days and the actions of others and of course my own, seem almost barbaric in comparison to modern life but that was just the way it was.

I hold no malice towards my father or old grumpy chops, they did what they thought was right at the time and that in a way justifies it, but the headmaster, now that's a different case entirely! He's long gone now, but certainly not forgotten! He was undoubtedly psychotic, relishing in his daily round of vicious corporal punishment. If there is a God, let's hope he has banished the old sod to have his arse grated, daily, with a rough file and salt rubbed in! Followed by his balls being roasted over hot coals until they burst! Not that I feel any ill will towards him! Honest!

Thank goodness the world has moved on, not always for the better, but scenes like I have illustrated are now highly unlikely in schools and most homes, instead of being the norm.

I trudged into school the next day, unable to sit comfortably or pick up things, but I did my best to get on with enduring my prison time until I could escape once again. Not really a good attitude to have if you wanted to learn anything but as I thought I already knew enough, I couldn't see the reason for me to stay.

At least I had a chance to see Erin and maybe if I was lucky, I could walk her home after school. Fate was to interrupt my life as it has done frequently since, but this time it had the effect of making me a local hero.

It was break time and I was walking with my friend Joe, around the edges of the playing field at the back of the school, the wind was blowing a right hooley and we were trying to decide whether to take shelter under a tree or run for the school. Our minds were made up when an almighty gust gripped us and threatened to pick us up and drop us out at sea. Just a second or so later we heard a loud crack, like a gigantic whip and a huge part of the tree we were standing under crashed to the ground.

It knocked me off my feet, so, for a moment I just lay there, branches all over me, wondering if I was trapped. Wriggling around a bit, I was able to move a little at a time, until I was safely out from under the branches.

I stood up and looked around, then up at the tree to see where the huge branch had come from. I saw the split in the trunk and I remember thinking "That was bloody close!" It was then I suddenly remembered Joe. Where the hell was he? I called his name over and over but there was no reply! There was nothing for it but for me to crawl back under the tree and look for him.

Getting back under was almost as tricky as getting out and by now it was raining heavily, the water pouring down through the branches like someone spraying me with a hose. I was already soaked through and it was very difficult to see, the water kept getting in my eyes and as I was on my hands and knees my hands got more and more muddy. As I wiped the water away, I plastered mud all over my face and into my eyes. To make it worse my face was being badly scratched and I could feel blood running down my cheeks. Just when I was ready to give up, I felt Joe, I say felt because my vision was by now almost zero.

I talked to him but there was no response and I couldn't feel him breathing, he was pinned down and I think that was what was stopping him. I shouted for help, but I knew it was unlikely to come, as we went there because it was an area that not many frequented, especially in high winds.

It was the day I thanked God for being a big strong lad, because I knew I had to get the tree off his chest or he would die there, pinned down. I stood up the best I could amongst the tangled foliage and wrapped my arms around the offending branch.

I remember screaming with effort as I put my back and legs to work, straining with every fibre to make the damn thing move and then suddenly it shifted, not a lot but it gave me hope that I could do it and so I redoubled my efforts and used power I never knew I had.

The branch moved and I moved and together the offending object was shifted enough to release Joe. He was still unconscious but I managed to pull him out from under. He was breathing again and I did something we were told never to do in circumstances like this; I picked him up in my arms and carried him back to the schoolhouse; over the muddy field that had taken on the texture of an Irish rugby pitch after a rigorous international, slipping and sliding in the mud, once or twice down on one knee but I never dropped him.

As I approached the school there was an obvious search party about to depart to look for us. Someone dashed out and took Joe out of my arms and I remember falling headfirst into the mud. I'm not sure if I could have walked another yard.

To be honest I'm not very clear on what happened after that, somehow, they got me home and I woke up in my bed with my mother sat beside me. Apparently the first thing I said was, "Is Joe alright?" My mum nodded with tears in her eyes. I hadn't seen my mum cry before and I wondered if I was in trouble again, but she was just glad I was ok.

The trauma took a few days to recover from but at least I had the bonus of not going to school. When I did return, I was a hero, not the usual idiot causing mayhem. The local paper had picked up the story and made me out to be a superman for lifting the tree off Joe and carrying him in those conditions, all the way back to the school.

He had multiple broken ribs and a punctured lung, but he made a complete recovery, so there was a happy ending. Even old grumpy guts shook my hand and congratulated me.

As a footnote to this incident, you might like to know that my report card said, and I quote, "Niall is not much good at academic subjects but he can lift things". I smiled when I read it and I have often quoted it in interviews. If only to show where I started and how much I improved over the years.

Unfortunately, Joe was killed crossing the road a couple of years later, it was almost as if he was meant to die that day, under the tree and somehow, I helped him cheat death, at least for a little while. I still remember him as he was, a gentle, wickedly funny boy who loved to run and climb and get into mischief. A perfect companion for a boy like me and I will always miss him!

With my three brothers, my four sisters and my parents all crammed into a small house, quiet time was very rare and sometimes it only came late at night when the rest of my family were sleeping.

I would lie awake, trying to rationalise some of the irrational events in my life, a pointless exercise that only further served to torture my young mind. I made plans that were all destined to evaporate by light of morning, but it did give me a sense of control of a life of chaos and inevitability that was laid out before me.

It appeared that my destiny was to work on the land or the local trawlers, raise a large family and die, scraping a living barely above the poverty level, perpetuating the life of my father and condemning my own children as well.

There was no way my young self could know that I would transcend this existence and create a life full of everything I could ever desire. All I could see was what was right in front of me and I despaired of it all except for the possibilities with Erin.

Saturday afternoon was usually my time to knock golf balls on the beach, but one never to be forgotten day, I had arranged to meet Erin for a walk. Sitting on the seawall, eyes fixed firmly on the horizon, I imagined the two of us, leaving for America and a life out west, a life portrayed in Technicolor in so many films. Full of adventure we would climb mountains and build a cabin and ... my thoughts were forgotten as Erin suddenly sat down beside me.

"Far away with the fairies, were we?", she taunted in her soft floating voice.

"Just dreaming", I replied.

"What about?"

"Oh ... stuff. You know".

"Not really, but that's ok".

We sat there quietly for a moment or two, looking out to sea on a glorious day, the sun dancing on the water, glinting like diamonds in a jewellers' window, the gentle crash of the waves doing their best to retrieve the beach on the eternal journey back and forth. If there was ever a heavenly day, this was it, it's still a goto day for me, after a lifetime of days, the tranquillity mesmerising and promising so much.

We decided to walk along the seawall, as the tide was rapidly coming in, talking about goodness knows what and looking at each other, every now and then and each look saying far more than we could elucidate. I picked up the odd sizeable pebble and launched it out over the sea and she followed suit, although not as far, still seeing it plunging into the water with a mighty splash. Laughter was the mood of the day and everything seemed right with the world. Elvis … we talked about Elvis, I just remembered that.

I must admit to feeling a little jealous of this handsome young American singer with the wobbly legs. Erin talked about him in a way that I hoped she thought about me, mind you I will admit I was never much of a singer, my father used to say my voice was like the noise made by a piece of coke caught under the door.

Walking as we were, along the seawall it was very flat but we came to an area where the hillside took over and became steeper and more uneven. At that age we took the hill with gusto, accelerating as we climbed, laughing towards the top. I'm still not sure whether Erin tripped on purpose, but I suddenly found myself reaching out to stop her falling and taking her hand in mine, a hand I kept hold of as we finally reached the summit. I felt a sense of elation that surged through me, holding her hand as we stood atop of that hill and marvelled at the vista before us. I should have kissed her then, but my young confidence was still to grow and the moment passed for a short while. Holding hands was still an enormous achievement in my young life and the feeling of togetherness was new and sensational. It never occurred to me to ask if she felt the same, I just assumed she did. Maybe if she reads this book, she'll let me know.

We sat in the dunes on the hill, protected from the wind and warmed by the sun, content in our own little world. To my surprise she lay back on the sand, arms above her head and eyes shut, this time the moment was not allowed to slip away and I leaned over her, blocking out the sun. She opened her eyes and looked straight into mine, my blood pressure must have gone through the roof, but I admirably stayed in control and leaned in closer and kissed her, eyes closed and heart open. Again, I have no idea whether it was good for her, all I know is life was never going to be the same. I had tasted manna from heaven and I wanted more.

We stayed for what seemed a lifetime, cuddling and kissing, two innocent children learning to be adults and enjoying the lesson, until the sun started to fade and we left our piece of heaven and made our way, still holding hands back to the seawall where we started.

Our houses were in different directions and I offered to walk her home but she was adamant that she could walk home on her own, I felt she was holding back something from me, but I couldn't fathom what it was, so I let it go. As she was about to leave, she stood really close and kissed me, not me kissing her, but her kissing me, so I knew it was a feeling we both had and that was proof, if proof was needed.

I watched her go and stood there until she went out of sight, a wave of her hand as she once again disappeared around the corner.

There was a massive impulse to run after her and never let her go but I knew that was wrong and I resisted the temptation by running as fast as I could down onto the beach, where the tide had just retired from, jumping and shouting like a lunatic. Not caring who heard or saw me, eventually stopping and making a reluctant journey back through the narrow streets to our house and the cacophony that passed as normal.

Our walks were often repeated and we must have traversed most of the County that beautiful summer, those hobnail boots were well used as we sauntered high and low, laughing and talking about anything and everything, creating a special time that still has a resonance whenever I stop to look back.

2. FARMING, FUMES, WOOLLEN TRUNKS AND MORE GOLF

During that summer I started to work for a local farmer about three miles away, over the fields.

Occasionally I worked late and it could get quite dark as the sun sank below the trees. This might not seem difficult but to anyone who has had to walk meandering footpaths over undulating fields, three miles is an awful long way in the aforesaid hobnail boots. It was easy to wander off route and end up in a bog or the edge of a fast-flowing stream, that was too wide to jump. I often ended up making unintended detours, adding long distances to the already difficult journey. I would arrive home shattered and after washing off the mud of the day's work and the added detritus of the journey, I would be too exhausted to go out and enjoy myself. When I did get to bed there was no lying about daydreaming, straight off to sleep, only to be woken early for breakfast before I started out again.

I did this six days a week, leaving only Sunday to meet up with Erin, although our walks were getting shorter, my legs longing for a break. Something had to change.

After a couple of weeks of my tortuous journey, the farmer's wife, who could see I was struggling, suggested I stay at the farm, instead of going home each day, an offer I jumped at and the next day I moved in for the summer. There was a spare room for me to use, a luxury I hadn't expected and when I came into dinner that evening, there was, in my eyes, a feast laid out at the table. It was normal for them, but paradise to me and helped to open my eyes to what life could be like. They had a son a few years older than me and he had left for University, hence the opportunity for me. Talk was often about him and how well he was doing with his studies. I think it was obvious they didn't expect him to return to the land, but they seemed ok with it and were ready to let him make his own way in the world.

I was amazed at their supportive attitude and their unselfish approach to their son's future. More life lessons for me to consider and store away for future use.

The work was hard and plentiful but the rewards were so much greater. I was used to grafting but this showed me that you could expect reasonable rewards for it. This attitude has stayed with me ever since. I still toiled hard but made sure I was well rewarded and I treated those working for me similarly.

Another aspect of my temporary new home was the family dog. We had never had a pet, there were enough mouths to feed, so to add a hungry dog would be ridiculous.

Smacker, as he was named, was a working dog, a bit of Collie, a bit of everything else I think, always happy and wagging his tail, smacking it against the door or the wall or a bin. I'm sure he knew what he was doing. It was an amazing sight, watching him take instruction via whistles and word commands, rounding up the sheep. He would dart in and out of the flock, barking and bullying them into going in the direction he had been commanded to take them. That dog must have been one of the happiest creatures on the planet, you could see that he loved his job with every fibre of his being, if he had wagged his tail anymore, he would have taken off like a helicopter. At night he would lie at my feet, by the fire, as he snored and made tiny little barks as he herded sheep in his dreams. I really missed that dog when I eventually, reluctantly returned home, the summer almost over and school once again intruding on my happiness.

Mischief was never far from my mind and during my last few days on the farm I was working on the tomato plants in the huge glass construction that contained them. Every now and then there was an outbreak of greenfly.

All the windows and doors of the glass house would be closed and we would release smoke canisters that would kill the greenfly. We wore masks to protect ourselves as the smoke was very thick and the last thing you wanted to do was breathe it in. These canisters were the size of a small can of tonic water and easy to conceal, so I slipped a couple into my pocket for future use that at the time was unplanned.

My brother Seamus, who I had forgiven by now, came with me to the local cinema, the one I had been banned from. Remember? Well, they kindly lifted the ban and gave me another chance.

I was never one to hold a grudge but banning me meant missing some great films. They were then related to me by friends who had watched them and I was very jealous.

So ... canisters in pocket, Seamus and I took our seats near the front as we always did, except he went to one side and I went to the other. We had a pre-arranged signal that when the trailer ended, we would simultaneously pull the rings on the canisters and roll them under the seat in front letting the natural slope of the floor take them right down to the front of the cinema.

Good plan but fatally flawed. As soon as we rolled them under the seats they caught on the feet of the person in front and the cloud of smoke came out from under the seat and immediately enveloped us in a guilty cloak.

There was utter pandemonium, people were screaming and coughing, not necessarily at the same time, jumping over seats in their panic to get out. Some idiot shouted fire and the panic became even worse. The house lights came on to show people pushing and shoving to get out while they could. Clothes were torn, fights broke out, sweets originally destined for consumption became the source of ammunition in retaliation for some perceived slight, escalating as wars do, until the boxes that once contained the goodies were hurled as well.

Hats came off from the old ladies sitting in the aisles reserved for OAPs, as they withdrew their hatpins and used them as lances on any poor unsuspecting person who dared to enter their private space.

One person even hung precariously off the balcony by one hand, swinging to and fro, like Tarzan on a vine. Quite what he was thinking at the time I couldn't hazard a guess, except to think his exit might have been blocked and in his panic, he did something really stupid, that he immediately wished he hadn't.

One idiot was stupidly trying to exit via the screen that was displaying a film showing an open wide prairie scene that in his state of panic he must have believed was real, until he met it with his nose and found it was a boundary. No problem, he had a pocketknife, like all of us and he utilised it to good measure by slashing the screen, only to find a brick wall behind it which he stabbed at furiously, breaking his knife and cutting his fingers to the bone, leaving him standing like something out of a horror film, blood gushing everywhere.

This rapidly unfolding farce was made even more surreal by the thick smoke that lay at seated shoulder height throughout a large area at the front of the cinema.

Unfortunately, I just sat there, mesmerised, stunned by the absolute mayhem exploding around me. All it needed now was the Keystone Cops and the scene would be complete! They accordingly arrived, in the guise of stewards who knew me well! It was evident to them, bravely fighting their way to the source of the smoke, that I was again guilty of 'malicious mischief', as they called it.

As was usual, I was frogmarched out of the cinema and onto the street, with explicit instructions, to "Never", and it was expounded in a much louder and more dramatic form. "NEVER! I REPEAT! NEVER, EVER SET FOOT IN HERE AGAIN!

My ban this time was for two lifetimes, the idea being that if some idiot lifted it and let me in, I would still be considered banned and thrown out unceremoniously.

Seamus kept his head down, as usual and escaped without so much of a mention of his name by me. I should have known better because, true to form, when I returned home, still laughing at my revenge on the cinema, my father was waiting for me. You guessed it; Seamus had ratted on me again! The little sod! Who needs enemies when you have a brother like that?

Once again, I'll say nothing more about my punishment, not wanting to offend the more squeamish reader.

The next morning, everyone was quiet around the house, an unusual and unnerving silence greeted me as I turned up for breakfast! Before I could eat anything, I was sent across the fields to fetch water for drinking. When I arrived, I realised the cows had been around and the water was very muddy. It was not a unique happening and I had no option but to wait, stomach rumbling due to lack of sustenance, until the water cleared, before filling the buckets. Can you believe it? How did we live through that?

Everything these days is so hygienic, with use by dates and all, there was none of that then and we drank out of a dirty well! I made three trips that morning to fetch water, as if I wasn't punished enough the previous night. Seamus did his best to hide from me for a week! What a brother!

To bring in a little extra money, mum used to work as a cleaner, part-time at the golf club. As if she didn't have enough of that looking after us lot! One day she arrived home with a message for me to attend the next day as they needed a local caddy for a gentleman visitor and someone had recommended me. I was to be clean and tidy, so my mother said, but that was probably what she would say anyway.

I arrived at the golf club, spick and span, with my best Elvis style hair, slicked back yet flopping over my eyes. It was a look I had acquired since Erin professed her love for him.

As caddies, we were never allowed into the club house, but went around to the small area occupied by the ground staff, at the rear until we were called.

I could hear a lot of chatter coming from the front of the club, which was unusual, because it was normally quieter than in church during prayers. Well, you've probably gathered by now I rarely kept my nose out of an interesting situation, so I sidled up to the throng milling around a person who I guessed was some sort of celebrity. Being taller, even at my tender age, than most of the members, I could see a blonde-haired young man, taller than me, smiling and chatting, mostly to the lady wives of the members. He caught my eye and excused himself politely from the ladies and approached me.

"You look like you might be my caddy!", he said with a sweet lilting voice that seemed almost effeminate and held out his hand. Now that was strange because most members or guests used to practically ignore me until they needed a club or some advice about the course. I shook his hand. A much firmer grip than I had anticipated greeted me.

"What's your name?", he inquired.

"Niall, sir!", I replied, politely as I possibly could.

"My name is Duncan Mulberry!", he offered.

"Good to meet you Mr Mulberry, sir!", I countered, again as politely as I knew how.

He leaned over and whispered, "You can call me Duncan, when no-one's around".

That had never happened before either. Duncan Mulberry, I knew the name but couldn't think where I had heard it. Perhaps he lived locally and my father had mentioned him, yes, that was probably it.

"Play much golf sir?", I inquired.

"Not a lot to be honest Niall. Only here because my fiancé's father is Captain of the golf club this year and I think he wants to show me off".

"Sorry sir but should I know you?", my innocent request seemed to please him.

"Do you listen to the radio much Niall?"

"Not really sir, if I'm not working, I'm out doing something. My father listens to the radio, now and again. Are you on the radio sir?"

"I am indeed Niall. I'm a singer. My records are played on the radio a lot. Are you an Elvis fan?", he asked, nodding at my hairstyle.

"I am sir, or rather my girlfriend is!", suddenly realising that it was the first time I had referred to Erin as my girlfriend to anyone. "Just did this to please her really".

"Nice job", he muttered as he turned to speak to another lady, who was obviously a fan.

He was once again engulfed in a female scrum that formed round him.

"Bloody glad I'm not famous", I thought. "All those old women round me. Yuck!" I expect most of the females would be in their thirties but to me of course that was ancient.

Eventually we left the ladies and joined the rest of his four ball on the first tee.

I took out the 5 iron and gave it to Duncan, who gave me a short glance and took the club.

His opponents played off before him, all trying to hit their one irons as hard as they could, finding the trees, bushes and other assorted hazards by trying too hard. Duncan used his easy 5 iron and hit it straight down the fairway, maybe not as far as the others, but he was in a safe place for the next shot and would not have to take a sly kick, as some did, to make his next shot possible.

There was much muttering and excuses flying around by the members but Duncan was as cool as a cucumber.

For his second shot I gave him a seven iron. He whispered, "Give me the six I can make the green from here".

I held out the seven and did not make a move for the six. Duncan looked at me for a second and then took the seven iron from me. His next shot was short of the green and a bit right. He could see that if he had used the six iron, he would have made the awesome greenside bunker, as it was, he had a simple chip on to the green to an accessible flag.

The others were getting a bit rattled by his conservative play and tried even harder, landing in the dreaded bunker or even overshooting the green into the bushes beyond, a land of no return.

Duncan could hardly contain his smile and was very gracious in his remarks to others. "Oh bad luck!" or "Almost".

His chip onto the green left him about two feet from the flag for a tap in par that he took with ease.

The members wrote numbers onto their cards that came nowhere near Duncan's four and the muttering went on.

Golf's a game of risk and reward but also game management and Duncan beat his playing companions by a country mile, His father-in-law was proud of him and said so a number of times throughout the match.

When it was all over, I departed to get his clubs cleaned and returned to his car. I had just shut the boot when he walked over to me.

"That was a very important day for me Niall and I couldn't have done it without your help", he said, holding his hand out and giving me five whole pounds. I had never had so much money in my hand in my life and for only a day's work! I was speechless! Duncan smiled and walked away, then he turned and said, "If I play golf here again, I'll be sure to ask for you".

"What a lovely guy", I thought and turned to walk home, with my earnings tucked safely in my trousers. I had only gone a few paces when I noticed a redheaded girl approaching from the club house, it was Clodagh. She was even more beautiful than I remembered.

"Hello Niall!", she greeted me. "How's Erin?" She smiled a knowing smile and pouted her lips, as if to say, "What's wrong with me?"

"Your cousin was very well the last time I saw her", I countered.

"Am I not pretty enough for you?"

"Of course, you are!", I stumbled, completely thrown by where this conversation was going.

"I like your hair", she complimented. "Very Elvis".

Now I was blushing again, unsettled and not knowing what to say next.

"Didn't you want to kiss me?", she tortured me with. Obviously, she had seen her cousin and they had talked about me. I wondered what else she knew.

We were saved by the Colonel who came to look for his daughter.

"Ah Niall there you are!", he said in his military way. "I told young Duncan you were the best person to caddy for him today. He was just singing your praises in the club house".

"Thank you, sir. I should have known it was you who recommended me. I'm very grateful".

"Nonsense Niall, you should know your own worth". That was the second time recently I had been told that.

The Colonel took Clodagh by the hand and led her back to the club house. As they turned to go in, she smiled and blew a kiss in my direction. Bloody hell. Now what do I do?

Confusion fuddled my mind for days, first I thought of Erin and then I thought of Clodagh and felt guilty, so I thought of Erin again. I was torn between two beauties who, for some reason unbeknown to me, were interested in the yokel that I was. My poor bedraggled brain was fit to burst and my hormone levels must have been through the roof, as I wrestled with my conscience and my desires.

Serendipity they call it, when chance events develop in such a way that they are beneficial to the parties involved! A lot of people like to think of it as fate, if so, what do they call Zemblanity, which is the opposite! I have asked this question of any number of my learnéd friends and they all say fate! It baffles my brain that opposites equal the same result! Whatever the reason, my first noted experience of this phenomenon took me completely by surprise!

It was rare for me to meet both girls at the same time and if I did, knowing I was on thin ice, I avoided them both. Until

… one hot day I decided to cool off by going for a swim in the sea. Swimming was something I was very good at, big powerful shoulders and hands the size of dinner plates, as my mother used to say.

It was only a shortish walk to the beach and somewhere along the way I would usually meet up with friends heading in the same direction. We were a noisy bunch, singing and shouting, pushing and shoving in the way only boys do, laughing sturdily at next to nothing and generally full of the joys of life.

Sometimes, someone would bring what passed as a football, a hand-me-down old thing with an outer skin that felt like it was made from a rhinoceros, with iron like laces that kept the inner bladder from bursting out. We would tear up and down the beach, like a buffalo stampede, kicking each other more times than the ball, tactically inept, all chasing the ball at the same time and God help the poor old goalie who got in the way. If we scored, we jumped up and down, kicking up a minor sandstorm, which swept off down the beach to cover dormant beach goers. Red faced boys with sweat running off them were a regular feature of the beach, but that day it was very different.

Zemblanity was conspiring against me, laying the groundwork for unparalleled embarrassment.

None of the regular lads were around as I approached the

beach on that beautiful afternoon. There were small gatherings of people dotted around the shoreline, but no-one of my age to gather with, so I found a convenient spot and took off my clothes apart from my trunks. I had been accustomed to second-hand clothes for many years but these trunks had seen better days! For years I wore perfectly good hand me downs, donated to the family by caring relatives.

On this occasion my mother had berated me for attempting to wear trunks she considered far too small for me. She would not let me out of the house with my trusty trunks, which admittedly were budgie smugglers, so she searched through a recent batch of second-hand clothes she had acquired from somewhere. "These should fit! Put them on!" Well, to be honest, I was dumbfounded! They were made of wool! I put them on and all I did was scratch! They itched like hell! Mum was insistent that I wear them and so, I had little choice!

My new unfashion wear was just about keeping my modesty intact as I casually walked towards the water. I was dying to scratch the interminable itch that was tearing at my flesh and doing my best to get into the water before I succumbed!

"Niall!", I heard someone shout. As I gazed around, to my horror I saw Erin and her mother, sitting on the seawall, about fifty yards away. I quickly waved back and was reluctantly about to go over, when I saw Clodagh there as well. "Oh shit! Now, what do I do?", I thought. This could be awkward, especially being cladded only in an old strip of wool that although it covered the essentials, burned like the fires of hell on a hot day!

I had no idea whether they discussed me or not, but I couldn't take a chance on approaching them both at the same time, just in case, so I waved and ran towards the water.

The chill hit me as soon as I dived in, but I gradually adjusted to it as I struck out towards open water. Foam topped rollers came crashing into shore on a regular basis and half the fun was swimming through them, disappearing only to resurface a little further out.

I knew I was being watched so I did my display of strokes, forward and backward, with Olympic prowess or so I thought.

Stopping to catch my breath and floating out there in the blue, something made me aware of the current flowing around my nether regions! To my horror, I realised that I was no longer wearing the woolie mammoth trunks that I so recently was disparaging. Suddenly the itchy covering became my most precious possession! I scanned the surface of the water praying that I might see them floating within easy reach. No chance, they were probably on their way to Liverpool by now, only to be found by some buoyant beachcomber and discarded as yukky old caveman pants. Oh, what I would have given to have found them, whatever their condition, to cover my manhood, shrunk by the cold water, but still visual enough to mortify me if I had to leave the sea anytime soon.

I dare not float on my back or for that matter on my front, so I kept swimming, up and down, up and down. As I scanned the shoreline, I was horrified to see Erin and Clodagh on their way down the beach towards me. No! No! This couldn't be happening! Normally, the sight of their nubile young bodies in tight fitting costumes would have been a boyhood dream but this was a nightmare of extreme proportions!

They both waved at me as they entered the water and I panicked, swimming further and further away, but the tide was on its way in and kept pushing me back towards the beach. From being dots on the horizon the girls were racing each other to get to me first, now what could I do?

Like two mischievous mermaids they circled me, splashing and giggling, looking so beautiful that at any other time I would have thought myself the happiest boy on earth, but this was different, this was hell on water. I fully expected the devil to appear in a cloud of boiling steam, complete with pitchfork, pointing at my nakedness and guffawing at the whole situation he had obviously engineered.

Just when I thought I would die of embarrassment I noticed Erin, the minx, with something in her hand. She held it aloft and waved it around. "Lost something?", she laughed!

"NO!", it couldn't be, could it?

"If they're not yours, I'll throw them away", she smiled wickedly and tossed them in the air, only for them to land in Clodagh's outstretched hand.

"Must be somebody else's trunks", she smirked, looking around and shouting, "Anybody lost their trunks?" Waving them like a flag at the end of a Grand Prix.

There has been many a night I have woken in a sweat to find I have endured a repeating nightmare based on this one experience. It is never resolved, leaving me embarrassed and a young boy again even now at my ripe old age.

Both girls, on an unseen cue, disappeared beneath the surface, my hands went down with the speed of light to cover my shrunken treasures but too late.

They resurfaced, giggly to each other. "Not much to make a fuss about, is there?", offered Clodagh, whilst Erin added, "Changing into a girl, are we?"

I really wished a whale would come along, a highly unlikely event this close to shore, but I desperately hoped the whale would swallow me whole, taking me far away! Somewhere, where I could live out my days, hiding from this humiliation.

The girls then started to throw their prized possession to each other, lobbing it over my head, high enough to stop me retrieving it. This seemed to be the best game they had ever played and they pursued it with gusto. There was only one thing to do and I propelled myself into the air, raising most of my body out of the water, catching my now prized possession and taking it down and into the depths, where I awkwardly but swiftly girded my loins, guarding my precious privacy.

"Hurray!", was the cheer from the girls, as my struggle was completed. Erin swam over to me and to my wonder and surprise, she kissed me and at that moment I completely forgot about my prior problem.

Before I could say anything, she turned and swam swiftly away from me. I was unaware that Clodagh was now swimming towards me and I felt a tap on my shoulder, I turned around and bugger me if I didn't receive another kiss. Was this heaven trying to make up for putting me through hell earlier, or was it serendipity fighting back? With a kick Clodagh was gone, following Erin back to the beach and I was once again left to myself out in the blue.

I never did find out whether they had planned it or whether

it was spontaneous but either way, I was a very happy though confused and embarrassed young lad.

My only question is, why does my nightmare never get that far? Only ever getting to the point of most embarrassment just as I wake.

By the time I got back to shore Erin and Clodagh were back with Erin's mother and preparing to leave the beach, so I retrieved my dry clothes and changed out of the offending trunks, promising myself that I would never go swimming again without the proper apparel and I never did.

I tried to catch up with them, but they were well ahead and I had to make do with both girls turning to give me a smile. They then linked arms and practically skipped away!

What a day for a daydream! What fuel for a repetitive nightmare!

For the next few days, I made sure I was nowhere near my twinned torturers by using any spare time I had, wandering through the fields, jumping streams, climbing trees and just being a boy. This would prove to be the last summer of my youth before I joined the adult race and started working for a living. For that last precious period, I went my innocent way, just wandering, revisiting and generally exploring the countryside.

One afternoon I was lying in the sun on a grassy slope

overlooking a small river, that gurgled and gulped its way to the open sea and freedom, when I heard a splash that made me sit up abruptly! I immediately came eye to eye with a young girl only yards away. She looked as surprised to see me, as I was her! Her last shot was still hanging in the air, briefly hovering over the water, then skipping along it to the opposite bank! An impressive feat that I thought only boys capable of. (I had a lot to learn!)

"Good shot!", I offered lamely as she lowered her arm, her returning smile beaming straight into my heart.

"Frightened me for a moment!", she said, throwing the stones in her hand to the floor and slapping her hands together to remove any dirt residue. She had quickly regained her composure and came over towards me, sitting down a few feet away, not in the least bit coy. Her long wavy brunette hair splashed over delicate shoulders, perfectly framing a slender face, with ice blue eyes, a petite nose and a perfect mouth. Not that I was staring, of course!

Boys must be like pollen to the bees, the way that pretty girls had come into my life without me searching for them. Here I was sat in the most glorious setting you could imagine, chatting to an enchanting girl who seemed to have little or no self-conscious feelings.

This summer was turning out to be a winner and I was totally unaware that it was because I was starting to grow up.

"Do you live nearby?", I enquired.

"I'm staying at Drakesford Farm, for a while with my aunt and uncle."

"I know Drakesford Farm. I worked there for a while. Lovely couple! Made me feel at home! Used to have a great time with Smacker, their sheepdog. Boy, could he run! I could never keep up with him! And he used to go to sleep at my feet of an evening and could the bugger snore! Sorry! Don't normally swear in front of ladies!"

"I'm not a lady! But I intend to be one, someday!"

"What a worker that dog was. In and out of the sheep, sending them this and that way until they ended up in the precise place the farmer wanted them. I loved that dog and I think he loved me! He was what I missed the most when I had to leave to go back to school."

She was very quiet and her face had a terrible sadness about it. I thought for one moment she was going to cry. Had I said something wrong? Quick! What was it? I saw her take a deep breath and then she said.

 "Smacker's not well. The vet was calling today to look at him." I could see she was crying now, softly and to herself.

"Oh no! Poor Smacker!"

"I loved that dog as well", she sighed. "Known him since he was a puppy and watched them train him. He was always around to greet me, big mucky paws and all. Ruined my clothes".

Quite a conversation killer really, but we bonded in silence and sat there for a while just listening to that little river happily going on its inevitable journey from its sojourn in our little piece of paradise, down to the parental sea.

"My name's Amy."

"Niall."

"I'm going back to the farm; do you want to come with me and visit Smacker?"

"Good idea", I replied, still wondering why I felt as if I had known her a long time.

I offered her my hand and she sprang to her feet; she was much taller than I initially thought, but still quite a bit shorter than the lanky youth I had become this summer.

"You're tall!", she blurted out. Strange that we should both be thinking similarly.

We were in no particular hurry to get back to the farm and for a short while, we even paused in places to admire the scenery, something I would not have done in previous summers, stopping to pick raspberries, growing in abundance and devouring them with a lust that would return every time I ate raspberries in the future, as anyone who knows me will verify.

"Would there ever be a more perfect day?", I thought to myself, temporarily forgetting poor Smacker. Of course there would be other days, but that was in the future and not yet on my timeline.

As if my poor young heart wasn't confused enough, Amy joined Erin and Clodagh on an ever-growing list of 'Friends', threatening to overwhelm me with its intensity.

I felt the desire to kiss her, welling inside me, but surely it was too soon. Thankfully for my turbulent libido, we arrived at the farm.

We went into the house and said hello to Mrs O'Shaughnessy, who gave me a big hug, much to the amusement of Amy and we spent a few lovely moments recalling my time at the farm. I asked about Smacker and with a tear in her eye, she said the vet was with him now. If I wanted to say goodbye, then I needed to hurry.

My heart skipped a beat! I hadn't reckoned on Smacker being that ill. How I didn't cry, I'll never know! I swallowed! Several times! That seemed to help hold back the tears for a few seconds but just as I thought I'd break down, I kept myself in control.

Amy and I sped out of the farmhouse and around to the familiar old barn in the cobbled yard.

Mr O'Shaughnessy was standing inside with the vet, under the light of a lantern. He looked up to see us but he was obviously deep in thought. Smacker was lying beside him, still breathing but obviously in distress, the vet with syringe in hand was about to inject but halted as we entered.

The words were hardly audible and that big tough farmer, used to sending animals to slaughter, was close to tears, but we understood his message and knelt together to smooth the hair on Smacker's head, gently saying our goodbyes, hearts bursting with the enormity of it. Smacker looked at us and licked my hand, recognising me immediately and almost as if to say goodbye. Now there was no holding back! I openly cried without fear of derision, feeling a burgeoning grief overwhelm me. Amy sobbed as well.

The vet looked at Mr O'Shaughnessy, who nodded silently and the syringe was applied gently to Smacker, who slipped away to chase sheep in heaven or so I imagined at the time.

Mr O'Shaughnessy, who had been holding Smacker's head all the while, gently laid him to rest on his blanket in the home he had known and loved all his life.

Amy and I walked out from the gloom in the barn into the bright world outside. The birds were singing, there was noise from cattle and sheep in the field. How could the world possibly be carrying on as normal when a tragedy like this had just happened? But of course, it did! It wouldn't be the last time I looked sorrow in the face and it never got better. The finality of death is something that dominates our lives as we get older, but even as a young lad it reached depths I hardly perceived existed.

I hugged Amy, this young girl I had only just met. It seemed like a lifetime ago and we both sobbed our hearts out unashamedly, clinging together as if life depended on it.

Mrs O'Shaughnessy must have seen us from the farmhouse and came out to comfort us. In the process she asked me to stay for dinner, something I had done frequently in the past, as you know and I gladly agreed. I was certainly in no desire to leave at this moment.

Although meeting Amy was a confusing addition to my friends, she was a very welcome one and she was only here for a day or two more. So, what was the harm? I just had to make sure I didn't use the wrong name when talking to any of them, it was that simple.

If only it was!

Walking back home over the fields, my belly full, the

surroundings rapidly fading as the sun disappeared over the horizon, I was full of hope and excitement. My young heart full to the brim, tears of sorrow for the loss of Smacker and smiles of joy at meeting a girl who unknown to me would soon disappear out of my life forever.

I wonder sometimes, what became of her? I imagine she became a force to be reckoned with, tall and sophisticated, full of life and eager to take on the world, an image I have carried with me for a great many years. I wonder if she will read this book and recognise herself. If she does, I hope she has lived a life as full as I have.

Did she realise the lasting effect she had on me? I doubt it! Maybe she reminisces about visiting her aunt and uncle, at the farm. Perhaps she tells her grandchildren about Smacker. Leaving out the sorrow of his death.

Maybe the image of a ruddy young Irish lad pops into her head, for a split second, conjuring up childhood days, when she threw stones across the stream. Who knows? Perhaps she may think of the second time we met? I haven't told you about that yet, have I? Oops! Getting ahead of myself. Again! (It's on the next page.)

I did eventually arrive home! Mum was a little worried about where I was, but with all the others running about creating mayhem she would have been distracted anyway. She listened as I told her about my visit to the farm and the fate of poor old Smacker. My sisters listened in and were soon in tears, even though they had never set eyes on him. This was partly from my telling of the story, but they also remembered my talking about him, when I worked on the farm.

There was no TV in those days so everyday stories about what we had been up to, were pounced upon by my sisters. The boys more or less had a free rein, but the girls did not, so they always hung on every word of our exploits!

Thunder and lightning paid us a visit that late evening, but thankfully, not until a good time after I arrived safely home. My father was not in the least bit worried about where I had been until so late, knowing my penchant for wandering. He never questioned me as he sat in his chair, pipe in hand, trying his best to ignore the hullabaloo that was ever present in our house.

With little time to dwell on my own thoughts until I lay in bed, when my brothers had finished with their fighting and bickering, the house relieved to be silent for a while, hugging me, keeping me safe in a world that was becoming more and more real to me.

I had arranged to meet Amy the next day, but it poured with rain, non-stop. It would have been quicker to go by boat ... if I had one, so I sat around or did odd jobs for my mother, all the time wondering what Amy was doing and whether she was thinking of me. Finding myself staring out of the window, lost in thought, I felt a sadness eating away at me.

It was a new feeling, a sort of longing that somehow gnawed at my whole body, a depression of sorts that laid a black cloak over my normally happy soul and kept out the light. Knowing Amy for such a short time couldn't be the source of my melancholy, could it? I didn't feel like this when I left Erin or Clodagh. I did miss them, but this was something much, much deeper, a sadness that overwhelmed me and darkened the world.

I wish my older self could have talked to the young me and offered some words of advice. I had no-one to talk to or ask advice of. All my siblings were younger than me and I never even considered my parents as sounding boards. So, I endured in silence! Had she left to go back to her home? Would I ever be able to find her again? Questions bombarded me, crowding my mind!

That was a long day! An even longer night was to follow, as I lay in bed listening to the storm outside battering the old house! I felt like I was dying inside! Nothing had ever felt this bad before. I would rather have faced the tyrannical headmaster in his worst guise as a torturer than go through that heartache! Sleep was a welcome visitor that was late arriving but welcomed with open arms.

Eventually the rain stopped. A new morning was beckoning and the world outside seemed brighter and full of adventure, even if precipitation still dripped from everything. As soon as I was able to escape from the house and my daily duties, I ran, yes RAN, hoping to find Amy where we had planned to meet. I slipped and slithered, as I splashed my way across the fields, a day late, but still hoping she'd be there waiting. She wasn't!

Deflated and generally low, I climbed a gnarly old oak tree that stretched out over the river below, sitting with my feet dangling over the fast-flowing water as it cascaded over the rocks. Oak trees, drying in the sunshine, can sing it seems. The wind gently coaxing the leaves on the still flourishing branches to caress me with a silky symphony of white noise, filling up my ears with melodies, soft and sweet, gentle as a whispering breeze. I was almost asleep when I was suddenly aware of someone nearby, pacing up and down, it was Amy.

"Hello down there", I shouted and watched her jump at the sudden intrusion into her thoughts. Laughing is not good when you are suspended above a river and I nearly lost my balance, grabbing on with both hands to steady myself.

"Careful", she cried. "I'm not diving in after you if you fall in the river".

With the agility of youth, I swung out of the tree and down onto the bank, to stand before her.

"I didn't think you were coming!", she offered.

"I felt the same, that's why I climbed the tree".

"I've been here for ages. Were you asleep?"

"Of course not!", I answered assuredly, although suspecting I may have been.

There was a moment when I wanted to grab her and kiss her but it passed whilst my faint heart pondered my next move. No reclining on the grassy bank today, the ground was still soaking from the previous day, so we walked, keeping to the path and avoiding large puddles. Two children, chatting and getting to know each other, eager to learn all there was to know. She loved books, especially those on America where she planned to live in the future. Films were also high on the list, romance and adventure being amongst her favourites.

The wide-open spaces and the promise of a fabulous life called to her like a siren on the shore, just as it did to me. We were kindred spirits!

Me? Well, my desire, as you know already, was also to

travel. I talked of standing on the beach and watching the ships sailing over to Liverpool, but my ambitions seemed to pale compared to hers. She was so together. So focused. Girls grow up much quicker than boys and it was obvious that she had a sophistication that I was yet to develop and that she was out of my league. I was yet to learn my worth in the world and it hurt to feel out of my depth, but it was another real-life lesson that I was unaware of at the time.

We paused at a small stone bridge, over the river. It had been damaged in the storm the previous night and in need of urgent repair before it collapsed into the swollen water. You could see right through the floor of the bridge, at the angry water cursing it from below, for daring to stand aloft. (At least for the time being!)

There was no way we were crossing that way and she turned back and walked straight into me. To this day, I have no idea whether her action was on purpose but we stood very close to each other, eyes darting and cheeks reddening, until she said, "Kiss me then".

My young heart did a backflip and I leaned forward and did as she requested. A gentle, almost butterfly like connection that was obviously less than she was expecting, as she leaned into me again and the pressure increased. Sweet as the icing on a cake, warm as … what am I talking about, you can't describe it in words! Most of you readers will have gone through this experience yourselves, use your imagination!

Think back to when you were thirteen going on fourteen and in love, or at least what masqueraded as love at the time. Yes, this wasn't my first kiss and yes there would be times later in my life when it wouldn't stop at a kiss but at the time this was as good as it gets and I was loving it.

Without realising it, my arms were wrapped around her and her body was pulled in close. No surprisingly, my body reacted in a fashion I would become familiar with, but there was no escalation, no fumbling, just innocence, enveloped in a warm embrace that has stayed with me always.

We held hands and walked for miles, exploring the glorious Irish countryside, planning to meet up in Dublin when we were a bit older. Talking of America and how it must be to live in such a country, one we had only seen through the eyes of Hollywood with its skewed version of life and love.

Idyllic days like that burn themselves into the memory, lying dormant until smells, sounds or sights, trigger instant recall and we flash back to relive precious moments in time lost to others but retained for a lifetime, nestled in obscurity buried deep but waiting to be caressed one final time.

Wishing that day would never end did no good at all,

because inevitably it did, closing too quickly on a short romance between children on the threshold of life, parted after the briefest of time by life's cruel twists and turns, never to meet again, except in my memory.

That last kiss and standing at the edge of the field before I climbed the style, tore at my heart insistently, urging me to go back but there was an inevitability to our parting that made me resist the urge to return and so I simply disappeared into the night, never to return to her.

If only! What a huge preface to a statement that is! How many amongst us has said it at some time or another? If only I had taken that job! If only I hadn't taken that job! The permutations are limitless.

One statement I think that would resonate with most people is, "If only I could go back in time and experience it all over again!" Of course, we can't, except that is, when we open our memory banks and concentrate on that long ago time when the world was perfect, or at least we thought it was. Anything was possible! We thought we would live for ever! To experience a kiss, a touch, a smile, an embrace. Once again be as happy as we have ever been! "If only!"

The next day was spent moping around the house, until my mum sent me out into the world, sensing I believe the melancholy that had shown its ugly head, once again! She believed that taking in the air of a fresh Irish summer's day would lighten my mood. I strolled down to my goto place, the beach where the inevitable footie was happening in its usual shambolic fashion, with lots of shouting and swearing, unless the local Father was passing, in which case everything went quiet until he was out of earshot. No-one wanted something being said at Church about the use of foul language, especially when the ecclesiastical stare was concentrated on us.

I didn't feel like joining in but got drawn into it when Patrick Mulligan called me a poof. I wasn't sure what a poof was, I doubt whether Patrick did, but it sounded offensive so I clouted him one.

We ended up rolling around on the beach, coincidentally just as Father Michael came strolling into sight.

You have never seen a fight stop so fast and football take place with such reverence that even the pious Father smiled. He knew far more about us than we realised at the time, chuckling to himself as he walked by, passing a blessing on us and going on his merry way. I didn't know until years later that he had volunteered to take the word to front line troops during the Second World War. "A hero without a gun", was one remark made about him and "The bravest man I know", was another from someone who saw him giving the last rites to dying soldiers whilst under fire, with total disregard for his own safety. A legend in

Ballytreeny and much revered.

Our dispute forgotten, Patrick and I spat into our palms and then shook hands! Then we raced each other, chasing after the ball, whacking it as hard as we could on every opportunity, spitting sand from our mouths and insulting anybody who got in the way. Just kept running and running, until we collapsed in a heap, exhausted but happy and I forgot for a while.

Much calmer and understandably exhausted, I walked the short distance home, slowly drinking in the events of the day, returning just as McDaffy's cows were being herded back to the milking sheds, shitting all over the place and forcing me to dance around the patties as we called them.

My father must have seen me coming and I suspect mum had told him about my mood because he put his arm around my shoulder, something he rarely did. "Come on son! You can help me mow the lawns at the Lodge".

My father had an evening job at 'The Lodge' where he would cut the huge lawns and tend the flower beds. The lady of the house only came there occasionally, treating it as a retreat from the city when she became bored with urban life.

Never staying long, she preferred to flit in and just as quickly flit out. Her existence was as alien to us as living on the moon. Of course, the upside was that she provided work for the locals and by that a means of putting food on the table and we were all grateful to her, but I doubt she even realised.

The house was huge by my standards and I couldn't believe there were so many bedrooms. Balconies overlooked the immaculate lawns, where infrequent guests would marvel at the vista, not really knowing how much work it took to maintain it and having no knowledge at all about the everyday plight of the working man.

I did wonder if I would ever own a property like it, but daydreaming, as my father would say, would not buy it for me. He of course was right, but hard work and a good deal of Irish luck did buy me a large house with a beautiful garden, membership of a fancy golf club and stars for friends. That, however, was a long way in the future and I set to picking up the grass cuttings and transporting them to the massive compost heap, out of sight in a distant corner of the gardens.

There was a serene feeling about working in those beautiful acres, calmness pervaded the place, the direct opposite of my usual way of life. Stopping for a moment I gazed around at all the wonder and caught a look of contentment on my father's face. It wasn't something I had been aware of before. He was obviously in his element, here amongst the blooms, being paid to do a job he would do for nothing.

It was a principle I tried to incorporate into my own job seeking, not always succeeding but striving to, none the less.

We didn't see eye to eye at the best of times and later in life we knocked heads often!

For that rare moment, I felt a connection with him. He had taken the time to show me his world outside the family, somewhere where he was just a man, not a husband or father. Which was his real identity? I'm not sure, but most of us have multiple personalities. The one we show prospective employers. Another for a person we have just met! When we are driving our cars! And plenty more! They all merge to create the complex people we are.

Walking home with my father after grafting with him was special to me. I was the eldest and I knew he was relying on me to bring in some much-needed money in the not-too-distant future. That evening it was just a boy and his dad, bonding over hard work and a job well done, striding along, our chests out and our heads held high. a father and his firstborn son declaring to the world, "Look at us. We're not afraid of hard work and we are proud Irishmen".

Writing this book has made me think deeply about the time I have spent on this earth, the things I have done right and the many more things I have done wrong. Some memories are easier to recall than others and there may yet be revelations I was not expecting. I was still at an age endowed with an innocence that prevented me from seeing the bigger picture, the poverty, the inhuman conditions that some had to endure. The enormous wealth of the few and the broken promises made to the masses.

So it was, with my unknowingly fettered eyes, I viewed the world with wonder and expectation, alive to my own experiences without an inkling that I was just about to step out of this protected zone and plunged deeply into the maelstrom of real life.

That last boyhood summer, with its treasure of experiences, disappeared swiftly after that memorable evening with my father. I briefly saw Erin on occasion, walking to church or shopping with her mother but we were never alone. Unable to further explore the emotions of youth! It would take almost a year before we would be together again and by that time I would change immensely and so would she.

The dreaded school days would soon re-enter my life and taunt me with short comings and exasperations, but it wouldn't intrude for long because fate was about to make its indelible mark.

3. UNEXPLODED BOMBS, SCHOOL, SNOWBALLS, GHOSTS & GRAMDMA

Summer holidays were rapidly coming to an end and school disaster days just around the corner, so it was important for us to pack in as many adventures as we could before the dreaded day.

Growing up as the eldest of four boys can be trying at times. First, you get blamed for everything, which in my case was mainly justified, but second and hardest of all you must let them traipse around while you play with your mates. It was my job making sure they got to kick the ball every now and then! Mind you, only just enough times to make sure they didn't cry, embarrassing you in front of everybody.

One memorable day, I was due to meet the guy's up Shiloh Lane, with the purpose of exploring the haunted house that stood just outside the village. It was rumoured that the house crumpled one night, crushing all the people inside, their ghosts still walking amongst the ruins. Local fact had it that the house had been built on top of a cave that subsequently collapsed pulling the house down, so no-one ever bothered trying to rebuild it.

All boys are obsessed by ghosts and exploring and I was no

exception, so when it was suggested that we investigate the ruins, I was in. There was only one problem, the bane of my life, my youngest brother Pádraig had to come with me by order of my mother, who was taking the girls shopping for new school clothes.

Younger than me by four years, he could barely keep up and I invariably had to carry him if we went any distance. He also seemed to pee more times than humanly possible, but I couldn't take the chance of taking him home wet, so he frequently delayed any expedition enough to cause grumbles amongst my intrepid comrades.

The only advantage in taking him with me, was the girls stopping us to look at Pádraig! He was a beautiful child, blond curly hair, bright blue eyes and a smile to charm the angels, as my grandmother used to say (remind me to tell you more about her later) but on this particular day there was a complete absence of females so he was not much use.

Shiloh Lane was not much more than a cart track in those days, leading to a small farm about a mile past the haunted house and so traffic along it was more or less non-existent. Why anyone would build a house out here away from the village was a mystery to us and only served to whet our appetite for adventure. A typical farm lane, it twisted and meandered like spaghetti thrown against the wall, over flood streams, the occasional forest of cow pats and horse shit (there was no cute name for it) which were skipped over with great skill whilst holding our noses.

The ruins could be seen, over the hedgerows, from about two hundred metres and our sense of impending adventure swiftly took over. Roger, the daredevil in our gang started the stampede by running as fast as he could towards our target destination. He was quickly followed by everyone else except me and my shadow Pádraig.

Tethered to my brother by maternal warnings, I watched as the guys disappeared around the corner, yelling and screaming at the top of their voices like a barrage of baboons. I was not happy but there was little I could do and anyway he needed another pee! Where did it keep coming from? I made sure he didn't drink a lot but that made absolutely no difference whatsoever.

We did eventually get there but all was silent and the boys were nowhere to be seen.

There was an eerie silence about the place, apart from the odd pigeon flying in and out of the increasingly fractured roof, that sloped as if in preparation for total annihilation. In the movies of course it was always a crow that was the harbinger of death, but for me a pigeon would suffice! They were almost the same size!

Where had the guys disappeared too?

Did the house eat them?

My imagination was now running wild with theories! We had recently seen a film called "Dracula" which frightened the crap out of us, although none of us would admit it! We walked home in groups, constantly peering into the shadows, convinced we were being watched. This wreck of a place would be perfect for Dracula to hide out in! No one came here! At least not until now! How I wished I had brought some garlic with me. The stuff grew wild in the woods! Should I go get some?

I told Pádraig to stay where he was and slowly entered the ruins, carefully checking around corners and listening for any ghostly sounds that might be emanating from an otherworldly source. All was deadly quiet, not even a bird singing or a pigeon cooing. For a moment I wondered if I had gone deaf.

The roof had almost disappeared and daylight shone through the partially collapsed floor above my head, casting an eerie beam of light that fed evil shadows into every corner of the room.

This was getting scary as the tension rose inside of me and it was heightened even more as a muffled sound echoed around the walls. It sounded like "Help", but it was so quiet I couldn't be sure.

Cold shivers started to run up and down my back as I heard it again. "Help" but fainter than the first. Thinking my theory about Dracula was spot on, I took a deep breath and backed slowly out of the ruins, carefully scanning the interior for spirit dwellers or blood sucking vampires. I could still hear the faint voice "Help".

Bursting out through the layer of greenery around the doorway, I tasted the fresh air rushing into my lungs, as I once more entered the realm of the living, spitting out the dust that had coated my tongue and invaded my nose. Still looking back at the house, expecting to be dragged back in at any moment, I whispered (I have no idea why I whispered but I remember doing it) "Pádraig!" There was no answer! "Pádraig!" I said it this time a little louder. "Pádraig!" I was shouting now and starting to panic. He was not where I had left him! Losing my friends was one thing, but losing my little brother would land me in deep shit!

"Pádraig!" I now screamed. What if that was him, I could hear inside the ruins? What if he was calling for my help? I had to go back in there and search for him, so that is exactly what I did.

Discarding my fear of ghosts and demons was preferable to facing my mother and telling her I had lost her precious baby!

Standing in that filthy mausoleum, sweat starting to mix with the ever-present dust, I stood and listened once more.

"Help!" I could hear it again, still faint, but clear enough to understand, but it didn't sound like Pádraig. Then from another direction I heard. "Help me!" Much louder and clearer, with a warbling effect that reminded me of another horror film I had seen recently. This was getting bad now, especially when a third voice, apparently from upstairs joined in the ghostly chorus.

"Help me Niall!" Hang on! How did the ghost know my name? Then the penny dropped! "You bastards! Come out I know you're there!"

Laughter suddenly erupted from all corners as the 'ghosts' revealed themselves.

"Got you sucker!" Roger shouted at the top of his voice, with the rest each making some sort of derogatory remark about my lack of courage.

"Alright you sods! You got me! Now where's Pádraig?"

"He was with you last time we saw him", chimed Roger.

"Come on! Stop pissing about! He's only little!"

"Honest Niall. We haven't seen him. Where was he last time you saw him?"

"Outside! I told him to wait there, but when I went out, he was gone".

There was no looking out for fiends in the shadows in my panicked flight into the outer world. I even tripped as I flung myself out of the doorway, almost disappearing into the thick hedge that was on a mission to block all access to this devilish, deserted dwelling.

Roger and the other reprobates slowly emerged from their hiding places, smirks now gone, replaced with worry for my errant brother. We reluctantly went back into the devil's domain and searched every conceivable hiding place, but he was nowhere to be found.

"Perhaps he went home?" someone offered, as we stood once more out in the sunlight.

"Doubt he would do that on his own", I said. "Let's search the ruins quickly. Roger you're the fastest. Run down the lane and see if you can find him".

With the plan in motion, we carefully looked around the outside of the ruins. It occurred to me that if he had entered, he couldn't have come through the front as I would have seen him, so I looked for a side entrance.

The house seemed to be in a worse state on the left side and I had trouble climbing over large chunks of masonry, so I figured he would never be able to climb over the obstructions, so we concentrated on places a small person could get into.

Someone, I forget who, spotted a tiny opening that seemed to be a semi-collapsed doorway, just about visible through the vegetation that had sprung up all around. Crawling on my hands and knees I could just about fit into the space. If the little sod was in here, I would be very grateful but I'd give him a thick ear when I found him. My knees were cut and bleeding, my neck was scratched by a convoluted briar, woven by nature into a natural barrier and my hair was full of spider webs! All his fault! Wait until I found him!

When I eventually made it through, I could see steps going down into what looked like a cellar, so I called out his name and almost immediately heard a reply. "Niall?".

"Come on out!", I shouted in anger.

"I can't! I'm stuck! My feet are caught on something".

"What were you doing down there?"

"I was exploring, like you said we would".

"I'm going to get the torch".

Back out I crawled! More cuts! More spider webs! My anger was growing with each laceration.

"Who has the torch?" I enquired, panting and rubbing the spiders out of my hair, not even bothering about my knees.

We did bring a torch! I knew that much. Roger was the only one to own such a thing and have batteries. But where was Roger? Of course! He was gone down the lane as fast as he could go. Probably back in the village by now! "Crap!"

To my surprise, Roger appeared, as if by magic! He had run a long way down the lane and met someone walking up from the village who confirmed Pádraig had not gone that way, so he came back. "Hurray!"

With the torch in hand, I crawled back into the cellar doorway where with a bit of wriggling I forced my way through and onto the descending steps.

Sitting there in the gloom I realised I was blocking the light from the door, but there was still some light coming in through the hole in the floor above. Obviously, there was enough light to tempt my daredevil sibling into carrying on regardless! With the extra light from the torch, I soon spotted Pádraig. He was just below me and crying softly. "Give me your hand and I'll pull you up", I told him but when I tried it was obvious, he was stuck firm. So, I climbed down as close to him as possible and tried to shift the rubbish around him.

"I fell in from the top of the stairs and when I tried to get out, I got my foot stuck", he cried.

"Don't worry, I'll soon have you out", I said with big brother authority.

I shouldn't have spoken so soon! When I found what his foot was trapped under, I froze. It was an unexploded bomb! I had seen pictures of bombs, so I knew what it was but it seemed huge, much bigger in real life. There was no way I could tell him what he was trapped by, without terrifying him, so I made a joke that it was a large pudding bowl that had fallen from the kitchen above and he believed me. Innocence of youth!

My only option was to remove some of the rubble under his foot and hope he would be released, without disturbing the lethal weapon in the room. The only reassuring thing was that it hadn't exploded when it went through the roof and the floors above so it should be quite safe now. Of course, thankfully, I knew nothing about how bombs deteriorate over time, so ignorance was bliss.

Our only saving grace was the material under his foot was wood, rotten from years of water seeping in from above and fragile in its composition. So, I made short work of it and gradually freed his little foot without disturbing the mother-load.

Picking him up in my arms was comforting for the both of

us and I slowly shuffled on my backside, up to the top of the steps where I let him clamber through first. I heard a loud cheer and clapping from outside as I wriggled my way out from our potential tomb.

Standing in the open air I suddenly realised what had just happened, feeling physically sick, shaking and sweating profusely, even as I ushered everyone away from our ghostly mission house. They were reluctant to go, but no-one wanted to argue with me when I was that determined!

After I sat Pádraig down safely a safe distance from the house, I took the guys to one side and told them what I had found. Of course, they didn't believe me, after all they had just tricked me so they quite fairly assumed I was getting my own back. No amount of swearing on various people and events could convince them that I was telling the truth. Roger being an alpha decided to look for himself, despite my warning that he was being stupid. It seemed an age till he appeared from the distant ruins but appear he did and we noticed he was running at full tilt. "The bastard was telling the truth. It's a bloody bomb! A big un!"

At this news it suddenly turned into the Grand National with runners tearing off and jumping anything that got in the way. If it hadn't been so serious, I could have wet myself laughing as they hurdled sheep and fences alike.

Pádraig was still totally unaware of what was going on and

just assumed it was a game, so we quickly followed the others back to civilization.

I did tell the local bobby about the bomb but asked him not to tell anybody that I found it, as it would get me in trouble and he of all people knew I had been in my share over the years, so he complied and said it was an anonymous tip.

I made Pádraig swear a pinky oath that he would not tell anyone about our little adventure, warning him that if he did, I would send the Boogey Man to get him in his sleep! Poor little sod probably didn't sleep for weeks, but it worked!

Stood in the garden a few days later I heard the most stupendous bang and I swear the ground shook. My mother came running out of the house and asked what had happened. I lied and said I had no idea. After all the truth would have got me in deep doo doo, so, I feigned ignorance and got away with it.

It was not until many years later at a family party that I related the true tale of the bang we heard and my mother said, "Where's your father's belt when I need it?" and then fell about laughing.

Ballytreeny was a busy fishing port in those days. I loved to walk down to the harbour and watch the men bring in the days catch. The sight of those tiny trawlers bobbing about, waiting to grab their berth was spectacular to my eyes, almost jumping out of the water to say, "My turn! My turn!", like tiny children impatient to be seen.

I can still smell the pungent aroma of fish, diesel and sweat that permeated the air and clung to any clothes you were wearing. My mother used to say, "Been to the harbour again, I smell!", followed by a stifled laugh as she pretended to hold her nose.

There was always a bustle about the area. Everyone had a job to do, or they would be miles away. No one went there for recreation! Except for me of course, but I did expect to be working there in the near future, so I did have a good excuse.

The fishermen worked long hard hours, but you could see the sense of pride in their eyes as they humped the boxes of fresh fish onto the quayside. I marvelled at all the different varieties of fish they caught.

Fate stuck its wanton neck again, as one of the skippers, who short of a man, saw me watching them. As I have said before I was a big lad for my age and he undoubtedly thought I was older, so he asked me to help carry the catch, which I did with relish.

These guys were heroes in my book, braving a treacherous sea, tossing about on a small boat, many miles from shore, without much hope of rescue if things turned bad, as they frequently did. I held them in awe and I expect it showed.

The boxes of fish were heavy but I got stuck into the job and the work was soon completed.

I wasn't expecting to be paid and was about to walk away, when the skipper came over and thanked me, giving me as much fish as I could carry, mainly cod, haddock or mackerel. He showed me how to pass a string through the gills of the fish and out the mouth, that way I could carry up to 20 fish.

Walking back home, fish over my shoulders, I felt like a real fisherman. People waved as they saw me coming up from the harbour, no doubt thinking I was fresh in off the trawlers and I did nothing to discourage the assumption.

Imagine the surprise at home when I arrived with all those fish. We ate well that night and after that, I made regular visits to the harbour to help the skipper and his crew.

One day the skipper, having loaded me with fish, asked me when I was due to leave school. I told him, not until the next year when I turned fourteen. He said that when I left school, I should contact him because there would be a job waiting for me on his trawler.

I was beside myself with joy as I took the fish home, this was my big break, a chance to ride the sea on a real trawler.

A romantic view of the life no doubt but one I was destined to do.

I told my parents what had been said! My dad looked at me good and long, knowing full well how difficult and how dangerous the life of a trawler man was, saying if it's what you want to do when you leave school, it's alright with me. My mother turned away, so I just assumed she was ok with it as well, not knowing it would have been one of her last choices. There had been a few untimely deaths in her family of young men on trawlers, but she kept it from me.

Fate seemed eternally on the march, as my father met up, by accident, with grumpy McGrundy and they inevitably talked about me. Old grumpy said, without prompting from my father, that to be honest the sooner I left, the better.

When my father told me I was elated! It was the answers to all my wishes! For once I couldn't wait to go to school the next day.

I grabbed the first chance I could, to talk to Mr McGrundy! At the end of the school day, I stayed behind until all the other pupils had left the classroom. Old grumpy was still cleaning the blackboard, almost lost in a cloud of chalk dust. I took a deep breath and approached him, just as he was cleaning the chalk residue from his glasses.

"Excuse me, sir. My father said he spoke to you the other day about my leaving school."

"Yes, Niall. We had a long conversation about you! Seems you want to leave and to be truthful with you, I think it is your best option. Normally I would promote learning as a pathway to success, but I think your journey lies in another direction. I have no idea what it is, but I doubt it will be boring! Go live your life your own way! I'm sure you will, at some stage, regret not paying more attention at school but you have a lifetime ahead of you to make up for it! Learning is not just for children! We all carry on learning throughout our lives, even doddery old codgers like me! Go seek your fortune or whatever it is you plan to do. I won't stand in your way. You still have a few weeks to go, so maybe you'll use them wisely. Knowing you, as I do, I very much doubt you will."

For once he seemed genuinely pleased for me and probably just a little bit pleased for himself to get rid of a complete pain in the arse that upset his class almost every day.

Walking home from school that day, I was full of mixed emotions. I was ecstatic that I could at last leave school but a sudden dread filled me with apprehension. Although I hated the place, it felt safe. All my friends were there. I had seen them almost every day for eight years and now I was unlikely to see any of them again for a long time, maybe never. Gone would be the school holidays when I was free to roam. Also gone would be the afternoons after school, when we played football on the beach, or caddied at the golf course. Erin would stay on a school and grow away from me, probably going off to University or something. I would no longer be a child.

Suddenly I felt the tears well up and I sobbed. My knees bent and I gradually sank to the ground, huddled over, bereft.

Father Michael sat down beside on the ground. He said nothing to me but I knew he was there and drew strength from his presence. I leaned against him, my tears still falling. His offer of a clean hankie was gratefully received, I dried my face the best I could and then blew my nose several times. For some reason he declined the return of the hankie and so I stuffed it in my pocket. Not once did he press me for a reason for the state I was in. When I was calmer, he stood, then placing his hand on my shoulder, blessed me, before walking slowly away.

After school, the next day, I ran down to the harbour to watch for the boats coming in. I couldn't wait to tell the skipper that I could leave at Christmas and there was a moment when I wondered if the skipper might have been humouring me.

It turned out he was very glad to have me on board and I

ran back home as quickly as possible to give everyone the good news. I had a job! They already knew I was leaving school. Two wins and no losses!

Just a few weeks to go until Christmas and my great escape, so not a lot could go wrong at school, could it. Could it? I should have known better, the devil on my shoulder wouldn't let me leave without at least one more skirmish with authority.

Snow was a regular visitor to Ballytreeny in the winter and there were no snow ploughs in the area. If the way was blocked, you had to dig through it yourself or climb over it. It was a pain to most folk, but to the children it furnished a super playground. Snowball fights were epic with rival 'gangs' stockpiling supplies of ready-made ammo, then hiding in wait until some poor unsuspecting victim wandered past. It would rain snowballs for a moment and no-one was safe.

Strategy was a major factor and we would try and outmanoeuvre our foe by sending in a decoy to draw their fire whilst sneaking up behind them. As soon as they had exhausted their supply of snowballs, we would open fire and then retreat quickly before they could make more. Of course, they did the same to us and it was anybody's guess who came off worst, but the main object was achieved, we all had a great time. It wasn't just the boys either, quite a few of the local girls, my sisters included would be 'volunteered' into making snowballs for the boys to throw, even throwing some themselves if we started to be overrun.

All the above was of course played out after school. "No snowballs to be thrown on the school premises" was the rule, break it and you were in trouble. Never one to worry about rules, I must admit to throwing the odd snowball at school. I was always extremely careful to make sure the teachers were nowhere near me at the time. Being a deadly shot was a hard-earned reputation and I was not about to lose my status, so I practiced as much as possible, head on a swivel, taking aim and firing.

Best laid plans and all that, but my reign of terror came to an abrupt halt, not through any miscalculation or unobserved teacher presence but because I hadn't yet developed the ability to see around corners.

Snowball in hand, pounded until it was a solid projectile, I surveyed the savanna for wandering wildebeest, like a lion looking for lunch and spotted one, just emerging from a waterhole and preening itself in the midday sun. I took aim, deadly and efficiently, dragging my arm back and preparing my shoulder muscles to unleash my deadly ammunition. I calculated and suitably adjusted for a crosswind, gave the order and dispatched the missile.

It's at moments like this when the world seems to go in

slow motion. Words were strangled in my throat! Desperate attempts to retrieve the winged object in flight were thwarted by the laws of motion someone once told me about and I instantly wished I had listened more. I was relegated to an observer of the upcoming target change. Just as the snowball left the comfort of my hand to hurtle onwards, old grumpy himself, no other, came joyfully around the corner of the building, oblivious to the onrushing comet heading his way.

I remember distinctly the smile on his face, it was a rare sight and either he had just received a pay rise or he had a recently successful bowel movement. Whatever the reason, he was smiling to himself, his mouth open, as if to congratulate himself on some high achievement! Open just enough to almost swallow the snowball as it hit its unintended and completely unaware target full in the face, or to be more accurate, right in his gob!

My arm was now frozen in the position of post projection and I felt my own jaw sag, dropping as if unconnected to my brain. Our eyes met, his red with rage, bowel movement a thing of the distant past, mine shrinking by the second as the realisation overwhelmed my lion's role and left me more like a deer in the headlights.

"O'Sullivan!! You little turd!" he spluttered. That's not fair I thought, I'm not allowed to swear, so why should he?

There was no point in running, he knew where I lived and I didn't want to risk him telling my father and then ruining my leaving plans, so I dropped my shooting arm to my side and waited for the onslaught.

For once I was saved by the school bell calling us back to class. I meekly joined the crocodile wending its way upriver to the relative safety of the classroom.

"You're for it now".

"Get a book down your trousers".

"Wouldn't wanna be in your shoes".

The consensus was that I would be condemned to the firing squad, blindfolded and executed, my blood running red through the mantle of snow carpeting the playground.

I sat there on my hands, as if to protect them from the oncoming assault they were bound to receive. The left hand blaming the right hand for the deed and the right hand blaming the brain, whilst the brain ... you get the gist of my dilemma, panic was setting in once more, my go-to feeling in this type of situation having been there so many, many times.

Enter McGrumpy, his mouth area bright red, either he had been eating pupils again or it was where my wayward warhead had smacked into him at terminal velocity.

I swear smoke was coming out of his ears and he was snorting like a brahma bull about to enter the arena. He took down the weapon of class destruction that hung on the wall, as a deterrent to all miscreants and swished it, time and time again, even once whacking it hard against his own leg and showing no sign of pain. There was a rumour he had lost both his legs in the war and that he had steel replacements fitted made from recycled fighter planes, but this couldn't be true, could it?

I was sweating in places that I previously had no idea could contain sweat glands, but sure enough little rivulets of water began to descend from all quarters until my socks were a soggy mess.

"O'Sullivan!!" the dreaded name call, only made by a judge wearing a small black hat, rang out across the classroom.

"Here! Now!" the command punctuated by more swishes of the disciple of doom, the horror of hands, the pummelling of palms … you get the point. I was now ready to shit myself to add to the watery mess in my shoes.

Standing up took most of my willpower and the rest focussed on a last-minute plan to run out the door, although that route was blocked by the headmaster who had sidled in on this one act drama. Step by slow step I approached my fearful fate, rubbing my hands down the legs of my trousers in the forlorn hope that it would decrease the upcoming pain, like prisoners to the guillotine, not even a last request being granted.

McGrumpy stood a couple of feet from me and looked up, yes, by now at thirteen and a half I was already quite a bit taller than him, my shoulders were wider, my hands bigger and maybe this swayed him. I have no idea. He launched into a monologue that has stayed with me ever since.

Whether he had thought about it before he came in to the classroom I'll never know but I'll relate his words to you and you can be the judge of whether he could possibly have composed it on the spot, which I believe would be the work of a genius, or he had prepared it, tested it and revised it, before stepping over the threshold, which still would have taken a mind far more erudite than the one I and most of the other pupils gave him credit for.

"O'Sullivan, you are the most frustrating pupil I have ever had the misfortune to attempt to teach and I say attempt because teaching has to be a two-way street or it becomes lecturing. You have successfully frustrated my best efforts, honed on hundreds of pupils over a great deal of years. Shrugging off multiple punishments as if they were badges of honour, causing mayhem in what I have always regarded as a place of knowledge and generally disrupting the flow of normal school life to a point where it has become unsustainable with your presence.

If we could have drafted you into Hitler's army the war might have been over in months with the chaos you would have caused. God help the rest of the world when you leave this hallowed ground! It is blissfully unaware that you are coming and totally unprepared.

I sincerely hope you are ready for this next adventure of yours, but whether you are ready or not, today you are on your way. The headmaster and I are convinced, there is little else we can teach you. Maybe this last talk will resonate down the years and have an impact on your impulsive behaviour.

You will regret, I'm sure, that you have neglected your education, others around you will sparkle with knowledge and you may flounder.

Concepts based on acquired knowledge will be lost on your uninformed mind and you will, if you want to succeed in life, need to make a belated effort to catch up with the civilised world.

We have done all that we could! We will undoubtedly learn from this experience! I just hope you do the same. Please pack up your personal belongings and leave this classroom for the final time.

Whatever you do in life, be good and ask yourself, would I like it if I was on the receiving end."

With those final words, Mr McGrundy left the stage, because it really was a proper speech, one I have permanently installed in a place of honour.

The headmaster followed out the door without a backward glance at me and then the class was in uproar.

I was struck dumb by the profound words of my erstwhile tormentor and tears welled in my eyes, refusing to leave my pride intact! Forlorn was the feeling that filled my consciousness and any thoughts of elation at never coming here again were buried below the rubble of my former cheeky confidence, laid low by the masterful oratory of old Mc Grumpy.

The rest of that day is a blur! I went about the business of packing up the few odds and sods in my desk. Then, walking slowly home in the snow, explaining as best I could to my mother that I had finished with school and then I ... well I ... to be honest I have no idea what else I did. Memory has failed to reveal what my father said, or my siblings and if there were any repercussions, I don't recall them. I still remember the words of my underestimated teacher and realise I was wrong and he was right!

I did regret not paying attention in school. I did feel inadequate at times, when more learned people spoke and I did make a concerted effort in later life to expand my knowledge and found I had a thirst for it that was hard to quench. Reading became a passion of mine and I devoured books like that lion I always pretended to be.

Mr McGrundy, I am sorry to have been the bane of your life, please accept my apology and know that your words will always stay with me. Thank you!

Escape from my futile educators was swift and warranted, with my Christmas holiday coming early that year, so I found myself wandering the shoreline, gazing out at the vast expanse of water, whipped up by winter winds, boiling as it crashed onto the seawall, sending spray cascading into the street beyond. It didn't worry me at all that I would soon be out there on those waves, riding through peaks and troughs that would threaten to swallow us whole. It didn't worry me because I hadn't yet experienced it. Ignorance once again claiming the day.

There was still an allure beckoning and mesmerising me, when it came to the sea, a primal call that is echoed throughout the world with sailors crisscrossing the globe carrying people and cargo to destinations most of us have never heard of and could never hope to see.

Winter was well and truly present with its blanket of snow covering the coast with a Christmas card scene that temporarily softened the harsh reality of life in rural Ireland.

I walked and walked, trying to come to terms with the fact I was no longer at school and would never be returning, not realising to this point that it would affect me at all, but it did.

A sudden panic set in, contemplation of a leap into the void that was opening up in front of me. Previously I had been able to define my life around school days and holidays, a regular pattern that, although I didn't appreciate it, gave me stability in a world of chaos.

To be truthful I felt a little lost, aware of my immediate path but mindful of the wider world opening out in front of me. Remember I was still only thirteen, a child really, no matter how big I was for my age, a child on the threshold of a wondrous journey.

It's tempting for me looking back to see my life through Guinness tinted glasses but it wasn't easy and the next year would attempt to break me, even kill me, although there was no way I could foresee it! There was this underlying realisation that my feet were on quicksand and it was waiting to swallow me up.

By chance I had wandered back to the Lodge where my father worked part time as a gardener. I peered down the drive at the winter wonderland within. Smoke was curling up out of the chimney stacks of the Lodge. Was someone in residence I wondered or was this really large house being heated to keep its resident ghosts warm?

There were many such ghost stories in Ireland, the land of storytelling. The Irish are proud of their myths and legends, perpetuating them in song and verse, with generation after generation eager to carry on the tradition.

I had never personally seen a ghost but I had heard the stories relating their comings and goings. My mind was receptive to the tales and I daresay on the lookout for real proof.

I was about to turn away from the Lodge when I saw a young person, couldn't tell whether it was a boy or girl, togged out in winter clothes, hat, gloves, scarf and boots, waving to me enthusiastically. I hesitated for a moment, probably checking if the wave was meant for me or someone else before I accepted it was for me. I waved in return, my ungloved hands taken from warm pockets and hoisted into the crisp winter air.

The wave changed into a beckoning gesture and me being me thought, why not and so I strode off over the virgin snow, leaving a trail a blind man could have followed. I began to struggle a little as I sank knee deep in to the soft and pliant covering, puffing and panting as I tried to lift my legs up and out of each self-made hole.

Because I was concentrating on the effort to walk, I had

taken my eyes off the person doing the waving and scanned the area to see if I was on track to their position. There was no-one to be seen! I redoubled my efforts in a last-ditch attempt to reach my destination, surely, I should be able to see them by now. No, not a thing and by this time I was almost to the front door. I looked back just in case I had walked straight past but again, nothing doing.

I was absolutely bewildered, my tracks from the entrance to the doorway stood out like ink blots on a fresh page, no other evidence existed of the waver's presence.

At that moment, a hand was placed on my shoulder and I almost jumped out of my boots. Turning to see what ghostly apparition was awaiting me I was surprised to see an elderly woman, probably at least forty, smiling benevolently at me.

"May I help you, young man?" she offered.

"Pardon me, ma'am but I saw a child waving as I passed and when I waved back, they beckoned me to come in. You can see my trail", I said as I turned and pointed. "But when I got here, I couldn't find the person. I'm baffled"

She smiled that smile again. "You are not the first person to see the child! The first time I saw him was when I was about your age, I saw him from a bedroom window. He waved to me and beckoned for me to come out and play but by the time I got outside he had gone. I did see him again, several times over the years but not recently. You're the first to talk of him for quite a while. What's your name?"

"Niall, ma'am"

"Well Niall, would you like to come in and get warm, I have some fresh cakes".

Not needing to be asked twice, I gladly accepted and followed her into the house, taking off my boots and coat and entering the parlour, as she called it. There was a roaring fire in a huge fireplace, spitting and crackling, consuming the logs like Lucifer in his heyday.

"My father tends to your garden ma'am" I offered.

"Does he? What's his name?"

"Brendan ma'am, Brendan O'Sullivan.

"Good man, your father, works hard and does a terrific job. Is that what you want to be, a gardener like your father Niall?"

"No ma'am, I'm going to sea. Starting on the trawlers after Christmas."

"How old are you Niall?"

"Thirteen ma'am … and a half"

"Isn't that very young to be going off to sea? What about school?"

"School's glad to get rid of me, I think. Incorrigible was the word they used or something like that. Long word. Not sure what it means, but my school report did say I was good at lifting things".

She smiled a gentle smile. I seemed to amuse her, my rustic twang seeming even more yokel up against her genteel brogue.

"You seem bright to me Niall, don't assume other people are always right about you! Only you know what is inside your head and only you are responsible for the things you do. I have a feeling you will do very well in this bright and wonderful world we live in. My grandfather was born not far from here, on a farm and like you longed to see the world beyond. He made a life for himself that he could never have dreamt of and had this place built. I've kept it going for many years in his honour. I sometimes think the boy we have both seen is my grandfather's spirit. He loved this place and once he had made his fortune, returned here to retire and died a very happy man."

We chatted for quite a while that day, this lovely friendly lady, trying to keep alive the vision her grandfather had.

The house is sadly gone now, erased from the landscape and lost to the march of time but it still exists in my memory, complete with ghostly waving figure. I felt completely different when I left there that day, the apprehension was gone. It may have been the cakes or the roaring fire, but I prefer to think the ghost of her grandfather inviting me in.

I'm sure he wanted me to learn of his successful transition from poor farm boy to rich entrepreneur, assuring me I would be a success in life and if so, he wasn't far wrong.

Talking about grandparents reminded me that we regularly visited our maternal grandmother, who lived about two miles from us. She lived in a small, detached cottage overlooking the beach in an area that was not thought posh at the time, but when I visit the area now it is rather upmarket. The house has been extended by the current owners and would have all services connected, unlike in my grandmother's time or mine come to that.

My grandmother always made a fuss of me probably because I was her first grandchild, my mother being the eldest of three girls and the first to marry.

My grandfather died when I was three and I have no memory of him, but pictures were everywhere showing a big beaming Irishman, with shirts that never quite fitted his muscular frame.

I loved to play records on the old wind-up gramophone that I was allowed to operate only with supervision, until I was about ten and fully grown up, as my gran used to say (She had lots of sayings, some hilarious to us kids).

"Eat your cabbage, it'll put hairs up your nose", or "Stop shouting, I can't hear myself drinking", were two of her favourites. There were many others, equally as barmy, but she did make us laugh. Whether it was intentional I am still not sure. Maybe a few more will come back to me as I write this memoir.

If we arrived a little early for dinner, we would be drafted into selecting a chicken, catching it, which was harder than it seems with her "free to roam" birds. Then observing her killing it by chopping the poor things head off and then helping with plucking it. It's no wonder people turn vegetarian.

Back to the records. While dinner was cooking, we would rummage through the carefully sleeved and delicate 78's (kids ask your parents what they were or probably your grandparents. Think of them as huge CDs made of easy to scratch, simple to shatter, child magnets)

There was one in particular titled "Music. Music, Music", you can find it on YouTube if you are interested, and we all knew the words and tune and belted it out for all we were worth, especially as our choir continued to increase every year.

Mum's sister Charlotte would arrive now and again from Dublin with her husband Uncle Ron and their son Dennis and the choir would increase even more. I'm still not sure where we all sat down but as kids, probably on the floor, making sure we didn't sit on one of Nan's cats of which there were a few. They wisely scarpered when we arrived and didn't come back until the place was quiet again.

There was always a full kettle on a swivel stand attached to the fire surround, ready to be swung over the open fire, soon bubbling away ready for the next pot of tea.

My Nan was always laughing and winding us kids up. I think she knew we would have to go home eventually and maybe she was getting revenge on her daughters for giving her a hard time when they were little.

On the other hand, perhaps, she was just a happy soul who loved her family and wanted to see them happy. Either way we loved her and the visits to that quaint old house.

Dennis and I used to play in the garden sometimes and marvelled at the big old mangle that Nan used to wring out her washing.

When we were younger, we tried in vain to turn the handle but as we grew older and stronger, especially if we stood on a box and jumped on the handle, we could get the mangle to turn. Great fun until Dennis was stupid enough to put his fingers in the mangle just as I jumped onto the handle. The scream could be heard in Dublin. At least that's what my Nan said as she clipped me round the ear. "What did I do?" was my useless vocal response. "You caught his fingers in the mangle!" which wasn't strictly true but I knew better than to argue with her for long and those clips around the ear left them stinging for ages. She was an expert clipper!

As I got older, I used to visit Nan on my own and we would sit and natter for ages, something I rarely did with my parents. I could tell her things I couldn't tell my parents and know she wouldn't snitch on me.

She also had some batty friends who drifted in for a cup of tea and a slice of her homemade cake. One of them, a lady called Thelma who was from Cork, so she kept telling me every single time she saw me, was particularly loopy. She would walk in, stand in front of the fire and lift her skirt to warm her backside, without so much as a by your leave. My Nan never batted an eyelid, taking it all in her stride and occasionally joining her in the ritual much to my amusement.

Thelma mangled words like I did Dennis' fingers, without intention and with no ill will towards the English language. A thunderstorm became a "Thinderstum", Frank Sinatra became "Frank Sumatra" a belly ache became "a billy doo" and that's just some of the ones I could understand. Maybe it was because she was from Cork but I doubt it.

I always thought my Nan to be ancient but if I do some maths at which I am getting better, she was probably in her early fifties when I was thirteen and now, at my time of life, that seems very young.

Nan passed away when I was eighteen and she was not even sixty, for me it was an awful loss. I still think my sense of impudence and fun is a direct result of being immersed in her world and I often see her looking back at me because my eyes are just like hers.

She taught me to respect women, as did my mother and woe betide you if you didn't. She checked out every girl I ever went out with and gave me an honest assessment of them, some undoubtedly meant to get a rise out of me, but I knew she always had my back and would die for me if needs be, as I felt for her. Miss you Nan.

4. CHRISTMAS, TRAWLERS, NEAR DEATH, CRAZY COWS & A FREE SPIRIT

Christmas is a lovely time of year, people are kinder, happiness is endemic and the air is filled with optimism, what a holiday, if only the rest of the year was the same. I used to think that every year and to a certain degree I still do.

There wasn't a lot to share with so many mouths to feed and bodies to clothe but we still managed to have a good time. Games were played hour after hour; tantrums were thrown and people sent to bed. Drunken friends and relatives passed through the house, on their way back or on their way to a party. Poitín liberally flowed out of vessels carefully hidden from prying noses both internal and external. If a guest arrived sober there was not much chance of them leaving that way, especially if my dad was pouring the alcohol.

Even Father Michael stopped by for a taster, at least that's all he said he wanted, but to be honest he was already three sheets in the wind before he stepped over the threshold. He could sing a bit could Father Michael and knew all the filthy words too, getting him started was not the problem, getting him to stop was. His saving grace was, that one more parishioner to see and so he would eventually make his way out the door, sometimes after failed attempts to exit via the pantry.

Our neighbours were just as poor as us but their door and ours was always open. No one would steal from you! There would be more chance of someone breaking in and leaving something for you. If someone fell on hard times, we shared what we had, especially if there were kids going hungry. It was a different time, no social services, no welfare, just a community bound by a common code of decency.

That Christmas was a memorable one!

In a few days I would be off to work on the trawlers, a working man at thirteen, bringing a wage into the house and helping to put food on the table. I felt so grown up, so mature, it was my last Christmas as a child, from here on in I was a man. How wrong can you be?

Festivities still echoed in my head that first morning on the trawlers, waking at two thirty am and making the walk down to the docks ready for the boat to go out at five. It was a powerful young man who strode out in the dark that day, full of promise, energy and lust for life. It was a different person who arrived home at eight thirty pm, shattered, wracked with pain and wondering how I would be able to do this day after day after day.

Arriving on the dock in jeans and a light jacket, I must have looked a proper landlubber. I noticed the stares as I shuffled from foot to foot in the cold morning air.

Paddy Walters, a friend of my father, called me over.

"You can't go to sea like that young Niall" and he disappeared for a few moments before emerging with a set of oilskins.

"Put these on, they'll do you 'til you get some of your own".

They were way too short for me and smelled like the bottom of the sea had puked over them, but they were good enough to get me started and until I could afford some better ones. Most of the guys were friendly, having a laugh and a joke before the work started, the craic as it was known. One or two you were told to stay well clear of, drinkers and fighters, nasty natured and quick to temper, but I was well protected and most of them knew my father and would not want to cross him.

I felt like a real trawler man in my ill-fitting apparel, no more walking across fields carrying water for the house. Hurray! I reported for duty and the first job I was given was … you guessed it, carrying water from the tap outside the public toilets back and forth, back and forth until the boat's freshwater tanks were full. It didn't stop there though, when I got to the quayside our boat was moored further out into the harbour and the only way to it was to walk over several other trawlers. Now, carrying water on solid ground is quite easy, even over rough pastureland, jumping from a static quay onto a trawler shifting about like a … nearly said what the sailors said it was like, sorry, use your imagination! Then once I had traversed that obstacle course, I had to synchronise my leap onto another moving boat often swaying in the opposite direction. Repeat this a few times and you see why it is foolish to fill the buckets right up to the brim. By the time I emptied the contents of the bucket into the water tank, I had spilled a good portion. I had to learn this skill very quickly, there was only a small amount of time to complete the task and the skipper would be furious if the tanks were not full, we had to leave with the tide as it was a tidal harbour.

With the job completed I was told to stand to one side while they cast off. I would learn how to do all these highly skilled jobs eventually but on that first morning I was still a novice. Breakfast was being cooked and the smell of bacon wafted beautifully under my nose with a fragrance never to be matched by Chanel. I took my turn and picked up my breakfast, tucking into it. This is the life!

The ocean waves, a hearty breakfast, sat amongst fellow seamen. One or two of them eyed me up and smiled, they were obviously glad to have a big strong lad like me to help out on board.

I had scarcely finished my breakfast when we left the shelter of the harbour, the small trawler hitting the open sea and the swell lying in wait for us, sneakily loitering surreptitiously behind the seawall.

Wham! The boat was tossed in the air, I swear it was completely out of the water! What the hell! Now we're falling into a hole and my stomach is in touch with my neck. Oh shit! Look at the size of that wave about to hit us, we'll never survive that! Bash! Water came cascading over me like Niagara Falls as I held on for dear life.

All around me men were going about their work or sitting quietly biding their time until they were needed. How could they be so cool! We were about to sink! My breakfast didn't like it either because it decided to abandon ship, but before it could do that it had to abandon me, which apparently it did with a degree of excellence that left those around me, jumping out of the way with a dexterity I had yet to learn.

I thought I was dying, I had never and I mean NEVER felt so ill. If we weren't so far out at sea I would have jumped overboard and swam back but this was not feasible, so I clung to the seat and puked until I thought the next thing I'll bring up will be my arse!

Until you have experienced a trip like this you can have no idea what fishermen have to go through and to be fair, we hadn't gone far yet and just when I thought it was getting better the boat would suddenly lurch to one side, gravity taking over and dropping us like a stone, only to be countered a few moments later by a movement in the opposite direction as violent as the former.

There was a fair share of mickey taking going on and one old hand was very vocal about a young lad he knew being washed overboard on his first day and being found weeks later tangled up in the fishing nets, eyes gone, tongue gone, testicles ripped off, only one ear remaining, oh and one leg amputated above the knee. His mother apparently couldn't identify him he was that disfigured, she only knew him by the shiny new belt she'd given him on his first day at sea.

By this time death seemed a very good option and one I was ready to welcome with open arms but of course I survived, quite how I have no idea, but I did.

There was quite a bit of singing and to be fair some excellent voices. Mostly they were shanties or Irish folk songs and the odd pop song,. I joined in during later voyages but I could see the odd wince when I got carried away. Everybody's a critic! I thought I sounded pretty good but as I found out later in life my ears lied to me.

That first voyage was one of the most difficult experiences I have ever had. I had to endure it because there was no way off the boat. That's a metaphor for life that I have applied many times since, sometimes you just have to hang on and ride out the storm as it usually dies out in time.

I did work hard that day, partly to make up for the bad start but mostly because there was an easy rhythm to the work when the fish were hauled in.

Watching and learning, that was 'on the job' training as they call it today. Very few words were exchanged, a look, a nod, a demonstration or two, that's how the first day went and I was glad when it was over.

The work of course does not end when the boat ties up at the harbour, the fish have to be boxed and humped off the boat and over to the yards and then I had to make the long walk home, by which time it was dark again.

My parents must have smelled me coming from a mile away, I stunk to high heaven but I did bring fish for them to have the next day, so that was one saving grace. By the time I had washed, all I wanted to do was fall into bed. Did I feel like I was a man at last? No way! I felt like I was a thirteen-year-old child. Which I was. Going to sleep that night was no problem, getting up at 2.30am was and so it went on.

My left eye sometimes refused to open fully on those early rises, try though I might to force it open, it stubbornly refused to comply. I firmly believe that one side of my brain was still sound asleep, the side that worked my left eye. Thank goodness I didn't have to shave at that age or one side of my face would have been covered in cuts.

It was also important I let my siblings carry on with their beauty sleep, so I tiptoed around getting dressed in the dark. That may sound easy but if you have never done it, give it a try. Tell your family you are carrying out an experiment and let them judge your prowess. Different colour socks? Absolutely! Shirt buttoned up one hole out with the resulting collar up at an angle and probably inside out? More than likely! Trousers on back to front? Two legs in one trouser leg resulting in a forward roll, colliding with something really solid? High probability! Shoes on wrong feet? Hair at all angles? Definitely!

There were times when I longed to be back in school tormenting grumpy guts, eating breakfast without throwing it back up a few minutes later.

Waking as the sun shone through the window instead of moon walking like a zombie risen from the grave, craving human flesh. My temper was not good at that time of the morning! I would often kick a wayward can down a deserted street, listening to it clattering along, hoping I had woken someone else at this god forsaken time! Selfish I know, but it was an outlet that gratified me and I performed it with gusto.

We talk about the practise of sending young boys up chimneys or down mines, but you rarely hear anyone mutter about young boys on trawlers. I know it was my choice but looking at it now, I can see the dangers involved, but it was my way out and because of that it justifies my actions.

Back on the quay I went straight into water carrying mode. I was getting very efficient at hopping from boat to boat and back again, very fortunate to have long legs that were getting stronger by the day.

We sailed with the tide and for a while there was little for me to do, apart from sit around and gaze over the water. Breakfast was soon on the go but it was a meal I never ate, even without the greasy food inside me I would still be seasick and was for most of my time on the trawlers.

During the winter months all the trawlers would fish for cod, whiting, and haddock, but other species would also be caught like plaice, ray, herrings and prawns. These all had to be separated and boxed and if we had time to gut fish it would fetch a better price at market. No one had a set wage in the fishing industry, it was all based on shares of the profits.

Crew members would normally have one share. I received a half share but was expected to do the same work as a man.

When the owners were paid for the catches, a certain amount went to the bank towards financing of the boat, then there was the cost of the diesel and other operating costs. The rest would be split into shares and paid out accordingly, but the owner would have at least 4 shares. No one ever knew how much they had earned until Saturday. The price of fish at market would be crucial to the final profits so, if fish was plentiful, we got less, which sounds ridiculous and when the weather was really bad and we couldn't get to sea, you could end up at the week with nothing. The average I received was £3, but one week I made a massive £7 which was more than my dad was earning. I was king that week but that was a one off. Whatever I earned was a bonus to the family and certainly helped.

The dangers of working on the trawlers was brought home to me when I had a very lucky escape that could have cost me my life.

Part of the skipper's expertise was knowing where the fish were running. We would arrive at the desired position and all the crew would assemble on deck waiting for the order to set the nets. The boat would be rocking from side to side, a natural expectation out there on the sea but every now and again and not predictably the boat would lurch as a heavy wave struck the bow.

In my early days on board, I spent many times on my rear

end, legs in the air, like a drunken sailor on shore leave. As I said, it was difficult to anticipate the adverse motion but gradually my mind and body were trained to react in such a way that I at least stayed on my feet, usually by anchoring one foot and moving the other to compensate for the boat movement. I noticed others doing this and eventually it became second nature.

On this memorable occasion, we were ready to set the nets and the marker buoy was out. The idea is that the ropes that are tethered to the nets are run out over the port side making sure the following nets would not snag on the propeller. It was my job to shout to the other crew members as the remnants of the rope disappeared over the side.

Now these nets were very heavy and took the effort of three strong men to manipulate them, so it was important to get the job right. I was concentrating on observing the ropes when we were suddenly hit by a heavy wave. I did my nautical dance and shifted my one foot to keep my balance, this time successfully and without doing a backflip.

I was momentarily pleased with my newly acquired sea legs and didn't notice that my adjusted foot had landed smack in the middle of the coiled rope just about to uncoil and go overboard.

The first I knew of a problem was when I felt a grip like nothing I had ever felt before, grip my lower leg and as I looked down, I was horrified to see the rope wound up my leg like a snake about to devour me. I was about to go overboard wrapped in half a ton of rope as a diving companion and I froze with fear.

The stories of people being lost at sea and turning up weeks later either in nets or washed up on shore suddenly became a reality. All this in a split second! I expected the worst and could do nothing to change my fate.

Luckily for me an alert crew mate had spotted what was happening and acted on impulse, chopping my leg off! No that's not what happened! That's what flashed through my mind though as I saw him dash towards me with a large knife in his hand.

He somehow grabbed the rope and to this day I have no idea where the man got the strength from! He held the rope with one hand, which was an incredible feat of strength considering the rope already expelled was trying to drag the remainder overboard, whilst attempting to cut the rope with the other. It was impossible for him to do both things and he dropped the knife and held onto the rope with both hands, his cheeks puffing with effort and the muscles on his arms bulging as if they were about to explode. Within a few seconds other crew members saw what was going on and ran to help, cutting the heavy rope and releasing my leg.

Meanwhile the boat was still steaming ahead for the nets to be deployed, as the skipper wasn't aware of what was happening.

I honestly believed I was going to die that day. Lost at sea at thirteen, what a waste, I could see my mother and sisters crying at the news and my father, ashen and grief stricken.

Jimmy Astley the guy who saved my life was quite badly hurt in the rescue, tearing arm muscles with the superhuman effort he made and I was astounded when we spoke about it later. It appears he shouldn't have been in that position on the boat at that crucial moment. His job was to help manhandle the nets overboard and should have been the other side of the wheelhouse. Why he was out of position we couldn't figure, he had no explanation and I was so grateful I didn't query it. If he hadn't been there, I wouldn't be writing this book! I wouldn't have had the wonderful life I have had and would merely be a statistic in maritime accidents.

To Jimmy Astley I say, thank you for saving my life, it's a debt I can never repay and you have my eternal gratitude for your selfless act.

That incident is still as vivid to me today as it was all those years ago. Realising you are about to die and with no chance of escaping the reaper, there is a terrible acceptance of the awful consequences. My heart leaps towards my mouth as I write and a cold shiver, flits over my body, like the souls of the deep are still trying to drag me down to that watery grave. That long ago day, when the hand of fate intruded on the reaper's foregone conclusion, by rescuing an Irish child who was destined for more.

Somehow or other I stuck that job for almost a year, determined not to give up but just as determined to get out.

There were of course, magical days when it was great to be alive and out on the sea, the sun playing silver patterns on the water like so many laser beams, scattering amongst the peaks and troughs.

I recall a truly memorable day, when someone spotted a school of whales just off the bow. Spectacular is a poor word to describe their magnificence. Up close to these masters of the ocean you start to get a feeling that they live a joyous life. A happy family, frolicking in the water like huge baby seals, looking like they are having the best time ever. The sheer size of them is breath taking, almost defying belief. Enormous, placid creatures, roaming free on an endless journey around the planet, stopping off here and there to show us simple folk that we are just frail human beings, bobbing up and down on a plank of wood and completely out of our depth.

They were very aware of us and put on a show of immense proportion that I will remember for the rest of my life, writing this today brings a smile to my face again as it has done many times before. If you have never witnessed a pod of whales, then put it on your list and remember I told you so.

Another more bizarre situation I experienced is hard to believe but well documented in the Irish papers.

As the harbour is tidal, we sometimes had to anchor up outside and wait for the tide to turn before docking. This time wasn't wasted as we gutted the fish ready for market, increasing their value and meaning a bigger payday at the end of the week.

There I was gutting fish like the pro I had become when I saw something glint in the entrails I was removing. Imagine my surprise when I cleaned it off and found a perfectly preserved ring with what looked like diamonds in a cluster. Not a big ring as such and I doubt very expensive, but undoubtedly it meant something to someone.

All those Hollywood movies started me thinking of how it got into the sea and over the next few days I imagined a number of scenarios.

Two slightly older people were stood on the deck of an ocean-going Liner. Tension in the air crackled like errant electricity striving for an earth whilst words of anger flowing from the woman's clenched gleaming white teeth lashed the unwilling ears of the handsome man stood in front of her. She accused him of things my young head barely understood, spitting out her words, those sputum coated missiles of anger, in a staccato burst that rattled and assaulted his guilty posture.

With a single motion she grasped the diamond ring he had given her many years before and with a grace that belied the flashing in her eyes, launched it, like a seasoned pitcher, over the safety rail and into the briny wind beyond.

They both watched as the ring quickly lost momentum and made a rapid descent before disappearing into the waves below.

Frozen like a bad internet connection they stood there transfixed, her with a hand to her mouth stifling a cry, him with the realisation that things could never go back to what they were. Whilst the sparkling ring slowly sank towards the bottom of the sea, only for a curious cod to gulp it down in one.

That was one of my favourites I played over and over in my youthful imagination. Oh, to be blessed once again with that innocent internal cinema, untainted by life, relationships and reality.

At the skipper's request I handed the ring to the harbour master, who passed it to the local sergeant, who passed it to the 'Lost and Found' at his station. Somewhere along the chain of custody, someone must have mentioned it within earshot of a local reporter from the "Ballytreeny Scout", the paper that carried stories about the folk in our area. I was interviewed and photographed for the paper and an article was duly printed on the front page no less, telling the tale and asking for the owner to come forward.

The chances against the owner of the ring reading the article were vast but the "Dublin Star" picked up the story and suddenly it was national news. A string of claims was made and reported but they were not able to give the details of the inscription on the inside of the ring.

It went unclaimed for months until someone from Liverpool claimed it and gave exact details of the engraving.

The woman had apparently been swimming and had forgotten to take her engagement ring off and was very distressed to have lost it at sea, never expecting to see it again.

A cousin of hers in Dublin heard she had lost a ring and sent her a copy of the paper, never believing it might be hers but just to give her a ray of hope. It was nothing like I imagined but still rewarding to know she had it back and she sent me a postal order for two pounds which was a nice bonus for me.

One of the worst days out on the trawler came without warning as a storm descended on us just after we hauled in the nets, full of fish. The clear sky vanished into the black of night within seconds, winds blew like howling from hell, whipping up the water that threw the trawler around like a child's toy. Spray hit us from all directions, while we struggled to tie down everything on this impossible rollercoaster.

One after another we were knocked off our feet, lucky to stay on the slippery deck and not ending up washed overboard. Lightning suddenly lit up the boat with arc lights brighter than the sun, blinding us and added to the terrifying conditions.

There were cries of desperation and terror from crew members, including me, as we worked to make safe our catch and prevent nets and crew from disappearing over the side.

One violent pitch sent me into the air, both feet flaying, desperate to make solid contact. I came down hard on one knee, the searing pain shooting up my body and if I screamed, no-one would hear me above the howling wind.

Rolling on deck I cracked my head against something, it was so dark, I had no idea where I was but thankfully, not in the sea.

Another jolt, another clap of thunder threatening to burst my eardrums, was quickly followed by the most spectacular light display I have ever seen, momentary but monumental! It left my eyes blind and my senses numb!

My stomach lurched as the boat once again dropped like a stone, then soared like the lava from a massive volcano exploding beneath us, propelling us it seemed, out of the water and freefalling back down again.

There was an awful sound of breaking timber and it seemed the boat would crumble into a thousand pieces, smashed and broken like a child's toy underfoot, but somehow it held together, testament to wonderful Irish boat building.

There were a lot of suddenly religious people on board, instant converts praying for their lives, me included as we hung on for dear life, all thoughts now firmly concentrated on personal survival. I would love to say there was a sudden reprieve but the fact is the storm took quite a while to pass over us and the return to normal seas was slow to come, but we hung on, united in peril, staring death in the face and once again surviving.

When I stood on the quay that day, I felt a relief that almost made me cry, how I didn't fall down on my knees and howl like the wind had been doing earlier I don't know. Maybe it was the pain still causing me to limp that prevented it, who knows?

It was a long slow walk home that day! Should I tell my mother about the storm? I knew she worried about me every day, so telling her would only increase her daily suffering and I somehow kept it to myself. Putting this experience in writing is once again stirring up old, almost forgotten trauma that populated my nightmares for years. It may very well cause me more disturbed nights but I'm glad I have managed at last to put it in writing. Let it serve as a message of gratitude to those who risk their lives on the sea every day to keep the rest us fed.

Small boats like this go out every day, no matter what the weather, crewed with brave men who toil with small reward to bring fish to our tables and I salute them.

One of my problems that went unobserved by me was the overpowering stink of fish that followed me wherever I went.

Despite constant washing (Forget about hot showers! That was never about to happen in our house). I apparently always stank of fish. When you worked in it day after day you became so accustomed to it, you totally ignored it.

I wish someone had told me before I went to the pictures with Erin on our first date for almost a year. There had been absolutely no time for dating or anything else come to that, I was either working six days a week or collapsing in a heap on my day off.

One of those precious days off I was forced to go to church and I caught a glimpse of Erin with her parents. One of my sister's giggled and handed me a note that she had obviously read as I could see it was hurriedly rewrapped. It said to meet Erin at the pictures later that day and so I had no choice but to pull myself together and walk to the cinema.

I arrived early to see who was on duty on the door. If Freddy or Paddy was on, I would not be able to get in as they were instrumental in getting me banned but as luck had it there was a new guy in town and he'd drawn the short straw on the door.

Erin arrived looking stunning in an emerald-green frock with her long red curly hair cascading down over her shoulders. I must have had my mouth open because she said, "Catching flies" and giggled as she clasped my hand.

At least I had some money these days so I bought our tickets and we went in and sat down.

Almost immediately I noticed people in front of us, turning

and looking around, not necessarily at me but just around in general.

The nose twitching came later and now they were looking at me, including Erin. "What is that smell?" she exclaimed as she too wrinkled her nose.

"What smell?" I inquired.

"That awful smell of fish. It's terrible!"

"I can't smell it" I offered.

"Well, it's coming from over …" she had stopped midsentence as she leaned into me and sniffed.

"Niall it's you who stink".

"What! Can't be I washed this morning and these are my best clothes."

By this time people were moving seats. It meant we had the area to ourselves but it seemed Erin was about to move as well.

"I'm sorry Niall, but I can't stand it. It's making me feel sick, I have to move" and move she did.

As quickly as that our brief romance died on the vine, smelling like rotten fish. I walked out before the film started and the irony of it all smacked me in the face as I saw in large letters the name of the film we were about to see "MOBY DICK".

My embarrassment was complete and I walked home determined to pack in the trawlers as soon as possible. I was fourteen and I thought my life was over, but of course it wasn't. Fresh adventures were only just over the horizon, pleading with me to seek out new pastures and I did, but not before almost scrubbing my skin off trying to get rid of the smell and asking random people if they could smell fish!

I will be eternally grateful for the trawler job, perilous though it was. School quickly became a distant memory as I fought, on a daily basis to stay alive (or so I thought at the time). It was my introduction to the working world and the camaraderie of colleagues. To be suddenly immersed in such a tough way of making a living, made me appreciative of my subsequent advances.

Walking away from the dockside that last time, I was relieved but felt rudderless again! What do I do now? My heart leapt a little and I felt choked as I glanced back at my recent residence, bobbing up and down, inviting me back. But there was no way I was ever going out on a trawler again! NEVER!

It was heaven not having to get up in the early hours, I didn't spend time trying to walk in a straight line after a day's work and I didn't have to worry about the smell! All I had to do now was find another job.

You would think I'd had enough of the sea but I was still dreaming of travelling and so I tried to join the Merchant Navy, only to be told the minimum age was seventeen. So, it was a job on land for a couple of years.

In those days, most jobs came to you via personal contacts., so I asked all and sundry to put their feelers out.

My father was friends with a local businessman with three large greenhouses. Terry Swarbrick was a swarthy man, built for the land but with a good business brain. He grew tomatoes and salads and as I had some previous experience, he gladly took me on. Again, it was six-day week and I was only paid £3 10s per week but it was constant and I was my own boss.

I had to plant 15,000 tomato plants and tend to them until they were ready to harvest. It was tedious at times but I was never one to complain. I just kept my head down working until the task was finished. It was a good time to learn about self-motivation and caring for large scale crops, something books are slow to teach. Terry left me to get on with things and rarely showed his head in the place which suited me down to the ground. There was only one small hiccup during my time there and it had nothing to do with tomatoes!

Terry had a cow that he milked every evening after work, a job he seemed to look forward to. He said it was calming after a hard day's work. I doubted this, but everyone is different and each to his own as they say. The hiccup came one Friday afternoon! Terry stuck his head into the greenhouse, without coming in, just sort of leaning in using the door as support.

"Niall ... I'm taking the missus away for the weekend. Can you milk the cow and deliver the milk to Mrs Griffiths next door? Thank you." With that he disappeared, not waiting for an answer, nor instructions as to how to milk the cow, nothing.

I stood there flummoxed, a little bewildered and just slightly miffed as I was going to try and get into the cinema that evening to see a John Wayne film.

As Terry was off on his toes, I was stuck with the job, so after finishing for the day, a little earlier than normal, I went round to where the cow was kept.

Now ... some people look on cows as being stupid ... docile ... placid creatures even. Wrong! They are evil manipulating monsters with one wandering eye that follows you across the yard. It was like being watched by a wonky surveillance camera. One eye staring into the distance while the other never let its gaze on me waver for a moment.

I found the clean bucket and placed it somewhere near the post I had planned to tie the cow to. Wrong! To all who want to know, secure the cow to the post THEN fetch a stool and the bucket.

It's true I had seen milking many times but this was my first time actually doing it.

I walked slowly over to the cow as it stood calmly swishing away the flies with its tail. The wonky eye watching my every move. Reaching out to grab hold of the rope tied loosely around its neck, I slipped on some manure I had failed to see, because I was watching the wonky eye.

Before I knew it, I was almost under the cow, udders staring me right in the eyes. With that, the cow shifted its body mass and the huge udders, full of milk, smacked me full in the face, followed by a sudden burst of milky foam that soaked the front of my shirt.

As I jerked back, I put one hand down in the manure, instinctively and involuntarily picking it up! With my body mass shifting now I did a pirouette on my back and ended up right under the cow and just under the sewage pipe it used as a backside. The smell was a hundred times worse than the fish and I did question between expletives what on earth Terry fed her on.

There was no retaining my dignity, it had long deserted me,

running down the lane screaming and definitely smelling of cow shit.

I ventured once more to the domain of the wonky eyed cow and this time I looked where I was stepping.

Careful to avoid the all-seeing orb, I grabbed the rope around the crafty bastard's neck. There was a bit of grunting and groaning, mostly from me, but I managed to secure the cow to the post and at this point I will address the wisdom of putting the bucket at the post before I got the cow.

I stepped back proud of my achievement in tethering the monster before me, only to spy said bucket firmly secured by one large hoof planted firmly inside it, straw and shit mixed in even quantities all around it.

The wonky eye looked at me and I swear it winked! Or maybe the right word is wonked!

As it said in my school report, I was good at lifting things, so I wrapped my right arm around the bovine appendage and tried with all my fifteen-year-old might to shift it. I sweated and I swore, I cursed and cajoled but there was no shifting the beast, it was quicker for me to get another bucket.

"Stupid cow!" I shouted! "Stay there!" as if it had much choice, tied to a post with its leg in a bucket, but give it precise instructions I did. It was a little bit like a golfer watching a little white ball that he had struck with fury, now heading directly towards the water hazard and shouting to it "Get over! Get over! GET OVER!" Word of advice to all golfers "THE BALL NEVER LISTENS ITS TOO FAR AWAY!"

I flounced off, wiping my shit-stained hands down my trousers, trying to get the worst off before I picked up a clean bucket. The barn door was open and I marched into the dark interior and promptly fell over a bale of hay smacking my head on something moving in the dark only to receive a sharp dig in my side by a bleating demon that passed for a goat. There was only one thing to do, backtrack!

Of course, I then fell over the bucket I was looking for, but at least I'd found it and could complete my task with the mooing monster.

Stumbling back round to the tethered cow like a sailor on shore leave, I stopped abruptly. The wonky eye was still running surveillance but it had a definite glint in it, almost a smile as my eyes caught sight of the original bucket, now safely on its side without a cow's leg in it. Yes, I admit, I swore! Bless me Father Michael but I swore!

Then I realised I didn't have the stool! Oh, good god! I was off again. Sorry Father Michael!

I gave up then, turning the original bucket upside down, sitting on it and putting the fresh bucket under the udders. Of course, then I realised I had to wash my hands before milking. More swearing but I was learning from experience. I moved the buckets well out of reach of the wandering legs and eyes and sprinted to the washroom and cleaned my filthy hands.

The cow, on my return, gave me a bored look as if to say for goodness' sake man get on with it! A woman would have done it hours ago!

Things were looking up and the bucket was slowly filling, but of course the cow was still feeling petulant and kicked out at me, knocking the bucket over and I was again on my knees trying to save the contents from mixing with the sewage carpet I was knelt on.

There wasn't much more than a pint or so of milk left, so, I swiftly topped it up with an equal amount of water and took it round next door.

My appearance and farmyard fragrance must have been off putting as Mrs Griffiths didn't linger to chat with me, grabbing the bucket and I believe holding her breath, she disappeared back into her kitchen.

The next day I made an arrangement with the farmer next door to milk the cow for the next three nights, which he did and I never heard a thing about the watered-down milk.

With Terry and his family away, I was on my own picking tomatoes as they ripened. Easy enough job you'd think, pick it and grade it and move on, simple, but not for me. Sometimes I wonder whether the Reaper is messing with me, for slipping through his grasp on the trawler. Out of the corner of my eye I saw a blackbird appear from nowhere, having somehow penetrated my defence system and descended onto the tomato plants. Profanities rained down again as I ran across the greenhouse to where the bird had landed only to see it disappear up into the roof space.

Some of the ripe tomatoes were ruined where the bird noshed on them and these would have to be thrown away. I had worked very hard and long hours tending to these plants and there was no way I would let a bird randomly destroy my crop.

I grabbed a step ladder and climbed up to see where the bird was getting in. A pane of glass had been moved aside to increase air flow and the netting covering the gap was prised open by the enterprising avian burglar. No problem! Just pull the wire back over the gap and re-secure it, properly this time.

As with my milking fiasco, it would have been better if I

thought about it first before rushing into action, but I was only fourteen and hadn't understood caution when I first encountered it. It was still a concept that was only vaguely familiar to my teenage brain.

Balancing on the upper regions of the step ladder, wobbling a little, but well in control, I gripped the offending netting and steadying my footing, gave it a massive tug.

Certainly, it would have been a better plan to test if it was caught up or not. In this case, NOT. With the net showing little if any resistance, the tug I gave it was far too strong and my arm raced back across the gap with the net following on swiftly!

So swiftly, that my arm ran along the pane of glass above and I felt what appeared to be a sharp sting. More expletives as I grabbed my arm to see what had happened, my fingers wrapped around it and then blood started to ooze out and run down my arm and drip off my elbow at a faster rate than the milk from the cow.

I was really lucky! Somehow, I didn't faint and fall off the ladder into the tomatoes but I suppose, dear reader you would have found that funnier! Go on, be honest!

I ventured a look at the cut and it was about four inches long which in my panic looked like my entire arm was about to fall off.

Being alone on the site, the only place I could go was next door to Mrs Griffiths, she of the watered-down milk and turned up nose, but I had no choice, wondering if I could make it there before my blood supply ran out.

The more I hurried the more the blood seemed to pump and I arrived at her door practically exsanguinated, kicking at the door as both hands had another priority. No one answered immediately so I kicked again and again, dust and dirt flying around from the doorway.

Just as I was about to give up and sit down to die, Mrs Griffith's eldest daughter Frances opened the door, expecting to see bailiffs or the like and finding me half dead, with a blood-soaked arm outstretched and a goodly supply running down and staining her doorstep.

Luckily, Frances was a real farm girl and took it all in her stride, wrapping my arm in towels and helping me to her car.

She didn't even seem to be worrying about my blood ruining the upholstery, as she rushed me to our local doctor who was luckily in at the time. The nearest hospital was over twenty miles away through windy old lanes and it might have been touch and go, getting there in time.

We are talking about the mid-fifties and surgical practices were not what they are now. Doctor Hoffman cleaned the wound and immediately started to stitch it up, without anaesthetic, causing me to border on passing out with the pain. It seemed an eternity but the doctor finished a neat job and I sat there, only then noticing that Frances was still holding my hand in hers. She must have been a strong girl because I surely squeezed her hand like the grip of Hercules when I was being stitched, but she didn't complain. She was the only one at home that day and was about to go shopping, so once again the Reaper was thwarted, he must have been sick of revising his list of recruits when I was mentioned.

Believe it or not I was back at work the next day, working with my arm in a sling, keeping a vigilant eye out for the accursed blackbird but it never reappeared.

The only good thing to come out of that latest testament of my resilient resistance to the Reaper, apart from the wicked scar on my arm that later in life I attributed to many manly things and absolutely nothing to do with a blackbird, was a chance meeting after I had been to have the stitches removed, incidentally something else that made my eyes water.

So, there I was newly scarred and forever peeping at it when I nearly walked into a pretty girl walking the other way.

"Hello Niall!" she said, standing really close and not

attempting to move away.

I hesitated, one because I was still not the most comfortable around girls, but also because I had no idea who she was.

"I'm Imogen ... Billy O'Connor's sister".

Now I remembered Billy very well, we were in school together but I didn't remember his sister at all. She was very pretty, with hazel eyes and long dark hair pulled back off her face and tied in a ponytail. Surely, I would remember someone this pretty!

"Oh ... Billy's sister ... right!" I said, unconvincingly. "Of course!"

She smiled, a knowing smile and looked right into my eyes and I mean right in, as if she was looking for the inner me. It was a gaze like nothing I had seen before or since. There was a serene calmness about her and she chatted away, asking about my scar, that I had been gazing at earlier and generally conversing like we were long lost friends. Openness comes to mind as I recall the moment, no walls or barriers of any sort in her persona, sweet and flowing without guile or pretension.

I was struck with her immediately and we strolled along together, it's only now I realise she must have changed the direction she was going, in order to walk with me. Her laugh was unforced and genuine, matching the flow of our conversation, her aims and hopes, my scar and ... nope, not a lot more I suspect. She was younger than me by a year or so but light years older than me in truth. I thought she was incredible, so full of life, so in touch with her own reality. This was not some schoolboy crush, this was me meeting a superior being, someone who existed on a higher plain. A butterfly talking to a frog and taking time to listen to his infrequent croaks.

During my life I have been lucky to meet some extraordinary people, comedians, singers, writers, sportsmen but not one of them had the qualities that this young Irish girl had.

I don't say this lightly but there was something saintly about her, ethereal almost, untouched by pollutants, free as the air we breathe to wander where she wanted, when she wanted.

If she had kicked off her shoes and danced barefoot through the lanes I would not have been surprised. Dancing to music that came from within her, arms waving above her head in a rapture that captivated each and every one she met.

Imogen was a perfect human being, the most perfect I ever knew and I feel privileged to have spent that afternoon with her.

A few days later I was stunned to find out she had been taken from her family! Someone said she was not normal and had to be sent to an Institution. At the age of fourteen I came face to face with a world that rarely touched me, Big Brother manifested in the name of sanity.

What did these people need to do this for? Ripping a young girl from her family and locking her away because she was different. A tender, gentle creature without malice sentenced to life imprisonment for not conforming to the norm? It must have been a nightmare of epic proportions for her, not understanding what was happening, caging a free spirit and throwing away the key. I imagined her, alone and frightened but still exuding love with every breath until her spirit was crushed by the norm and she withered inside.

I never heard of her again, apart from my parents discussing her one day when they thought they were alone. She was deemed mad and needing help. I wanted to scream from the rooftops but to my shame I did nothing, consigned her to my memory and got on with my life. I know I can't rescue her or the many others who were looked on as different but I can use this book to let the world know she existed and that she was a very special girl.

Life for me in those distant days was very much a seesaw existence as you have probably gleaned so far from this memoir. The highs and lows changed position at seemingly random intervals with a velocity at times that left me breathless.

Erin, Clodagh, Amy, Imogen all touched my life briefly and moved on, teaching me valuable life lessons and leaving me with a desire to continue meeting the fairer sex whenever I could. A task I relished and worked hard to perfect.

5. FOOTBALL, RECLINING REFS, TRAGEDY, BIKES, CRAMP & CAROLINE

Another of my passions was Gaelic football and I used to play for a minor side every Sunday, they had a junior side but because of my size I bypassed them straight into the senior side. In Ireland in those days if you played Gaelic Football, their association would not allow you to play soccer, but being Irish we had a novel way of circumnavigating the rules, we just signed up with a different name. No one on our team would rat you out but if an opponent recognised you, you had to be sure to recognise them because it then became "If you dob me, I'll dob you!" and so a kind of détente existed that ensured preservation of the status quo.

The lads I played football with were, shall we say, enthusiastic! Some of them, however, lacked the finesse we admired in the players we read about in the papers. Sometimes, fuelled by alcohol and cigarettes, they would charge around the muddy old field we called a pitch, kicking lumps out of the opposition and anybody on our team who got in the way, even the poor old ref.

Talking of the ref reminds me of an incident that had both

teams in tears, of laughter I might add. We were playing the Dublin Dodgers, a big lump of a team that worked best at close quarters, elbows and fists flying, plus the odd heavy boot to the ankles. They were a team with a fierce reputation at corners.

Our ref, Danny Milligan knew of the Dodger's tactics and tried to keep an eye on them the best he could, but they were sneaky bastards and would shout disinformation to the ref to distract him. "He's fouling me ref!" was a favourite, as was "lookout ref!" Each remark causing the ref to look away from the activity around the goal mouth.

On one memorable occasion, 'Kipper' their winger was about to take a corner, when all hell let loose around our goalie. Danny intent on performing his duty stood transfixed near the goal line, whistle in mouth, producing numerous short sharp signals warning the Dodger's about their behaviour. Meanwhile 'Kipper' hearing the whistle, thought he had clearance to take the corner and duly launched one of his trademark rockets into the penalty area. Danny with eyes firmly on the Dodgers had no idea the ball had been launched and when the cries of "Lookout ref" came, he totally ignored them, continuing his vigilance, thinking they were distraction tactics.

The ball caught the totally unaware Ref right in the back of his head with such a wallop, he did a somersault that would have earned him ten points at a gymnastics event! Whilst simultaneously blowing the loudest and longest whistle we had ever heard on a football pitch.

I kid you not, when the ball hit him, his head jerked forwards and then down to his chest, causing an equal reaction by his body to tumble towards the floor, his legs folding in the tuck position, as he rolled in mid-air, finally landing on his back in the mud with a splat!

It served as a starter gun for spontaneous laughter by all onlookers. He lay prone on the floor, still blowing his partially mud immersed whistle, although he was spark out, legs twitching in a spectacular display that would have been envied by any Irish Dancer.

We knew he was still alive because the whistle was sounding as he breathed in and out.

Being the sympathetic bunch that we were we rushed to his side and tended to him.

Hang on a minute, that's not true, we couldn't help him because both teams were doubled up with laughter! Foe leaning against foe, all divisions forgotten, bound by the hilarity of the performance of the only authority figure on the pitch. It didn't help that the few spectators we had, mostly fathers and brothers, were also helpless with laughter.

How long it took for Danny to come round I have no idea,

but that somersault was the talk of local football for a long while and is probably still being retold, with the exhibition now scoring 11 out of 10.

There was also a minor problem when we eventually restarted the game as Danny, bless him, kept blowing his whistle because he thought there were two balls on the pitch at the same time and it didn't help that some smart arse on the touchline actually kicked a second ball on just to confuse him more. I don't remember the score of that game but the memory of that somersault comes back often to give me a chuckle.

It seems there was always something going on at our football games. We did have a spare ball but sometimes it was flat and before it could be inflated, the laces had to be undone to expose the inner tube. This took quite a long time and should have been done before the match but of course it rarely was.

We should have known better because our pitch was on reclaimed land that bordered the coastline and one touchline ran perilously close to the cliff edge and if the ball went over it took some brave volunteers a long time to get down to the beach to retrieve it. Danny the ref was having a particularly difficult day with our fullback Fergus, a wild-eyed boy who was as wide as he was tall, from a family well known in our area for their fighting, drinking and general lack of discipline.

That piercing whistle went off one too many times in the direction of Fergus and he took a run at the touchline kicking out at anything in the way and connecting with the first-aid box that sat innocently in the way of his flailing boot.

The unsuspecting box suddenly burst in a shower of ointments and bandages that flew in all directions, the remnants of the splintered box travelling the furthest. The only remaining item where the box had previously resided was the brass handle that we carried it with. Spectators and players joined in the hunt for the dispersed contents while Danny tried to send Fergus off! But of course, Fergus was having none of it, as he felt he had done nothing wrong on the pitch. Danny, being the bravest person he could be, stood up to Fergus and pointed off the pitch, so Fergus true to form took a massive swipe at the ball, sending it high in the air. We all watched it gradually fly out over the cliff and disappear into the great unknown.

Suffice it to say there was utter turmoil, Danny kept blowing his whistle and pointing towards the touchline. Fergus's family came running to aid him, surrounding the ref, grabbing his whistle from his mouth and threatening him with all manner of physical harm, whilst the rest of us looked on.

I must at this point give Danny his due, he wasn't a big bloke but he wouldn't be intimidated, standing his ground and finally a furious Fergus complied with his instructions, leaving the field along with his family.

You guessed it; the spare ball was flat so we had to wait while it was inflated. What with the flat ball, the shattered first aid box, Fergus being sent off and the disappearing ball, it was a long time before the match restarted and again the score is lost to time but who cares about the score.

It was important at the time but after all these years it's all the little asides that come to mind.

When the match was over, we would return to our changing room, which was a dirty old semi-derelict hut without a lock on the door and wash ourselves down, both teams!

Two huge tin baths had been filled with hot water from a neighbouring house who we had an arrangement with. The din was ear shattering as ribald remarks flew between fellow and rival teammates, with laughter the loudest. Until that is, one of my teammates, Derry, who was the joker in our pack surprised us with a bucket of ice-cold water, leaving us screaming abuse while he stood there laughing. He did that time after time and we knew it was coming but he was clever enough to wait until our guard dropped.

Another of his party tricks was to sneak up behind you when the ball was on the opposite side of the pitch and yank your shorts down, leaving your dangly bits wafting in the breeze much to the merriment of the onlookers and bending down to retrieve them only resulted in another cheer.

If only he had done that to the opposition, it might have been a good tactic.

I still see him when I return home! He still retains that cheeky smile and a twinkle in his eyes. I shudder to think what his grandchildren are like.

Because I was the tallest by far, I usually ended up in goal, a position that suited my build but not my disposition. I always preferred to be running around, usually because it was too cold to stand still but goalie was usually where I ended up.

It was not the best place to be at times. I would stretch my arms and pluck the ball out of the sky and an opponent would react by grabbing my unprotected undercarriage giving a good firm squeeze, resulting in a dropped ball in more ways than one. My elbows came in handy when wreaking my revenge later in the game.

Diving hither and thither in the muddy goal mouth meant that my kit was filthy by the end of the game and like most young lads I took my kit home to my mother to wash! As if she didn't have enough to do! It was always spotless for the next game. There was a massive following for Manchester United football team in my area and all the kids followed the scores and collected pictures and press cuttings of their favourite stars.

Billy Whelan, an Irish International, played for Manchester United and was a massive Irish hero that we all wanted to emulate, at twenty-two years old he was only just starting on his career path but he had every Irish kid wanting to be him. He had scored 52 goals in 100 matches, over a period of three years, which is an amazing return that not many can beat, winning two league titles.

On the morning of the 7th ^{of} February 1958, I was on my way to work and I saw one of my friends, Andy, going in the opposite direction. Andy looked terrible as if he had been crying, but he was a big strong lad, older than me, that I played football with. He stopped his bike and just looked at me, horror written all over his face, his shoulders down and hardly able to speak. In broken sentences, punctuated by deep, gulps of air, he told me about the Munich air crash and that the Manchester United team were on board. Andy didn't have all the facts, but he did think that they were all dead, something that was revised later but still numbing to this day.

I went to work in a fog, unable to process that my hero Billy Whelan was dead, it couldn't be possible. He was a star! Things like that don't happen to famous people! A feeling of utter despair shrouded me for weeks, the details slowly emerging and stories of heroism amongst the players as they desperately tried to save as many passengers as possible.

The world was in mourning for all those brilliant young players, no matter what team you followed this was universal sorrow.

Newspapers were devoured daily as the survivors told their harrowing stories and news of some who survived the initial crash, dying later from their injuries.

We didn't play much football. To kick a ball would be to trivialise such a monumental catastrophe. We sat on the seawall, the beach waiting patiently for us to run around, kicking up sand and occasionally the ball, but it would not be used. Someone sat on the ball!

If you had a Man United shirt, which only the richer did, you wore it.

Pictures cut out from papers, passed around our group, sometimes wet with tears. There was no derision of someone who cried, we all did it at some time or other. It was like we had all lost a close family member.

Goodness knows what it felt like for their friends and family. Unbearable I would think! It was many years ago and a lot has happened to me since then, but every time I see an anniversary event of the tragedy I hark back to that vigil on that lonely seafront, across the sea from Manchester and my heart bleeds. For those who lived through it and followed that young, brilliant team of exquisite athletes, who lost their lives in such a disastrous way, it was a point in their lives where the world just stopped and the sun wouldn't shine and there was no future worth thinking about. Father Michael dedicated the next Sunday service to a remembrance of those boyhood heroes and families huddled together, mothers hugging boys who normally would frown upon such action, tears flowing freely from young and old alike, as we all prayed for their eternal souls.

Life for us, of course, would carry on. Night would follow day and summer would return to our lives, but at that devastating time, not one of us would have believed it.

We did gradually return to normal, the job at the greenhouses was upgraded to add two more even larger units growing tomatoes and salad plus several acres of Tulips, Daffodils, Hyacinth and Iris. This extra work was too much for me on my own so I asked Terry if he would give a job to Seamus (should have known better from previous experience). He said if I was happy to teach him, then to go ahead.

For a while it worked out very well, we both worked hard and the crops responded in kind by outstripping expectation.

We were earning steady money so we decided to each buy a bike that would then save us bus fares. There was a bike shop called Clancy's in Ballytreeny so we walked down to have a look in the window.

A sky-blue racer had pride of position, all chrome and sparkling paintwork and I was hooked.

In we went, two scruffy local lads with eyes bigger than their pockets to be greeted enthusiastically by Bryan the owner. He was smooth was Bryan, made sure he had one foot on the door to stop you getting out. It was a bit like Hotel California! We tried cheaper bikes but we always kept coming back to the racer in the window. Seventeen pounds was an awful lot of money and we had no collateral but, in those days, they knew where you lived and so, you could buy on a cash per week basis with a no interest deal, but you couldn't haggle about the price.

They had two bikes, in the same model and in different colours so Seamus and I signed on the dotted line, not bothering to read what we were signing. We both agreed to pay 5 shillings per week until the total sum was paid, in other words 34 weeks!

We rode out of that shop like kings! I have bought brand new expensive limousines since but I could never better the feelings I had that day, my own bike, brand new, all shiny and as fast as the cobbled streets would let us pedal.

There is no feeling in the world like zooming along on your bike, through country lanes you would usually be walking, wind in your hair, carefree, full of joy at this wondrous experience. I can feel it now, rolling back the years and perched once again on the saddle of that first new bike. Exhilarating! Legs pumping with the exuberance of youth! Free as a bird to roam wherever we liked! What a special day that was!

Every Saturday I made the trip to the bike shop and gave Mr Clancy my five shillings, proudly meeting my commitment to repay the debt. It was only after about six months or so that he said to me, "When is your brother going to start paying?" I was absolutely gobsmacked, having no idea that my brother had not paid a single penny since we picked the bikes up. I should have known from the start that this would happen but he was my brother and I always gave him another chance.

I had no choice but to tell Dad. It didn't give me pleasure to rat on my errant brother or to listen to our father berate him for letting the family down.

He was marched down to the shop the very next day and found to be twelve pounds in arrears so an arrangement was made to pay a £1 a week until the full £17 was repaid, which he agreed to, reluctantly but he only paid for a month or so before he defaulted again. This was a pattern he was setting for the rest of his life and I was powerless to help him change course.

My brother although feckless had a knack of getting away with things! He was undoubtedly charming and always looked like he was repenting even though inside he was probably laughing like a drain!

A good example of the above happened at the end of the tomato season. The boss was away on holiday with his family and we were left to clean out the greenhouses and prepare them for salad planting. All went well at first, it was hard and dirty work but we kept at it and were surprisingly ahead of our schedule, or what passed for one.

In the yard there was an old tractor and Seamus thought it might be fun to take it for a ride along the beach. It was a bit old and rusty and not in good nick at all, but he got the thing to fire up and off he trundled, without telling me of course.

I wondered where the hell he was and searched the premises looking for him, totally unaware of his acquisition and destination.

Not being with him, I'll have to tell you what he relayed to me about what happened and knowing my brother, you can either believe it or put it down to his skewed selective memory.

Chugging along the lane down to the beach in the old

tractor, he saw a couple of incorrigible friends of his who willingly climbed on board. They had recently seen a war film about the Desert Rats fighting Panzer divisions in the desert and so the old creaking, rattling tractor became a makeshift imaginary tank complete with daring crew. With sticks as guns and using impromptu vocal utterings mimicking the sound of rapid fire, they charged the 'Tractorvator', as they called it, down the grassy bank and onto the beach.

Now as we know and they probably forgot, tanks run on special tracks that allow them to distribute their weight and get traction on the sand, so they can travel at a fair old lick.

Old tractors, laden with teenagers, inevitably experience a rapid halt when they come into contact with soft sand, as its occupants quickly found out.

To add to their dilemma this particular area of the beach was known for its tendency to be more like quicksand, due to the quite vicious tide having a nasty undertow. Before they knew it, the old tractor was sinking rapidly.

The 'Tractorvator' was immediately deserted by the 'Rats', shouting bizarrely, "Abandon Ship!", as they obviously got their films mixed up.

They stood there helpless as the wheels disappeared into

the sand. After a short while, standing there scratching their heads and other parts of their anatomy, they came to a consensus of what to do! The only thing they could agree to do was run to the garage nearby, owned by one of the boy's fathers and ask for a tow truck.

By the time they returned to the scene of the crime, all scrunched into the cab of the truck, the tractor was nowhere to be seen! Open mouths caught flies for a while, until the tow truck driver asked where the stranded tractor was!

"It was here when we left!" my brother uttered!

"Well, it's not bloody here now!" was the angry reply.

"Some bastard's pinched it!" The irony of his statement was lost on my brother!

Just as they were about to go look somewhere else for it, just in case they were in the wrong place, there was a loud groan, like a dying tractor. The area of sand where they left the 'Tractorvator' shook and dropped a few inches. There was a sudden realisation where their transport had disappeared to!

"You'll never get that back, lads!" was the truck driver's opinion. "That tractor is sunk completely under the sand!"

Seamus came back to me, cap in hand, terrified he might

lose his job and also worried he would have to pay for the tractor as well as his bike. I did call him a few choice words but I doubt they registered on his brain! Let's face it, I wasn't the best role model for him, was I? Looking back now I realise he was only emulating his big brother's love for a laugh.

I worried for days after, wondering how I would tell our boss and if I would get sacked as well. As it turned out, he was happy to believe that Seamus took the tractor and gave it a run to keep the battery working, especially when he must have claimed on his insurance, because a little later a new tractor arrived and we both kept our jobs. My brother got away with it again!

You thought I was a bit incorrigible, didn't you? Go on, be honest, I've got broad shoulders, well my brother thought I was a real rebel! Me, a rebel? He always saw me as the big brother who was always getting into trouble.

My reputation at school was still there long after I left, as a boy who openly defied authority. He saw me as someone without guile! Someone who was not afraid to perform dastardly deeds and own up to them. So, he was gobsmacked when an incident, that I have just recalled, happened after work one day.

The business was going really well, the boss had even more greenhouses built, employing a local builder called Bob. I know! Bob the builder! Who would have guessed? But that was his name! Bob was the proud owner of a Ford Prefect car, pale green with cream upholstery and matching hubcaps. This car was a status symbol for the builder and he kept it pristine, especially when going to church.

It was Good Friday a very important date on our calendar, but due to the nature of our products, Seamus and I had to work until 6.00pm. Bob was also on site checking up on his workers' progress. I asked Bob if he would give us a lift to church, it being much quicker than riding there on our bikes and then we would get the bus to work the next morning.

The bastard said no! Turning his nose up at us yokels, as he called us! Pointing out that we would mess up the plastic covering still protecting his seat covers. The twat!

We were getting ready to leave at 6.00pm when he drove past us on his way out, an exaggerated wave of his hand aimed at us in parting, followed by a "Toot! Toot!" on the horn. Reciprocation was made by Seamus and me with vigorous hand movements of our own!

We started our hurried cycle journey knowing we would just about make the church in time if we were not delayed, so off we went.

About two miles into the journey there is a relatively steep hill that twists and turns as it climbs up the ridge, before descending down to the coast and Ballytreeny. Imagine our delight when, halfway up it, we came across bungling Bob, head under a propped-up bonnet, with greasy hands leaning on the wings around the engine compartment.

Bob saw us coming and shouted, "Give us a push, lads!" Well, you can imagine the reply! "Go forth and multiply!" is the polite way of saying it, as we peddled past as fast as we could.

Seamus was laughing so much he nearly fell off his bike. We stopped briefly and looked back down the hill at the exasperated Bob, shaking his fist at us. "God was obviously looking down!" said Seamus, piously.

"Not a lot to do with God" I replied, as we started to freewheel down the other side of the hill. "After he refused to give us a lift, I pissed in his petrol tank!"

Seamus wobbled most of the way down the hill and had to make an emergency dash for the bushes before he wet himself. For one day we bonded as brothers and incidentally, just in case you were wondering, we did make the service on time, but not surprisingly, Bob didn't!"

My brother realised there was a crafty side to me that he was not aware of, which he reminds me of whenever the story, extremely embellished, is trotted out for unsuspecting guests.

One by-product of going to Church was that there were always girls around, parading in their finery, aloof and out of reach of scruffs like us, at least usually! I was growing up, almost seventeen, tall and muscular with a shock of hair and I noticed they took more notice of me this year than last.

We were milling around outside, after the service, Father Michael greeting us all, an individual remark for each and every one.

There has been a lot of adverse publicity over the conduct of catholic priests in recent years, but not so much about the ones who were the rock on which our community relied.

Father Michael was an exceptional man, brave and strong, but also calm and insightful, with a wealth of knowledge that he needed to trawl on many occasions, especially when I was around.

"When are you going to stop growing Niall?" he inquired with a smile, looking up at me with wonder in his eyes and then he added "Niall ... never forget, no matter how tall you are, keep your feet on the ground like everybody else".

At the time, I was not sure what he meant by that remark. Was he being funny? I know now of course that he was passing on a life lesson about staying grounded as a human being, but at the time I just replied, "I'll do my best Father!" in a vain attempt to sound like an adult and failing badly.

We spilled out of that holy place, pausing with the Father as we left and then entered the increasingly bustling crowd swelling in the grounds around the church.

Caroline was known to me, a friend of my sister's, but to be truthful I had never bothered with her very much, her being at least a year younger than me, so probably coming up to sixteen at the time. I spotted her walking with her parents and I was struck by how grown up she had become, as tall as her mother by now and still growing, a bright red bow in her tight brown curls.

I knew she was looking at me, just couldn't quite get eye contact and then it happened, just for a split second and she blushed. Not enough for her parents to notice but my keen, girl watching radar had picked up the faint traces and amplified them to readable levels.

Funny the skills boys attain when they almost reach seventeen.

Circling the pack like a lion on the prowl, I slowly edged closer and closer to her, finally standing and striking a nonchalant pose a couple of feet away, surreptitiously listening in to the family conversation. "Hello Niall!", it was

Caroline's mother. "Busted!" I thought.

"Hi Mrs O'Connell"

"Your mother says you are doing very well for yourself, running a tomato business, all on your own".

"It's a start!" I ventured. "Salad stuff as well when the season is right".

"I'm leaving school soon!" said Caroline, who I now turned to speak to.

"I couldn't wait to leave!" was my comment.

"I'd stay on if it was possible, but dad's not too well and I need to get a job. Anything going at your place?"

"I'll ask for you. The business is expanding all the time so there may be. I'll check!"

"Thank you, Niall. That's very kind of you".

As luck would have it, someone stopped to talk to Mrs O'Connell, so she politely turned away, leaving me with Caroline and just out of earshot.

"Do you fancy going to pictures with me one night?" I asked in a shy sort of way.

She laughed and I thought she was going to shrug me off but she said, "I thought you were banned from the cinema!

I was there when you set off the smoke bombs! Better than the film! We laughed for hours at the way they frogmarched you out, banning you for two lifetimes, you, spluttering your complete innocence but with guilt painted all over your face. Classic! Of course, I'll go with you! If only to see you turfed out again."

"Brilliant!" I commented, taken aback by her honesty.

"Only problem is, how do you get in? Perhaps I can smuggle you in, in my handbag!" she giggled.

"We could go into Rush on the bus they haven't banned me!" I countered.

Quick as a flash back came the retort "Yet!!"

"Smart arse!" I flashed back, only to regret it immediately, but she laughed and I knew she was cool.

"When shall we go?" she inquired.

"How about next Friday night? I'll check what's on." I offered.

"Oh … I have to go now but just one thing more!" and she moved in much closer and sniffed at me. "I thought Erin was exaggerating, you don't smell like the bottom of a fish barrel. So that's good. I was a bit worried".

With that she turned and mouthed, "Call for me on

Friday!"

Wow that was a chance meeting that got better and better. She sounded like a girl looking for a good time and I was the boy to give it to her. I'll tell you later about the date. I need to figure out which bits to leave in and which bits to leave out. Let me ponder and I'll come back to it.

Ok I've thought about it over a cup of tea and I've decided to let my story tell itself and then edit out the bits that could harm the innocent ... or the guilty ... depending on my mood and of the mood of my editor in chief, who, as a strong female, restrains my sometimes-vivid imagination from running away with me, as she often thinks I make things up. As if?

Friday raced up on me! I was buoyed by anticipation, sending my blood running and causing me to hum to myself as I walked up to Caroline's house. This was new to me, going right up to the door, knocking and waiting, not just running away.

Mrs O'Connell opened the door and invited me in.

Mr O'Connell sat in a chair by the fireside, reading his paper, appearing calm that some boy was about to take his precious daughter on her first date at the cinema and in another town to boot. He looked up from his reading and lowering his head like a bull about to charge, stared at me over the top of his glasses, nodding in my direction.

No need for words, the sentiment was clear. "Upset my daughter and you'll have me to deal with", as he returned to perusing the news.

"Caroline … Niall's here for you!" Mrs O'Connell shouted up the stairs.

In a moment Caroline appeared, already in her coat, a small rose-coloured beret at a fashionable angle on her head.

Walking to the bus stop, she took my hand, bold as brass, my heart skipped a beat and I had to swallow hard, good start I thought.

There was a small queue, made up of people we had known since birth, so we just stood closer together, still holding hands and moving our fingers around in a frantic underground battle of supressed love, exchanging occasional glances with a knowing glint.

The rickety old bus set off at a pace that belied its years of service, pre-war I suppose. Paint peeling and seats that had seen better days, artwork formed on the surfaces where multiple arses had slid up and down, during excursions to and from Ballytreeny.

I must admit there was little automobile traffic in those

days and it's a good job, because the bus lurched from side to, brushing hedgerows, first on one side, then on the other. The odd branch of a tree made a noise like chalk on a blackboard, as it came into contact with the flying bus.

It did make things interesting as the forces at work on our bodies, caused us to slip and slide on the already bum polished leather seats. Caroline's body was frequently pressed up against mine and she didn't seem to mind at all. Woo-hoo!

Alighting from the donkey's years old charabanc, we strolled like a couple who had done this many times and it felt so right, she was so easy to be with it was delightful.

For once I didn't have to peek at who was on the door of the cinema, although I did think for a moment that there might be a board with pictures on it with, "Ireland's most banned people" as a heading but thank goodness they had forgotten to display it that day,

The film was Norman Wisdom's "One good turn" and we settled down to watch it, still hand in hand. So far so good, but what is there with cinemas and me?

There is a scene where Norman is mistaken for a famous Orchestra Conductor and steps on stage to subsequently cause a musical riot. If you haven't seen it, just do a trawl of YouTube and you're sure to find the excerpt.

Well to cut a long farce short, we started to laugh, not just me, not just Caroline but the whole audience and soon the place was rocking. I was in such a good mood; the laughing overtook me and I might say Caroline. We were in a total state of euphoria, laughing until our sides hurt, crying, literally, tears pouring down our faces. The big problem was, we didn't know how to stop and the audience were now laughing at us and it got worse and worse, until the inevitable happened and I was ejected, closely followed by Caroline.

In normal fashion, I was banned for life and to make matters worse they banned Caroline as well, which made us laugh even more. We never did see the end of the film but we bought fish and chips and sat on a park bench and scoffed the lot.

It was a magical evening and to put the icing on it as we were sat on the park bench, I put my … hang on … you don't think I'd tell tales like that do you? You should be ashamed of yourself and anyway my editor in chief, bless her cotton socks would edit the hell out of it, so there.

All I can say it was a memorable night and I got her home at a reasonable time and we kissed at her doorstep, just before her father came out. Lucky that! More about Caroline later.

Life was about to change again for me in a big way, fulfilling my boyhood dream of sailing off to distant destinations, exploring the world that exists out there across the sea.

I had made job applications but had never received a positive reply, until, on the evening of Friday the 16th of September of 1960, I dismounted from my bike, having cycled home after work and football practice, to find my mother standing at the gate. She seemed excited for me, holding something in her hand, which she presented to me with a big smile and a look of apprehension that it was hard for her to disguise.

It was a telegram from Irish Shipping, asking me to report for duty at their Dublin office the following Tuesday morning. I read it and reread it, wondering if the words would somehow change and it was all a mistake, but of course they didn't and it slowly became reality.

I was leaving Ballytreeny, for all I knew it would be for good. This newfound reality was beginning to make me wobble a bit, reasons why I shouldn't go began sneaking into my thoughts, questioning my resolve. My mind was in turmoil, I remember shaking as I sat there, it was probably adrenaline but it did unnerve me.

That night I was supposed to be meeting Caroline for another trip to the cinema with a view to seeing the whole film, this time without being thrown out for laughing too loud.

I would have to tell her about my plans, preferably after the film, just in case she threw a wobbly and got us banned from the only remaining cinema I could get into.

We were going to see Ben-Hur, the famous film starring Charlton Heston with the wonderful chariot race that caught the world's imagination, not something to laugh at so it was safe enough to think we wouldn't be banned again.

Picking her up at home I went through the same rigmarole as the previous time with her father, all the time thinking "How will he react when his daughter comes home crying because I'm leaving Ballytreeny for ever?" I felt like a dead man talking as I replied to his searching questions with a confidence born out of terror. Thankfully, she deigned to appear just as I was running out of bravado and rescued me from his inquisition.

We sat on the bus, holding hands, swaying with the motion as we hurtled around the narrow roads, with me staring ahead, not wanting to meet her eyes, afraid that she might see right through my façade and confront me in front of the other passengers.

Luckily for me, bonkers Bryan O'Casey (we called him "Bonkers" because he was known to do random things that made us laugh and I know it's not PC but it was a different time) was sat immediately in front of us and he whiffed. I say whiffed to be kind; in fact, he stank. I can hear you asking, "What of?" Caroline sat there with the fingers of her left hand holding her nose as tightly as possible. When she tried to whisper to me, she sounded like a nasal Daffy Duck. She was asking me what I thought the smell was. All I could do was shrug my shoulders, as I had no idea. We sat squirming in our seats until I noticed Jocko, a Scottish kid who had come to live in Ballytreeny a few years ago, laughing with another lad a few rows back.

I let go of Caroline's grip and made my way towards the back of the bus and the sniggering Jocko.

"What's the joke?" I enquired.

"That plonker!" he replied pointing at Bonkers Bryan.

"What's he done now?"

"Run out of Brylcreem!" laughed the boys in unison.

"What's funny about that?"

"It's what he used in place of it" Jocko said before collapsing with convulsions.

His mate said, between laughs "He used LARD!" and then descended down the laughter lane that leads to total disassociation with bodily functions, farting loudly enough to make people turn round in their seats. The pair were now laughing more than we did before we were ejected from the cinema, they were in danger of soiling the seats they were sat on.

"We've changed his nickname to 'Fathead'" howled Jocko, before clutching his crotch with both hands and leaning heavily on his mate sat next to him.

Caroline was watching the whole time and I beckoned for her to leave the seat and come to the back of the bus, which she did, hanging on to the handles suspended from the roof, doing her best to stay on her feet as we rounded yet another hairpin bend.

She collapsed into the vacant seat and I laughingly explained to her what the smell was and the new nickname that Bryan had obtained.

Soon all four of us were convulsed with waves of laughter and other passengers, not knowing why we were laughing, were laughing with us.

Norman Wisdom would have been proud of us, it was infectious and by the time we descended from the bus I was exhausted, only to start again when the bus driver asked us to tell him the joke, we were all laughing at and none of us could for laughing.

Steering clear of Bonkers Bryan and his lardy hair we found seats in plenty of time before the lights went down.

"You were quiet earlier on the bus!" observed Caroline.

"Here we go" I thought.

"Been working hard and then Soccer practice, guess I was tired" I lied whilst praying the film would hurry up and start.

"Thought for a minute you were going to break up with me" she countered with.

"Oh God" I thought "Now what do I say".

"Of course not, it's just …"

Saved by the lights! The commercials came on and we were distracted by all the fine things on offer. I sat in my seat, sweating a little and thinking of what I was going to say later.

After about half an hour, either the sweating in the cinema and the laughing on the bus, or playing Soccer after a hard day's work, or a combination of them all, I suddenly felt the worst case of leg cramp in my short life.

My right leg was cramped from my hip right down to my toes and the pain was excruciating. With one involuntary movement I leaped up into the air, scattering the popcorn that was safely residing on my knees over the row of people in front.

Balancing on my left leg I tried to ease the pain in my right by pressing hard with my hand but that just felt worse. I was told many years later by an un-forgetting Jocko that I shrieked out like a banshee caught in a threshing machine, dancing like a lunatic on a pogo stick whilst peppering everyone else with God knows what.

It might have been funny for him but anyone who has suffered from severe leg cramp will know it is extremely painful, probably worse than giving birth, so my male friends assure me.

Caroline was mortified! She had no idea what was going on and as a deeply religious person, she thought I had been possessed by demons. The evidence was plain for her to see, the pagan dance, the swearing, the anointment of all around with popcorn, she told me later that she said a silent prayer, afraid to touch me in case the demons attacked her too.

Once again, I was escorted out into the foyer, but they were very helpful, understanding what the problem was and reassuring Caroline that it was cramp and not demonic possession.

When the pain finally calmed down to a point where I could stand on two feet and had ceased to swear loudly, we were allowed back into the cinema and thankfully before the main film started. In those days there was always a 'B' film before the big feature. The usherette was even told by the manager to supply me with a few drinks to raise my fluid level and thus go some way to preventing more cramp chaos.

We did settle down to watch the film but I caught Caroline looking at me every now and again to make sure demons had not returned to my compliant body. The film was awesome!

Laughter did return later as we were waiting for the bus home. Jocko and a few of his mates descended on the bus stop, almost crying with laughter and between snorts tried to explain why but failing every time they pictured what had happened.

All became evident when Bonkers Bryan turned up. In the heat of the cinema the lard must have melted because his hair had collapsed around his ears! His previous bouffant look having somewhat slipped from its former glory to look like a cart horse's tail after a day in the field. The memory still makes me laugh after all these years, thank you Bryan for being beautifully bonkers. I like to think you went on to be a visionary in some obscure field of research and I hope I am right.

As we were walking the last few yards to Caroline's house, I took a deep breath and stopped walking. I took her hand and spoke softly and I hope sincerely about my imminent departure. She started to cry and that upset me. I was way out of my depth and for once in my life I was lost for words.

Seventeen is no age to have to deal with turmoil like this, but I had to, there was no stepping back. She asked me, between sobs, whether or not I was coming home … ever!

I couldn't answer her! I was off on an adventure to who knows where and for as long as it took, but that statement would be too much of a hammer blow and I really liked her. I promised I would be back soon and I would write to her every day until then but of course I knew I wouldn't.

I left her on her doorstep, watching me go, sobbing quietly to herself, a tiny white handkerchief mopping up the salty tears of a teenage goodbye, caused by a boy who was obsessed with ships and faraway places, a boy who would return a man, alas not one to be involved in Caroline's life again.

I'm sorry if I hurt you Caroline but I was only a kid and the call of adventure was far too strong, we had a laugh while it lasted and I hope you look back on our time together with some affection, especially if you read this book.

6. OFF TO SEE THE WORLD, SEA-SICKNESS, A FAMOUS FOUR, NIAGARA FALLS & FIREWORK FOLLY

It seemed to me that although I was saying hello to a new adventure, I was also saying a lot of goodbyes. I truly believed I was never coming back and in the same way that leaving school hit me unexpectedly, leaving the farm where I had tended and nurtured so many plants, left me with a heavy feeling in my stomach.

Saturday was a normal workday for me and I cycled the route knowing it was my last time to do it. The lanes seemed unusually beautiful, decorated in their autumnal colours, as I tried to take in every second, even the smells emanating from all sorts of country life, wafting over my brain waves, consigning them to a memory vault for future reminiscence.

When I told my boss about my plans, there were no recriminations, no pleading to stay! He looked at me and told me he had always known I was a dreamer and that I was destined to strike out for far horizons. We sat together for almost an hour, me spouting about how I would see the world, with him interjecting with gems of knowledge gleaned from his personal experience and reflections on how his life had taken tangential detours on its way to his final destination. There was always a job for me if I decided to return but he accepted that it was unlikely and he wished me luck and good fortune.

What I did for the rest of the day, I have no recollection. Maybe I worked hard to get jobs done, which would be the way I would act now! Perhaps I daydreamed, hopelessly lost in a fog of expectation, anxious to be on my way, not looking back but forward to a future on the high seas.

Only one worrying thought crossed my mind! "Please don't let me be seasick!"

Saying goodbye to my mother was the worst part, her eyes red and puffy, she tried her best to hide it but I knew she was heartbroken to let me go. I was her eldest child and although I'm sure she loved us all equally maybe it was a sign of what would happen with all the others in the not-too-distant future.

Whatever it was, she never said, only hugged me for a little longer than I expected, kissing my cheek as she let go, her tears touching my face and running down to my chin.

If I close my eyes, I can still see her standing there with my sisters, all clinging to each other, huddled in an embrace that bound them to my heart. My father and brothers had left for work with only a cursory remark, my father wouldn't have known what to say and I think my younger brothers were a bit envious of my impending independence.

I turned and waved as I rounded the corner onto the main road, my heart pounding with expectation and to be honest, little regard to what I was leaving behind. Adventure was out there taunting me and I was going to damn well find it and make it my own.

Sitting on that old bus, once again, waiting to depart, my small battered old suitcase safely stowed, I aimlessly gazed out of the window at the clamour of cottages, all higgledy-piggledy and random. They were constructed without any reference to planning permission, in days where you built what you wanted, when you wanted, how you wanted and bugger the rest.

If you owned the land, it was ok and nobody cared. A sort of patchwork art that defied logic and became a picture for the ages.

My careless gaze was interrupted by the vision of a beautiful girl, half hidden in the shadows, tears in her eyes and a partial wave that seemed to be the most she could do in the state she was in. It was an unmistakeable Caroline, who had not wanted to endure a physical goodbye, merely letting me know how she felt. My hand gradually came to life in response to her parting wave, the bus noisily moving off, gears crunching. Our eyes locked in a final goodbye for a split second that burned itself into my retina, closing a chapter in my life, sweet and innocent, but deep and loving. Something I would try to replicate and fail to come anywhere near for many years.

I had been to Dublin enough times to know my way around, but it still filled me with awe. The crowded streets, shops, traffic! All things that were absent from sleepy Ballytreeny.

Everyone seemed in a hurry! I was one of the few to look up at the towering buildings (I hadn't been to New York at this time!). How could anybody live that far off the ground! Didn't they get nose bleeds?

The overwhelming feature was the noise level! It was deafening to my sensitive ears! I honestly put my hands over my ears at one stage to get a little relief from the cacophony. Nobody stared! Nobody took any notice at all! In Ballytreeny, someone would have queried my actions!

I would learn quickly not to base my expectations on a Ballytreeny datum point.

It was another new experience walking into an organised office in the big city. People were beavering away, charts were being updated, phones were ringing and small groups of people were congregating in offices. This was a huge machine and I was about to become a small cog in its ever-changing mechanism, small but important enough to be paid £6.00 a week, which at the time was good money.

I was directed to a desk on the far side of the office, under a clock that displayed multiple time zones.

A young man sat, looking like everything I would have expected from a professional manager. Good dark suit, clean starched white shirt, neatly assembled tie, close cropped haircut, clean-shaven.

In other words, everything I wasn't.

It's quite amazing going back over your life like this, because you remember things that you have pushed into the recesses of your mind. Things that set standards for later in life and this young man, unknowingly left an indelible impression on me about how to be presentable. It's an image I have subconsciously used numerous times to judge others and even more importantly to judge myself.

Having introduced ourselves, he asked me to take a seat and proceeded to talk about the job as a Deck Boy, the pay and conditions before asking me to sign my name. I immediately reached for the pen to sign on the dotted line. Another life lesson was about to be given, one which was to save me from a jail sentence later in life (maybe in the next book) as he put his hand over the page to prevent me from signing it. I looked up in alarm, wondering if I had offended him but he smiled and said, "Don't you think you should read it before signing it?"

In my haste of course that had never entered my head. Sheepishly, I picked up the form and read it from top to bottom and then signed it.

Apparently, it was normal for ship's crew to send part of their wages home each week and he asked me if I would like to do that.

I asked him to send £5 of my £6 per week to my mother and he smiled.

"That's a lovely gesture, but you'll probably need more than a pound of week in your pocket"

After a short discussion we agreed on £4 to my mother and £2 to me, which was quite a lot more than I had kept before.

There were some days I wish I had kept more for myself, but I had no real idea what lay ahead. To be honest, I don't think that neatly turned-out clerk would know anything about what deck boys got up to but you are about to find out. Hope you have your sea legs on, we're off on a journey to exotic places, well Liverpool to start, not quite exotic although compared to Ballytreeny anywhere is.

The formalities over, I was instructed to take my papers and report to the First Officer on board the Ramona Wave at the North Wall Dock. Walking along the wharf, looking at the ships being loaded and unloaded by hand and crane was fascinating. It was all part of the big machine, doing its bit as the interface between land and sea. I held my head high, knowing I was part of this, whilst also making sure I didn't obstruct any of the frantic activity.

The Ramona Wave was a fine-looking ship and I was proud to walk up the gangway to my new life aboard her.

I was asked my business by the person on watch and sent up to the first officer's room. Now, that's ok if you know where it is, but of course I didn't and having never been on a ship before I must have looked a right square peg. Luckily enough a guy named Percy, who turned out later to be the ship's carpenter, took pity on me and showed me to the right place, for which I was very grateful.

It wasn't the easiest place to get to for me, as by now I was over six feet tall and I think the ship was made for people six inches shorter. I seemed to duck a lot and I think Percy had a small chuckle at my expense.

I introduced myself to the first officer, who read my papers and asked me a few questions to see how green I really was.

I must have seemed like the Jolly Green Giant, star of many ads in years to come, but I need not have worried because he was a good man and from rural Ireland himself.

"It's a good life, if it's for you, but it can be a bad one if it's not." A statement I found confusing at seventeen but perfectly clear at this distance in time.

He took me aft to the crew's quarters and to my cabin, which although it had a bunk bed, I had all to myself.

To someone who has lived all their lives crammed together with seven siblings and my parents in a small house, this was heaven. MY OWN SPACE! There was a small dressing table and a chair with washing facilities. I'd never known such luxury and they paid me! Wonderful! Toilets were nearby and I didn't have to go outside for them either! Whoopee!

The mess room was where the crew ate their meals and was located mid ship and I was just in time for lunch. There was a lot of chatter going on amidst the clatter of knives and forks, mostly by older men who didn't even look up at me. Thankfully, there was one lad about my age and the first officer introduced us before he left. His name was Liam and would become a very good friend of mine and a rascal to boot, so I was in good company. Hail fellow well met and all that.

Liam took me to the galley where there were two cooks and a steward showed me the menu saying order what you want and it'll be served to you in the mess room.

It was hard to believe that all I had to do was order something and it would be brought to the table. Breakfast, lunch and dinner! Every day! I'd never had it so good and to be fair there were few complaints about the quality or quantity of the food served to us.

It transpired that we were sailing that night to Liverpool and then onto Glasgow, a trip that seemed a dream only a short while ago. That was to be followed by the big adventure itself, across the Atlantic to St John's, New Brunswick, Montreal, Detroit then across the Great Lakes to Port Arthur and Fort William.

To be perfectly honest I had never heard of some of these places and had absolutely no concept of where they were or how far it was to get there.

Liam gave me a full tour of the ship and finally left me with the Bosun on the Fore Deck whilst he went to the Aft Deck and I watched as the crew took in the ropes that tethered the ship to the quay.

We gently moved away from land as a tug pulled us carefully but purposely out into the river Liffey where we uncoupled, making our way into the Irish Sea.

My adventure had begun and that's all I thought about, whilst at home my mother and sisters wept and I can only imagine what Caroline was going through. I look back now and think myself callous and shallow but, in my defence, I was living my dream and for me this was the most important day of my life.

Standing on the deck of the Ramona Wave, as we moved further and further away from Ireland, the possibilities were endless and I had never felt so energised. The fresh salty air hung on the spray that showered me with welcome, as if anointing me into a seagoing fraternity. Freedom was the overwhelming feeling, an anticipation of what was to come. No barriers I couldn't break down! No insurmountable problems I couldn't solve, I was free. FREE! There were no tethers to bind my exuberance or walls to confine my ambitions. Exhilaration leapt unfettered through my youthful daydreams and anything was possible.

I stood quietly on that dampened deck watching an orange sun dissolve into a darkening sea on an epoch that has never lost its magnitude and it still rates as one of the best days of my life.

Reluctantly I eventually went down to my cabin, clothes drizzled with damp, but elation overruling every other emotion and sat in MY cabin, in MY space, not wishing for the day to end. Sleep came reluctantly to claim my boyhood dreams and weary from my adventures I slipped into a deep sleep to once again relive a magical day.

Bang! Bang! "What the hell?"

"Come on Niall! See you in the mess room" yelled Liam from the other side of my cabin door.

It did take me a few moments to realise where I was, the motion of the ship confusing my still sleeping brain but soon reality kicked in. It was a good job I didn't instinctively jump out of bed as I decided to sleep in the top bunk! I decided against the bottom one as I knew I would have been hospitalised with concussion, if I sat up too quickly!

Getting dressed as quickly as I could, I joined Liam for breakfast. I was wary of eating because of my trawler experience but I seemed to be doing ok, seasickness although making subtle prods, an overpowering gnawing hunger in my stomach was more urgent. So, I tucked into bacon and eggs and followed it with a large mug of tea. There seemed to be a constant flow of men through the mess, chattering and laughing for the most, each with a job to do on board and confident in their ability to do it, whereas I was still to learn exactly what was required of me.

Walking onto the deck from the dim interior into that beautiful sunny autumn morning, I was rather surprised to find us anchored in the Mersey River. We were waiting for a tug to take us into the dock and nothing could happen until it arrived, which apparently would not be until midday.

There wasn't a lot I could do so I borrowed a pair of binoculars and scanned the Liverpool horizon for landmarks.

It is amazing and I have related this to you before, dear reader, but when looking back like this you can recognise points in time that shifted your lifeline. This was really the first time I wished I owned a good camera. There was so much activity between us and the Liverpool skyline and I had nothing, apart from my memory, to record it with.

It took me a while but I did eventually buy my first camera, a story in itself that I'll probably tell you later and I have never been without one since. My life and that of the people around me has been captured, first on film and then on disc, all because of a passion born that day on the Mersey.

The tug did turn up at midday and towed us into the harbour and I hardly missed a moment of the journey, a wide-eyed Irish boy living his dream, black and blue from pinching himself, thinking any moment he would wake up and be back in Ballytreeny.

Liverpool got closer and closer and higher and higher, cranes and warehouses dominating the skyline, with the city sitting invitingly in the background. Frantic but controlled activity surrounded the ship as we came alongside the quay and secured in our berth. The gangway was put out and a number of people came aboard to talk to the Captain. I made myself scarce and went below to find Liam.

Having checked his room and found it empty, I went to the mess room where Liam was sat, mug of tea in hand, reading a book.

"It's all happening up top!" was my lame comment, knowing Liam had seen it all before.

"Yeah. Nothing for us to do really!" Then, after a short pause, he put down his book and with a mischievous look said, "Unless we get a pass and go ashore."

"Is that possible?" was my naïve comment.

"Of course! As long as we ask nicely and get back before morning".

"What are we waiting for?" I queried.

"Got any money?"

In my excitement I hadn't thought of that! "Not a lot really, how much will I need?"

"Depends on what we do £1 ought to be enough!"

Just a short note dear reader, beer cost ... wait for it ... one shilling per pint at the time, so £1 went a long way.

"I only have six shillings" I lamented.

"Don't worry" said Liam as he carefully closed his book and got up from the table. "I'll lend you a pound until pay day".

Remember, this is a guy who had only just met me and was treating me like an old friend. I quickly said thank you and we set off together to ask for permission to go ashore.

The Officer looked at us, with a smirk on his face and offered us some advice.

"Liam, you've been ashore in Liverpool before, but Niall is a novice. If you're going, you need to keep an eye on him.

Don't come back carrying him unless that's the only way he'll come back and for god's sake don't lose him. Now bugger off, before I change my mind!" The last part was said with a big grin!

We quickly disembarked amidst the frenetic activity on the dock and made our way through security and out of the gates, where we stood scanning the surroundings for a bus stop.

"Over there!" shouted Liam and we trotted off to catch the

next bus into the city centre.

Now this was a bus! It may have been grimy but it was fairly new, probably no more than ten years old. It had a bell that people rang when they wanted the bus to stop. How exotic!

I must have looked like the tourist I was, nose pressed firmly up against the window, straining to see everything before the light went in the next couple of hours. I needn't have worried because as the daylight disappeared, so the city transformed into a magical display of electric illumination. There were signs everywhere, offering a multitude of items and experiences, a lot of which I had never heard of and was reluctant to ask.

Pubs didn't open until 5.30pm so we wandered up and down the town centre, my mind overflowing with information.

We were walking down Mathew Street when we saw some yobs, at least that's what they looked like, humping instruments out a clapped-out old van and onto the pavement.

"Want a hand?" I shouted.

"Ok Paddy!" smiled a guy with a leather jacket with the collar turned up Brando style.

Liam stood back with a quizzical look as I tucked an amplifier under one arm and a guitar under the other.

I followed the other guys down some steps into a dingy cellar, illuminated by a solitary light in the far corner.

"Put it down there, Paddy" said the Brando guy and I obliged.

"Want me to get some more?" I asked him.

"Yeah! Why not? Got a bad back me anyway, so do your bit cock. I do love Paddies!" said Brando sprawling over a couple of rickety old chairs.

"He'll get you carrying it all. Lazy bastard" said a young lad about my age carrying a guitar. "He thinks he's god's gift to the world".

"So, I am! So, I am!" came the instant reply.

"What's he done now?" this time from a third fellow, bright eyed and fine features, who I thought was probably the leader.

"Got Paddy carrying all his gear! Lazy bastard!"

"I don't mind!" I offered.

"See! He doesn't mind. Now let him go and get the rest. Look at the size of him! He could carry the bloody lot in one go!"

Off I went back up the stairs to the street and picked up whatever else was available.

"New roadie?" said a guy carrying a drum case.

I had no idea what a roadie was so I said, "Yes!"

"About time!" he remarked "Give us a hand with this lot".

"Back in a minute!" I said as I disappeared back down into the gloom below with my precious cargo.

It didn't take long before all the equipment was being assembled before me. It was only then I realised Liam wasn't there. "Oh, shit I thought. I've lost Liam".

"What's up mate?" said the one who looked like the leader.

"I've lost my friend. He was just standing there".

Without another cue the guy picked up a guitar, left-handed, which I thought was unusual and started singing, making up a song about Liam "He was just standing there, I don't know quite where and before too long he disappeared, where did he go, I can't answer, he was just standing there".

"Hey that's good!" said the young guitarist and started to

play along, then the drummer. The bass player and Brando just looked on a trifle bored until Brando interjected "It has to be about a girl".

As quick as a flash the lyrics were changed to "She was just standing there." A pencil came out and Brando and lefty went over to the corner.

"It's what they do!" sighed the young guitarist "Every bloody time someone says something slightly different, it triggers them off."

In what seemed like a very short time the whole band were playing this new song. The words kept changing as it evolved, now it was about a girl of seventeen so I left them to it and went up to find Liam.

He was standing outside the club reading a poster proclaiming 'Star Acts' appearing tonight. "What stupid bloody names they come up with!", he offered. "Where do they get them from?" To my dismay I never bothered to look at the poster and read the name, but I can dream.

The club door closed with a slam and all we could hear was a muffled noise coming through some ancient air vents in the pavement.

I had a job as a roadie with the greatest band in the world, or so I like to think and I blew it because I didn't know what a roadie was!

We visited a couple of pubs and I noticed some very pretty girls and I chatted to one, but she couldn't understand my accent and I couldn't understand hers so that soon went flat, I think she thought I was Dutch.

It was great to be out and about in Liverpool in 1960, the place was absolutely bubbling with music and fashion, all created locally and some of it destined to take on the world and set trends that would reverberate for the next fifty years.

We found a café and had a frothy coffee. It was my first real experience of coffee. Sitting there, listening to songs we didn't know, being played loudly on a jukebox that people kept feeding money into, was like visiting Mars. Just the mechanism alone left me enthralled! A second cup and a fresh cake went down well. I was beginning to like this new life.

I would have loved to stop and experience more of that pulsating metropolis in those fabulous days, but Liam was insistent we return to the ship in good time and so we set off back to the docks and the Ramona Wave.

The ship was quieter, goods safely stored in the hold and everything prepped for the journey up to Glasgow and then across the wild Atlantic to Canada, starting another new chapter in my ever-changing life. We went into the mess room and this time I asked for a coffee! See how urban I was getting, already!

The trip up the west coast to Glasgow was a bit choppy, but otherwise pleasant as I settled into my new job as Deck Boy. I was working with the carpenters, of which there were two and doing odd jobs as required. Some of which were quite bizarre, not at all what I was expecting as you'll find out later.

Once again, when we docked, Liam and I got permission to leave the ship and so we set off to explore Glasgow. We had a shock when we walked past an area that was razed to the ground, utter devastation, as if a massive bomb had been dropped. We asked a local was this from the war and he said no, it had happened earlier that year. A bonded whisky warehouse with a million gallons of whisky and 30,000 gallons of rum caught fire. There was a huge blaze and the Fire Service rushed to put it out. Horribly, the alcohol exploded and 9 firemen were killed. It was a terrible tragedy and a reminder of the sacrifice made by members of the Fire Service, who run towards the flames whilst we do our best to avoid them. Very brave people.

The Glaswegians were very friendly to us, giving us directions and recommending places to see. We wandered freely from street to street, two young lads doing what us older people tend not to do and that is, explore without a map and without a specific destination. There was a true feeling of freedom in our meanderings, even jumping on a double-decker tram I thought was magical. For someone from a small Irish fishing port, Liverpool and Glasgow were mindboggling conurbations, stretching for miles. Crowds of people and traffic to be avoided. Shop windows displaying everything we could ever need but could never afford. All existing it seemed for our amusement.

We did venture into a pub or three and there we were greeted as kin folk, regaled with Scottish stories of rugby played against Ireland and the benefits of Guinness!

It was a weary duo that stumbled back on board the Ramona Wave that night, our legs with tired muscles only moving because the booze kept us going just enough to reach the sanctuary of our cabins.

The next day I spent writing a letter to my mother and then just lazing around all day as there were no duties for me to do whilst we were in port.

Some of the crew spent the day in Glasgow as we did the day before, but not wandering like us, as they had been there many times, picking up things they might need for the journey across the Atlantic.

One of the items they did bring back was fireworks, which as you can imagine were strictly forbidden on board, so there was a great deal of secrecy surrounding their acquisition. Some bright spark decided to let off a few in the mess and although we all enjoyed the display, the amount of smoke circulating made most of us retreat for the clear air on the deck.

The bright spark, who as you can imagine had consumed a few wee drams of whisky, brought the remainder of the fireworks up to the deck with him. Brandishing a large rocket, he said "Gonass slet his oft" or something similar. Before he succeeded in launching it, he slumped back in his seat unconscious and obviously in no fit state to launch a rocket.

There were a number of boos from some of the crew but no-one stepped up as rocket controller, until, you guessed it, I volunteered to be Von Braun.

"Go on youngster, see if you can get it to go over that tanker!" some drunken sailor said.

It just so happened that a very large oil tanker was slowly making its way up the Clyde to the oil refinery and passing us by a fair distance off the starboard bow.

What I was thinking I cannot recall, but it was obviously in keeping with other daft shenanigans that I had carried out in the not too distant past. I mounted the rocket on the ships rail and angled it out over the river just about where the tanker would pass. A crowd had now gathered around me and all were eagerly awaiting the imminent arrival of our target by shouting remarks to get a move on, as the slow-moving unsuspecting tanker neared our mooring.

The tension was building as the huge vessel inched into the sightline, breath was being held, bets were being made and some walked away obviously realising what I was about to do was very, very dangerous. As I said previously it was an OIL TANKER, why did no one older and wiser say "Don't do it son!" or "Don't do that it's a bloody OIL TANKER!"

Too late anyway! I had lit the fuse and stood back to watch. There was an almighty flash, a whooooosh as it left our ship like Superman on a mission to save the world and a trail of sparks as it sped through the dark winter evening. More bets were quickly made amidst shouts of "Get over you bastard!" or equally "Hit the bloody thing!" It seemed that opinions on the final destination of this missile could vary one way or the other and I suddenly thought "Oh SHIT, what have I done now?"

The rocket had reached its peak trajectory and was on its rapid descent, still trailing flames and on course to hit the tanker deck dead centre. If I had been aiming at that target it would have been a wonder shot but of course I was trying to go over the tanker.

"Oh, bloody hell!" I remember screaming as the rocket smacked into the deck and burst in a shower of colours that illuminated the tanker's superstructure and several crew members who were innocently patrolling.

There was pandemonium on the Ramona Wave as crew members vanished in every direction, all except me that is. I was transfixed, glued to the deck, immobilised by the enormity of the stupid act I had just perpetrated.

The tanker's crew were busy extinguishing any rocket debris whilst simultaneously shouting profanities in several languages, thankfully none of which I could understand.

If I thought that was that I was wrong! Unknown to me, the River Police were on their normal patrol and witnessed the whole incident.

I was sat in the mess with my regular mug of tea when the Police and our Captain entered, intent on interrogating the crew.

I knew it was my fault so I owned up immediately and took full responsibility, without divulging the name of the person who brought the fireworks on board.

The sack was the most obvious punishment, but because I had owned up and because of my tender age and maybe because the Captain realised other more senior members of the crew were as responsible as me, he let me off fairly lightly.

He also couldn't afford to sack crew when he was about to

cross the Atlantic the next day! I was giving a right old rollocking, fined a week's wages and a Disciplinary Report entered in my Seaman's Book.

I was a very lucky lad and glad I was still in a job and not being sent home to Ballytreeny in disgrace. I was also a lucky lad because, unknown to the officers I was slipped a few quid by those members of the crew betting on my rocket hitting the tanker.

It was one of the most stupid, idiotic things I have ever done and believe me I have done a lot!

So if you ever think of aiming a rocket at an oil tanker just floating past. "DON'T!".

There were times during that Atlantic crossing that I wished I had been sent home. We were bound for St John's when we ran into a storm. Now we have all been in a storm at some time or other! You know the kind of thing, where the heavens open and water falls by the bucket load, sometimes with a dose of thunder and lightning for good measure. You know what I'm talking about, so it makes me wonder why some learned person has not thought of a word to sum up what happens at sea. We call it a storm but the word is so general that it is like calling a Black Hole in space just another hole without any reference to magnitude.

There are categories of storms at sea and they are measured on the Beaufort scale from 0 being calm to 12 being a hurricane.

I honestly have no idea what the measured strength of ours was, but if we rule out a hurricane and call it a violent storm the waves could be up to 52 feet in height. Just for one moment imagine you are stood on solid ground looking up 52 feet to the top of a wave and then take this official description given to a violent storm into consideration.

"Exceptionally high waves; small- and medium-sized ships might be for a long time lost to view behind the waves; sea is covered with long white patches of foam; everywhere the edges of the wave crests are blown into foam; visibility affected".

It was terrifying! Huge waves (I didn't stand around with a tape measure to see how huge) were crashing over the bow of the ship and sending torrents of water frothing down the deck at God knows what speed. Whilst the ship danced around like a drunk at a free bar!

I did send a personal message from the end of my bunk to Father Michael asking him to intervene for me if it was my time to be called. Frightened doesn't even come close to what I was feeling. Waves hitting the bow sounded like thunder to us poor rats below and it was truly deafening and relentless. Sick to my stomach, my bowels in a knot and hanging on to any solid object that was secured to the ship.

For reasons of space the cabins were aft and the mess room midship and the cargo in between. The only way to get to the mess room was to go via the deck and that meant running the wave gauntlet.

A safety line was rigged on the deck and if you needed to cross you had to clip a brass ring that was attached to a belt that we wore, on to the rope that would hopefully prevent you getting washed overboard by the crashing waves.

I was terribly seasick for two days so didn't make the journey as many times as I probably would have but the times I did it was like no other experience I have ever had. I really did feel like I could be swept overboard at any moment and drowned.

We were stuck in the storm for days and at one time I honestly thought we would never see land again but I was one of the lucky ones. Some poor devils had to stand lookout for other ships while I was tucked up in my bunk being seasick. No one seemed to miss me and nobody asked me to work, which to be truthful I probably would not have been able to do, I was so ill.

The storm finally left us and went hunting for more poor

souls to torment, having wrung every drop of terror out of us, although the sea was still very rough and the ship was continuously rolling, a motion I still dread.

I felt well enough to vacate my bunk, although not up to mess food, when I was called to work below decks with the ship's carpenter. If I had known what the job entailed, I might have stayed under the covers and shoved my fingers down my throat.

"What could be that bad?" I hear you ask. Cleaning the bilges, that's what! The dirtiest, filthiest job you can imagine and more!

Ok, now you want to know what the bilges are, perhaps I should have written a reference chapter. The bilges are a gully, located in the bottom of a ship running from back to front catching any water making its way inside the hull.

The job was made many times worse by the fact that there had been grain in the hold and some of it had found its way to the bilges. With me so far? Good! Well, the aforesaid grain had swollen with the water ingress and had sprouted. Yes, even in those conditions, life goes on! There were tons of the stuff and that is no exaggeration. It all had to be shovelled into buckets and the buckets then hoisted up by hand once I had climbed up an 80-foot steel ladder out of the bilges. All this, whilst the ship rolled from side to side, doing its best to send me, the swinging bucket and the unwanted sprouting grain, plunging to a certain death in the bowels, where it seemed I belonged.

That job took three days to complete so you mathematicians might like to calculate how many rungs I climbed up and down during the process. Don't write and tell me the answer as I wouldn't know whether you are right or wrong, but I'll make a slight wager that if you laid all the rungs, one after the other on the ground, they would run right across the Atlantic, with a few spare.

At this length of time after these adventures I am airing, I feel safe enough that prosecution won't be credible, so I'll let you in on a bit of larceny that took place below decks.

One of the products being transported in the hold was Jacob's Biscuits, they were packed in tins, on pallets, that could easily be compromised. One or two of the crew would go down to the hold at night and remove tins from the pallets without it being visibly obvious and then distribute them to the crew until everyone had a tin.

I hid mine in the space under the bottom drawer in my dressing table just in case there were any cabin inspections. I have to say that the Jacobs Biscuits were very tasty and if Jacobs would like to sponsor me, I would be very happy to endorse their wonderful products. There are of course other products I enjoy if anyone is interested in my services. End of ad.

We eventually reached St John's after about ten days at sea, sailing into much calmer waters, sickness abated and my curiosity revived. The New World was spread out in front of me and I took every opportunity to view the landscape as we sailed around Newfoundland and into the Gulf of St Lawrence.

To say the coastline was spectacular is scant praise for a breath-taking sight that left me open mouthed with astonishment. Mountains so high they were covered in snow and a bank of swirling clouds rising majestically up from the water. It looked like a mythical home of the gods where magic was invoked every day and giants roamed the land.

Never in my life had I seen a landscape like the one laid out before me and I longed to own that elusive camera, so that I could keep a permanent record of this stupendous place.

My excitement revived I quickly forgot about the trauma of the crossing and between jobs you'd find me on deck scanning the horizon as we sailed into the vast St Lawrence River, down towards Quebec. This had always been my dream, sailing to distant shores, exploring the world and it was happening in reality.

It was hard to contain my excitement and noticeable to other crew members who kindly took time to point out various landmarks, especially as the river started to narrow and we passed Quebec City. If it was allowed, I would probably have set up camp on the deck.

I often thought of myself in terms of the settlers who came in small wooden ships, discovering this great land for the first time, their gasps of wonder as the long-awaited coastline came into view. How it must have been the fulfilment of their prayers to survive the long, sometimes soul-destroying voyage and go ashore, stepping foot on the promised land that they thought would never show itself to them.

Imagination is not the sole preserve of the young but I believe we older folk sometimes lose sight of the wonders that lay on that wondrous plain, allowing us to see things not as they are but as they could be.

The next port of call was to be Three Rivers (Trios Riviera's), a French speaking town in the Province of Quebec.

Following our established routine, Liam and I went ashore to explore the local area, with a loud warning ringing in our ears to stay out of trouble this time. Don't know what they were thinking. Me get up to mischief? How dare they?

In my short life I had never realised I was invisible, if I had I would have put it to good use, but here in French speaking Three Rivers it seemed I was. Asking someone for directions in English was not met with "Je ne comprends pas!" but with a complete absence of comprehension, as if we didn't exist. It was very surreal and as a sociable young Irishman, something that made me feel an alien, rather than a fellow human being, albeit with a different language.

Liam and I stood there, nonplussed by the outrageous attitude of the locals, as this would never happen in Ireland, we always made visitors feel at home, even if we didn't understand what they were saying. Sit them down and give them a pint of Guinness that was our policy! I bet sign language originated in Ireland, down the pub after ten pints of the black elixir.

After several attempts at communication, we gave up and just wandered the streets, trying to pronounce their names and guessing what they meant and that was how we were passing the time until we heard a few words of English.

"Are you lost boyos?" A small wiry man in denim asked.

"Thank God! I thought we were invisible!" I replied and the guy laughed as if he knew exactly what we were talking about.

"They're not too keen on the English here!" he offered.

"But we're Irish".

"And I'm Welsh, but we're speaking English and in their

eyes we are not welcome visitors. It's all down to history. You should check it out and maybe you'd understand".

We stood there nattering for a good half an hour, swapping stories of how we got to this remote location and then moved on to a local bar to check out the beer.

It appears our Welsh friend, Lloyd, was a native of Cardiff and had travelled all over America, working his way around until he found himself in Canada and a way of life he loved, so he stayed put.

To our joy, he had learnt the language and could order things for us without fear of being ignored and we settled in for a good time, even being joined by a couple of ex-pats a little later and surprisingly, a French Canadian who spoke perfect English.

It was the Canadian who thought that as Irish we should hate the English and have empathy for the longstanding feud with English Canadians but we had always thought of ourselves as Irish and had not been brought up to hate the English or anybody else to that matter.

At seventeen, politics is new and sometimes a little baffling having grown up free and allowed to have differing opinions. To be suddenly confronted by intransigent ideology was anathema to my young and malleable mind.

The opposing arguments rained down on us from both

sides and I have to say it was probably my first adult debate with any substance, even if I didn't fully understand all I was being told.

All in all, it was a great way to extend my education and to see that two people looking on the same world could see it from completely different viewpoints.

Another lesson learned and catalogued in my expanding library of life.

Walking back to the ship I muttered a few, "Bonjours" and nodded at the same time. Low and behold I was suddenly visible as I received a polite, "Bonjour" in return and I was invisible no more.

We met up with other crew members as we made our way back to the Ramona Wave, some of them laden with packages, most of which were cigarettes. I remember saying to James that if they smoke that lot below decks, we'll need gas masks and was surprised to hear that the cigarettes were not destined for personal use but for resale in Ireland when we eventually dock in Dublin. Apparently, the Dockers were always keen to purchase the contraband at a considerably higher rate than the crew paid for them.

Liam told me to buy some, but I didn't have a lot of spare money so I declined and then he made a statement that almost floored me, something no one had mentioned to me before.

He said I could buy cigarettes later in the voyage, after we had the chance of a great deal of overtime (more of that later, a story in its own right) and then said, "That's if we get back!"

"Wow! Rewind a little!" I ordered, putting my arm out and stopping his stride. "If we get back? What's that supposed to mean?"

It appeared that no one had mentioned the Great Lakes, where we were going, were prone to freezing over in the winter. If we were late on our voyage, there was a chance we would be trapped in the ice and unable to carry on. The ship would have to be manned by a skeleton crew until the big thaw.

This horrified me until Liam said not to worry as we would probably leave the ship and fly home, leaving the Captain and a select few to stay with the ship.

Fly home! That sounded brilliant and I found myself hoping that the big freeze would snag us in its grasp and I could fly back to Ireland, what an experience to tell everyone about. Me … on an aircraft!

The thought of being trapped in the ice was constantly on my mind during our immense voyage up the Great Lakes, a name that conjures up collections of water where you see both shorelines at the same time. Their name should be Great Seas because they are huge! Nothing like a lake as I would define one, some measuring over 350 miles long and 136 miles wide! It might be a good time to consult Google Maps and see for yourself the enormity of our excursion.

You may remember the offhand remark a little earlier by Liam, concerning overtime, well he was right and again another aspect of the job that no one told me about in advance. I'll let you be the judge but I'm certain that the practises I am about to relate would never get past Health and Safety rules in the modern world and I do wonder how the job is done today.

We left Three Rivers and made our way upriver to Quebec via a series of locks that would raise the ship to the level of the next section of river. It was an awesome sight and one there was no preparing for, just sailing into a massive three-sided box through gigantic open gates. The feeling of claustrophobia was overwhelming as I stared up at the walls towering above the ship, then the sound of heavy machinery as the gates slowly closed behind us, trapping the ship and me in a concrete pit. To top it all a noise like thunder echoed around the ship as the water from the level above cascaded into the pit and slowly, very slowly raised us inch by inch for almost an hour until once again we were out in the sunshine and at our new river level ready to sail on.

Of course, we sometimes arrived at a lock only to find ourselves in a queue, behind several ships waiting to go in the same direction as us, so when this happened Liam and I found out what our overtime meant.

I was instructed to sit in the bosun's chair. Now, this is not as you might think a chair that the bosun, a sort of crew foreman, would sit leisurely in whilst the rest of us worked. Not even close! It wasn't even a bloody chair! It comprised of a flat piece of wood with a rope through the middle that was in turn tied to a boom that could be swung out over the ship's side ready for the incumbent (me) to be lowered aft to the quay side and Liam forward.

If you were lowered from the centre of the ship the quay would be immediately below you but as we were being lowered forward and aft the side of the ship was not touching the quay side and we had to swing out further. If the ship moved, as it did often because until we did our job, the bow could come in or out very quickly and you could miss the quay side and disappear between the ship and the quay.

That's not too bad but if the ship then shifts back the other way you are caught between the two with the prospect of being the filling in a ship/dock sandwich!

The first time I was lowered over the side my stomach turned over and I nearly lost my breakfast! I plummeted down the side of the ship a lot faster than I expected. There was no safety rope to hold me in the chair, only my frantic grip on the suspension ropes.

My arse slipped off the wooden plank and I was now dangling by my arms and even at seventeen I weighed a fair amount, all muscle of course. I could feel the burn on my hands from sliding down the ropes.

It was like being back in old grumpy's class after a caning, only this time my life was literally hanging by a thread.

I imagined the headlines in the papers back in Ballytreeny. Boy sailor squashed to death between ship and jetty! What I didn't know at the time was that the old lags operating the boom were having a laugh at my expense and had deliberately lowered me too far. Just as I was about to be squished, I felt a sharp tug on the rope and I flew upwards and out of harm's way.

I could hear the bastards roaring with laughter way above me and I had to suck it up and try not to react. If I had reacted badly, you can be sure it would happen again but by ignoring it, they got bored and would not try it again, for a while at least.

Once down on the dock we had to secure the ship's ropes

to the bollards provided to stop the ship drifting, then sit around until it became our turn to use the lock. Sometimes the wait was for several hours and we would sit aimlessly waiting, bored with the task, until suddenly we would hear the ship's horn sound three times. That was the signal for us to jump up and undo the ropes tied to the bollards.

That bit was easy but the next bit was fraught with danger, as the now unrestrained ship was moving under the motion from the river. We were expected to run alongside and grab hold of a rope ladder slung over the side.

Sound easy? Just give it a try. First of all, drop the ship's rope and then run like hell towards the rope ladder, that was now doing its best to move away from you. Ever had one of those dreams where you're trying to catch something and it is just out of reach? Yes? Well, it's a bit like that.

We only had a few seconds to react before the ship left us behind so we had to make sure we got a firm grip on the ladder first and then put a foot on and hope for the best.

Climbing up was not easy but compared with what had gone before it was a relief. Liam and I scrambled aboard, out of breath and with sore hands but there were no cheers or clapping, just a crew going about its normal duties. Ungrateful lot!

The overtime, I hear you asking, well, on a few occasions we would be on duty, without sleep, for 2 days whilst going through the locks and that's where the overtime came in.

I was sitting on the riverbank one night, on a bollard when a ginormous moose came charging out of the woods and scared the crap out of me. There was absolutely nothing I could do, just stand there like a statue, staring into its fearsome eyes with it snorting its fury at me, whilst scraping its huge hooves across the ground as it made up its mind what to do next. In the background I could hear the howling of a pack of wolves and I realised the moose was probably more frightened than me, so I slowly sat back down and looked away from him. After what seemed a long time, I heard him trot behind me and he disappeared back into the woods. It was at times like that I realised how far away from civilisation we were.

Liam and I were sometimes there night and day waiting for the ships horn to sound, our food lowered down in a basket and if we wanted the loo we had to improvise and use the woods, which was ok during the day but at night it was a different matter. The woods in the dark are a hive of activity with lots of animals who sleep during the day and you never knew what you would meet.

There was also the occasional meeting with local people and some were very friendly native Indians. Having only seen them in Hollywood Westerns, it was great to realise they were nothing like the stereotypes we were brainwashed with.

They are quiet, elegant people, who, despite being forced from their land by an invasive army, still managed to have a massive pride in their traditions and way of life.

The girls were pretty as well but being kept at a distance from us! Sensible decision! It was amazing to find these indigenous were multilingual and none of it taught in schools! Bright and intelligent beings with immense sense of their own ethnicity. I was suitably impressed.

We moved on towards Detroit, with the weather changing daily, getting colder and colder.

Lake Ontario was stupendous 193 miles long and 53 miles wide and we sailed down the length of it. By comparison Ireland is only 170 miles wide.

To me, this huge body of water was mind blowing and of course it leads down to Niagara Falls, that awesome miracle of nature, famous throughout the world. A popular destination on most would-be travellers' lists.

I had heard of Niagara Falls and seen still pictures but nothing could have prepared me for such a magical place and for more than one reason.

Being given simple tasks to do by the carpenters was a

bonus to me, so when one of them gave me some planks of wood and a drawing, I was made up. I was in awe of these guys and their skill sets with their ability to repair things on the fly and change internal partitions in the hold at the drop of a hat, so it was great that they wanted me to build something for them.

I laboured on this barrel, for a few days, asking questions on how to craft the wood so that it curled around the central stays and the like, until it was not looking too bad.

Standing back and admiring it was a bit of a mistake because one of the crew saw me and said, "Better make sure it's waterproof, Niall".

I approached the carpenter and asked what the guy meant and he looked all serious and said, with a straight face I might add.

"If this barrel is going over Niagara Falls, it needs to be waterproof, as well as strong!" and then he walked off.

Niagara Falls? What was he talking about? Why would you throw a perfectly good barrel over Niagara Falls?

There was nothing to do but ask my good friend and fellow Deck Boy, Liam, if he knew anything about this strange remark.

Liam stood looking at me in a worried sort of way and

tipped his head from side to side and let out a big sigh, as if he was about to tell me a big secret.

"I shouldn't be telling you this because I know you'll worry about it!" remarked Liam in his best earnest voice.

"What?" I was keen to know.

"It's a tradition that all ships passing through Niagara Falls make an offering to the Water Gods".

"Water Gods?" I queried "What the hell are they?"

"It's probably bollocks but the locals talk about these spirits that inhabit the Falls and they say that if you don't pay tribute to them, you will have great misfortune on your travels".

"So, they're going to throw my perfectly good barrel over the Falls as some sort of pagan payment?"

"Not quite!" hesitated Liam and then continued, his serious voice now taking on an even more serious tone "There'll be someone inside the barrel".

"What? Who the hell would be daft enough to go over the Falls in a barrel that I made?"

Liam stood motionless and directed his eyes at the floor,

making a small shrill sound as air involuntarily escaped from his lips! Then he slowly looked up, taking another deep breath and I could see he was struggling with his emotions. Whatever it was he didn't really want to tell me.

He let a large amount of air out of his lungs and then launched into a sentence that chilled me to the bone.

"I'm afraid it's going to be you inside the barrel!" he exclaimed.

"No way! You won't get me in that barrel, I'll fight the lot of them before that'll happen".

"Don't worry" he said, "they'll get you drunk first before they put you in".

"Christ! You are joking! Surely the Captain won't let that happen?"

"He won't stop it! He didn't stop it when they put me in the barrel and sent me over the Falls".

This last statement was the nail in my coffin, there was no escape even the Captain was in on it. I knew there were some mad bastards on board as I had experienced in the bosun's chair, but this was way over the top.

"You'll be asked to write a letter to your family just in case something goes badly wrong, but don't worry, it rarely does!"

"Rarely does? By rarely, how many times has it gone wrong?"

"I'm not sure if there are any records kept of failures because it is highly illegal, there is even a local law forbidding it, but it still goes on. It's terrifying, when you go over the edge, that moment when you are weightless and falling, tumbling end over end, the roar of the water so loud it feels like it's about to crush your skull. Although. I think the worst part is the anticipation of that sudden contact with the millions of gallons of water churning around like a boiling cauldron below you, those final seconds when you wonder whether they are your last. THEN THE IMPACT!"

My blood ran cold at those three words and I felt my stomach about to reject the meal I had a few hours ago. Standing there, probably white as a sheet, I watched as Liam slowly left, noticing that he was stifling a cry and I thought I saw tears in his eyes.

I was like a dead man walking as I made my way back to the carpenters' area and my soon to be travelling companion made by my own hand.

Standing there staring at my handy work had started me

on a path I was previously oblivious to and now my future was being written in my own blood.

"I hear Liam has told you about the offering to the Falls", one of the carpenters related. "Shouldn't have done that. Better you didn't know until the last moment, now you're going to fret for days until it happens. Sorry about that!

We didn't want to tell you and upset you. Brought you a nice mug of tea, so sit down and relax. If you have any questions, I'll try to answer them."

Questions? Of course, I had questions but why bother, my fate was already sealed, there was nothing to do but write that letter to my family, just in case.

Now, I don't know if you've ever had to write a letter like this but it was one of the hardest things I've ever done. I knew that my family would be devastated to read it and I took hours writing and rewriting, crossing out, tearing up and starting again until I gave up and just let my emotions flow, hoping these last words would never be read out.

The next three days were horrendous! I worked on the barrel including coating it in tar to make it waterproof and fitting some leather straps inside to hold on to as I fell. There was precious little sleep to be had, the ordeal going over and over in my mind.

It was now the day before the offering was to take place

and Liam took me to visit Niagara Falls and I was gobsmacked. I didn't think that much water existed in the entire world, as if all the oceans had suddenly emptied their contents over the edge of a gigantic cliff. The noise was unbelievable and the ground we were stood on shook with the reverberation of the spectacle played out in front of me.

My return to the ship that day was made with great reluctance and I have to be honest I nearly took tail and ran! By some Herculean effort I made myself promise to do this thing, after all, if Liam did it and survived then so could I. Couldn't I?

The least said about that night's sleep the better, suffice it to say it was the longest of my life and I never want to experience anything like it again!

Walking up to the deck on that sombre day I remember thinking "A condemned man must feel like this!" but I held my head up high and kept going. There was a small gathering of the crew and no officers to be seen anywhere, as I grimly faced my open barrel.

"Have a drink. Young Niall", someone said and thrust a large glass of Rum into my hand. I wasn't very fond of Rum but on this occasion, I wanted to numb my senses as much as possible, so I accepted. As I did when the next glass was offered and the next! The deck was feeling very wobbly and I wondered if we had set out to sea again, so wobbly that my knees buckled and I felt myself falling. That was the last I remember of that day and the next time I was conscious, was the following morning, complete with the hangover from hell.

My head was banging like a gong and my mouth felt as dry as a camel's arse but I was alive. I'd obviously survived my time in the barrel and luckily, I was unconscious all the time. Brilliant! There was more banging but this time it was Liam, thumping on my cabin door.

"You awake?" he hollered.

I croaked some semblance of a reply and he came in.

"Guess I made it over the Falls ok?" I croaked meekly.

Liam started to laugh, a laugh that was echoing around my poor addled brain like an express train sounding its warning horn.

"What are you laughing at?" I exclaimed.

"You! You twat! There's no such thing as an offering to the Falls. It's a total wind up! I thought I almost gave the game away when you came to me. I had to stifle a laugh and turn away. I was crying with laughter and couldn't let it out.

They did the same to me last year!"

"You bastard!" I shouted at my supposed friend. "I believed you".

"I know. Brilliant, wasn't I?"

"Bloody Oscar material if you ask me!" and I started to laugh. What a shower of shit! They really took me in but it wasn't all over.

In the mess later on, my letter to my family, which I had given to Liam for safe keeping, was read out to the crew by one of the carpenters.

I won't go into the details except it made me cringe when I heard it read out loud and I did join in the laughter because the guy reading it was doing it in the fashion of an over-the-top hysterical woman. Not very PC now as I've said previously but those were different times.

It's easy to laugh now but it did take me a while to recover from my fake ordeal and it's something I'll never forget.

We continued our travels up into Lake Erie, which was even longer than Lake Ontario at 241 miles and up the Detroit River. It seemed amazing to me that America was on the port side (left) of the river and Canada on the Starboard side (right) the border running up the middle.

So far, I had only set foot on Canadian soil so when we

docked Liam and I once more set off to explore. I am not sure I had ever seen a town so full of life and energy before. Liverpool was hectic but life in Detroit seemed to be off the scale! There was a sense of things happening, a city bursting with talent, music on every corner, buskers and harmony groups everywhere, everyone seemed to be singing. It was crazy!

All the songs seemed full on, brassy even, in your face would be a modern expression, but sung with such enthusiasm you couldn't help but be grabbed by it. I immediately thought all of America was like this, which of course it isn't, but to an impressionable boy from Ballytreeny this was America and I loved it!

We noticed a crowd gathering and it piqued our interest, so we walked over to see what was happening. They were waiting to get into the Fox Theatre on Woodward Avenue. I asked someone what was on at the theatre and they shouted "Stevie!" I had no idea who Stevie was, but they seemed to love him! So, I persuaded Liam to come in with me and we could see for ourselves. The place was heaving and if seats were allocated, nobody seemed to bother. People were in the aisles, dancing in any space available, without even a suggestion of music playing. The stage area was roped off but I had a feeling that would soon disappear. You couldn't help but be carried away with the atmosphere and because I was taller than most, I had a great view of everything.

There was a sudden blast of brass instruments that created a mighty roar and people started to jump up and down, shouting and screaming at the musicians. The ropes as predicted soon vanished and the area around the stage became a pulsating mass of bodies, all sweating in time.

Onto the stage came a group of five young black men, perfectly turned out in matching suits, dancing in the most energetic way it was possible, driving the audience into a frenzy! The announcer, from side stage, shouted "Ladies and Gentlemen theeeee … Temptations!"

As if on cue, the audience roared again! The guys began to sing in a harmony so tight you couldn't fit a fag paper between notes! (for the younger ones who don't know what a fag paper is consult Google).

"Ain't too proud to beg!" they sang and the audience joined in, knowing every single word of the song and every note, even at one point singing the song while the band stopped playing and the Temptations just clapped in time. Wave after wave of singing reverberated around the old theatre, lifting the soul to ever higher states.

What a new sensation it was for me, I had never experienced music like this before. Irish music although fun and harmonic could also be a bit of a dirge at times, taking itself very seriously. This was a magic carpet ride of musicality taking my feet off the floor to fly with all the others.

There were a few acts on that day but apart from Stevie, the one I loved the most was Gladys Knight and the Pips. What a voice she had, absolutely sensational. Yet to become world stars they wowed the audience with class and style that set them apart.

"I heard it thru the grapevine" was sung along with so loudly I had to strain to hear Gladys, but the overall effect was electric and it still gives me chills. It seemed that song was an anthem to the audience and I could see why.

When they finished, I thought to myself this Stevie had better be good to follow that and he didn't disappoint me. I had no idea who Stevie Wonder was but when he came on stage it was if a hurricane had blown in. The energy he used performing could have lit the city for weeks. He was a walking, talking, singing, playing sensation that took the music and the audience to another planet, another universe.

Sweat was running off the walls and the ceiling then dripping back down on the audience but no one cared. They were here to boogie and boogie they did, it was totally unbelievable and I was in awe of this music they all called Motown. I have been to many concerts all over the world but nothing moved me like the show that day in Detroit City.

We left the building, carried along on the surge of sweaty bodies, out into the crisp cold air, not feeling the drop in temperature or caring, just a sense of euphoria that wrapped us enough to keep the cold at bay for a short while.

My ears were ringing from the volume in the theatre, not created solely by the band but in combination with the audience, so we found ourselves shouting to each other to be understood.

Just a short while ago we were in a French speaking city where we were virtually invisible, here we could talk to people and they listened. Everyone wanted to talk about the music, so we followed some of the crowd into a bar, where surprise, surprise, there was a band playing and very good too! They were loud as well, but no one cared, they just lapped it up.

That multi-cultural audience sang and danced, continuing what had gone on in the theatre. Even some of the acts we had seen came over and unbelievably began to sing for free in the bar and the night continued that way.

There were a few remarks about our accents, as people tried to figure out where we were from. They knew we weren't Canadian but we weren't quite English either. I don't think some of them had even heard of Ireland when we mentioned it, but it made no difference to anyone. We were there to enjoy ourselves and that is what we did, even chatting up a couple of rather nice young ladies until their boyfriends appeared and we discreetly disappeared.

Walking back to the ship we tried to remember the songs but all we could remember was the odd hook line and we repeated them until we thought we knew the whole song.

It was a crazy first time in America but one I have always treasured as a precious memory, never to be repeated but always to be remembered.

That heady day of musical indulgence was soon pushed to the back of my mind as we sailed on to Lake Huron, which was bigger than Lakes Erie and Ontario put together. With the temperature dropping daily we ran into a blinding blizzard of snow that cut visibility down to around 150 yards or so.

The bosun called me and told me to put on some warm clothing and take the lookout post for two hours.

Opening the door onto the deck was like opening a portal onto the North Pole. Everything not moving was covered in shrouds of white and the cold air smacked you like a refrigerated ex-lover. It had the effect of taking away your breath and forcing you to hunch up, gathering your clothing around you as tightly as possible.

I took over my post as lookout and was told to keep a sharp eye out for Lakers. They were ships of incredible length, some over 200 yards, carrying thousands of tons of grain across the Lake and into Quebec. We did not want to run into one of these giants in our comparatively small ship, so it was my job to ring a hand bell every thirty seconds or so, as a warning to any other ships in our area.

Sounds easy, doesn't it, well I can assure you that after an hour of ringing that bell, I was frozen to the marrow, hardly able to lift an arm and losing the feeling in my feet. My eyes were constantly being covered in snow and had to be wiped regularly, adding to the strain of keeping them on high alert for other ships.

By the time my two hours were up, I could hardly move, covered in snow and ice like an Arctic explorer. How did I ever find snow wonderful and exciting? Snowball heaven was far from my mind in this white hell.

Struggling to walk whilst doing an impression of the abominable snowman, must have been a funny sight but I doubt anyone was laughing as I fell through the open door leading to the cabins below. I was shivering uncontrollably, desperate to get the wet, icy cold garments off me in the comfort of my cabin, drying myself off and then collapsing into bed to get warm.

Sleep was a blessed release from my snowy ordeal and I stayed in bed for as long as I could, knowing I would have to do it all again soon.

It only got worse the further north we went, eventually sailing into Lake Superior, the biggest body of fresh water in the world. We rarely saw land as we made our way across this vast inland sea and siting of other ships was becoming less and less of a common occurrence. Maybe other ships captains had already taken the sensible option and left the region prior to the big freeze that was imminent.

Sailing into Port Arthur after the seemingly never ending 350 miles passage across, we gladly docked and were loaded with tons of wheat and other general goods including furs.

We once again went to explore, after wrapping ourselves in multi layers of clothes as it was -8 C outside. The Dockers were mainly Indian from the local reservation but they were very friendly and called us Irish Cowboys. It was these guys who said we stood no chance of getting back before the big freeze and were likely to get stuck out on the Lake. They told us of ghost ships that haunted the icy waters in the winter, crewed by poor sailors who had lost their lives, freezing to death but never quite dying. There was so much detail in their tales that a part of me believed them! I kept imagining meeting these ice clad corpses as they scaled the side of our ship!

They would find us easily, as we stood helplessly stranded in the unrelenting ice, swinging their bony legs from side to side as they rode on the bosun's chair.

It was a bit of a relief when we set sail on our return journey back down through the Lakes to the River Lawrence, a distance of almost 3,000 miles and then on to the great Atlantic Ocean and eventually home.

Lake Superior was kind to us and we made good time, without a snowflake in sight and then down into Lake Huron where it was a completely different story.

Thick ice had formed in large areas on the surface of the Lake and we had to be mindful of the many dangers in ploughing straight through it. The sound of breaking ice was constant and a bit otherworldly compared with the normal pounding of the waves.

I told you about the jobs I had to do on the locks during our incoming journey. They were hard! Add in the severe weather and the plunging temperatures and it became a living nightmare. Sitting on the dock in the warm weather seemed a distant pleasant memory! We shivered in front of a makeshift fire, until we were called to release the ropes and then run and climb up the rope ladder to the deck. When your hands are already numb with little feeling, grabbing a rope ladder and clinging on is bad enough, climbing up is a task too far! Somehow, Liam and I survived to tell the tale, sometimes only just.

At Lake Erie we joined a small convoy of ships slowly following an Ice Breaker that cut a channel through for us, a long and tedious trip but at least we made it back to the relative safety of Quebec.

We docked to take on more cargo, so we did our normal thing and went to explore, remembering that we would be virtually invisible to the populace. Some of the crew were going to a famous bar called Joe Beefs, so Liam and I decided to play it safe and go with them. We were drinking bottles of Labbatt's beer and I guess I got a bit too big for my boots, because I took the piss out of one of the crew who was not joining in the general mayhem. He ignored me for a while, realising I was drinking on an empty head, but I kept on and on.

The locals already thought we were savages when we walked in and were not surprised when they saw a big hairy fist catch me right on the chin, knocking me clear over a table behind. I would like to say I jumped up and walloped him back, but his blow had taken me by complete surprise and I lay there amongst the bottles of beer, spilling their precious contents all over the floor and in my drunken stupor apparently, I picked up a random bottle and drank from it.

Cheers rang out as I sat up, so I thanked everybody for their concern and apparently, promptly fell back into the mess of bottles, unconscious.

Liam said he carried me back to the ship but I doubt he could have picked me up, let alone carried me. It remains a mystery how I got back on board but somehow, I did.

When I woke the following morning, I wondered why my jaw was aching so much and a couple of teeth felt a bit wobbly. Looking in the mirror I could see the beginnings of a nasty bruise on my chin and slowly the events of the previous day came back to me. I felt ashamed that I had provoked someone to a point at which they would hit me and I went and apologised to the guy. He shook my hand and winced a little.

"You have a very hard chin!" he exclaimed and laughed.

I decided at that point to stay on board until the voyage was over, not an extremely hard decision seeing the weather was closing in fast. Our journey up the St. Lawrence River was still slow going because of ice, but we were lucky to follow in the path of a couple of much bigger ships up and into the Gulf of St. Lawrence. Soon we were rounding the awesome Newfoundland coast and then finally out into the Atlantic and the return trip across the Ocean to Cork.

Our trip back across the Atlantic was far less traumatic than our journey over! No big storms! A few large waves blotting out the horizon at times, playing havoc with my insides, put the fear of God up me!

Would I ever get used to this feeling of being totally at the mercy of the raging sea? Somehow, I doubted it, but studying the faces of my compatriots, there seemed to be an acceptance of the situation that I could not achieve.

Ireland! My Ireland! I realised how much I had missed it! The longing to see my friends and family and tell them of my adventures, grew the closer we got to home. I say home, although we would be landing at Cork, which was nowhere near Ballytreeny!

My resolve at staying on board dissolved as Cork came into sight and my desire to stand on Irish soil again took over. Off I went, this time with some of the crew to taste the Guinness once more and a right old time we had. Here we were not ghosted, we were returning heroes, back from the sea, Herculean travellers who had braved the Great Lakes and survived, or so we liked to think.

There was a certain amount of rivalry between different ships of which I was oblivious, being a newbie, so when some little turd came up to me, denigrating the name of the Ramona Wave, I was not best pleased! And he wasn't even Irish! Little Welshman, who would have been better off down the mines or so I told him as I picked him up off his feet, his little legs kicking out like an annoyed Leprechaun.

My crew mates thought this dangling dance of indignity, hilarious, cheers coming thick and fast, as did the fists as the diddy man's mates came piling in. There was pandemonium in the bar as chairs, beer bottles and small Welshmen, flew through the air, with the landlord screaming at us to stop! Little chance of that.

I had seen enough John Wayne movies to think this behaviour more than acceptable, but when the landlord, who had clearly had enough, waded in with a shillelagh the size of a cricket bat I decided to show the better part of valour and retreat!

Imagine my surprise, bumping into my cousin Dennis, as I made my escape.

To say I was amazed was an understatement! I hadn't seen Dennis in the years since I used to stay with him and my aunt and uncle during the summer holidays. "What are you doing here?" I drunkenly exclaimed as we hurtled out into the street.

"Your mother said you were on the Ramona Wave, so I kept an eye on the arrivals and then came to look for you. I went to the ship but they said you had gone ashore and I walked to the nearest pub and there you were. Fighting!" Dennis disapprovingly retorted.

My cousin, lovely guy as he is, was never the one to disobey the rules, as I discovered when we were children.

I was always up to some sort of tomfoolery but he would have none of it, preferring his books to my type of anarchy. I was quick to talk to the local girls but he held back, kicking his heels as I worked my silky charms. (That's what I thought at the time!)

"Let's get a drink!", I implored. Swaying a little as I tried to indicate a direction in which to travel.

"Not for me", he insisted, as he led me back to the ship, bending my ear all the way about how I was letting the family down. I thought, "He doesn't know the family like I do!"

Dennis persuaded me to ask for permission to spend the night ashore and off we went to his parent's house.

It might not have been too bad, but he told my aunt and uncle about my drinking and fighting in the pub. They were undoubtedly upset! My aunt read a letter to me that she had received from my mother, saying how worried she was about me being at sea and hoping I would come home to stay, soon. I knew my mother was unhappy at my choice, but it was so different to hear her words read out by my aunt, her sister.

To be truthful I had already decided to leave the ship when we docked back in Dublin, with a thought to joining another ship that was following a different route around the world, so I told my aunt that I would go back home for Christmas. The look of delight on her face was testament to the depth of her feeling and I was glad I told her.

There was still the little matter of sailing to Bristol, Liverpool and Glasgow before the adventure was over, so I joined the ship for this last lap with a spring in my step, eager to see Bristol, where I had never been before and also to revisit the other great cities once again.

As it was, I didn't see much of Bristol or Liverpool as I was needed to help watch over the unloading of cargo, assisting the carpenters with any subsequent adjustments to the hold configuration. Glasgow was my only chance of an excursion and even that had to be quick.

Liam was busy so I struck out on my own, trying to remember where we went last time and failing dismally. By sheer luck I passed by a second-hand shop and stopped to browse around. There was so much stuff in this shop it was hard to find a clear way through. It looked as if items were just piled in without regards to category or cost, maybe they were from house clearances. Wherever they came from there were millions of them. You could find practically anything you wanted from an old hand cranked record player to a tailor's dummy, most of it covered in dust and years old but I was fascinated. The owner saw me browsing and asked what I was looking for. Turned out he was Irish and from my area, so he was keen to hear about why I was in Glasgow.

I soon discovered he had left Ireland on a ship the way I did, but he didn't return. He had met a Glaswegian girl and settled in the city, bringing up a family, moving furniture for a living and eventually opening the shop with items people no longer wanted. While we were talking, I spotted an ancient camera, stuck at the back of a shelf and pulled it out to have a look.

"People do that a lot!", he said.

"Do what?", I inquired.

"Hide stuff they like at the back of the shelf, so no one else can buy before they come back. Trouble is they don't come back and the thing is left hidden."

The camera was a Leica, but that meant nothing to me, so he explained that they were a German company that made quality cameras. I asked the price and he looked at it for a moment and said £1. That was a lot of money to me and I must have looked a bit shocked, because he followed up with, as you're from Ballytreeny you can have it for 10 bob and I'll give you a roll of film.

My heart skipped a beat as I held the view finder to my eye and clicked the shutter! It was my first camera and I still have it. It was worth a lot more than I paid for it and I think he must have known that but he could see my joy and that was enough.

I spent the rest of the day taking pictures of anything that took my eye. This was the start of my love affair with the camera, a passion I still indulge in, having a library of thousands of photographs detailing the travels of a lifetime. Many people have asked me to populate a website with them and maybe I will one day, but until then they remain my personal visual memory bank, for reminiscing whenever I feel the urge.

The only regret I have is, I ran out of film before I made it back to the Ramona Wave. I couldn't take pictures of the crew and the cabin that had been home to me on our fantastic journey. Those pictures have to remain the property of my inner memory bank, burned on it by the intensity of the situations I had lived through.

When we finally docked at Dublin, I talked to the bosun, informing him I was leaving the ship with the intention of picking up another in a few months. I think he was genuinely sad to see me go. I had joined the ship a boy and in that short time I had become a young man, an inch or two taller, muscles on muscles and with a new outlook on life.

There were no barriers to what I could do, no limits to where I could go, just those that resided in my head and I was fast losing those. Life was decidedly on the up.

7. CHRISTMAS, CAROLINE, BIG BROTHER STUFF & SANDY ISLAND

I arrived home in Ballytreeny just before Christmas 1960, full of stories about my epic voyage and the wonders I had seen, without divulging the more potentially deadly jobs I had done or my escapades after a few drinks, of which my mother would not have approved. Sitting round the fire, telling my tales, embroidering them ever so slightly, was wonderful and brought me closer to my family than I had been in a long while.

My mother was keen for me to give up the sea but she never brought up the subject! She wanted it to be my voluntary decision, not out of guilt. When I said I was going to look for a job on land for a while, she hugged me and never said a word. She didn't need to! I could see the tears in her eyes.

For the first time I had some money of my own, not a lot but enough to allow me to go out at night and meet up with friends, usually around the pubs of which there were fourteen in Ballytreeny alone.

It was Christmas Eve and the pubs were packed with partying people, out to have a good time and I joined in with gusto, that is until I saw a familiar face across the room. It was Caroline and she was looking straight at me.

I hadn't been to see her in the couple of days I had been back. I meant to but never got round to it, so I was stunned when I saw her sitting just a few feet away. Her face was prettier than ever and my heart leapt at seeing her. She didn't smile, she just stared at me expressionless and statuesque.

I had promised to write whilst I was away but of course I never did! Was this payback for my neglect? Her stare was broken by a group of revellers entering the bar and when I next looked, she was nowhere to be seen.

There were people in my vicinity asking me questions about my recent adventures and I couldn't ignore them, so I had to stop looking for her. Out of the corner of my eye I caught a glimpse of her, almost hiding near the entrance and she was staring at me again. I smiled at her and she motioned for me to go over to her, which I did. As I approached, she slipped out the exit into the cold dark night, looking back as she went.

I found her outside, shivering! I went to put my arms around her but she moved away with a shrug that I wasn't expecting. My knowledge of girls was sadly lacking and I could feel I was about to be harangued over my poor education.

"You didn't write!" she noted. "You promised!"

"I …"

"Don't give me any excuses! You've been back two days and you haven't been to see me!"

"Well, I …"

Just as I was about to launch into an impromptu treatise on life at sea, one of my oldest friends walked out of the pub and put his arm around Caroline.

"I wondered where you'd gone!", said Freddy and then spotting me said, "Hiya Niall. Didn't know you were back".

"Couple of days ago", I said lamely, still looking at Caroline.

"Come and join us for a drink", he offered, still with his arm around Caroline.

"No thanks mate. Still a bit knackered after my time at sea. Kept me working all the time. No time to relax there, just work, work, work!

The family have kept me busy the last couple of days and there are people I should be going to see. People I've neglected!"

All of course aimed at Caroline, but I knew I had lost her. Freddy said his goodbyes and then holding hands with her, retreated back into the pub. For one withering second Caroline looked back and I knew what she wanted to say but knew she would never say it.

There was suddenly a black hole in my life, a gravity sucking monster that swallowed my small world, threatening to turn out the light in my life and it was my fault, entirely my fault. It would take me a long time to recover from that night and I wandered away from the pub and down to the beach, where I stood alone and cold, desolate and on the verge of tears. Young love can be hard on a boy or a girl come to that, when it ends abruptly and even more so when it was poignantly clear that neither of us wanted it to end, with just my young stupidity to blame.

If I could have gone back to sea at that precise moment, I would have, sailing as far away as possible. Looking out over the dark sea with the lights of passing ships visible on the horizon I had an ache that threatened to overwhelm me, whether it was for a love that I'd lost or for a long distant City I wasn't sure, but my legs wouldn't carry me anymore and I sank to my knees in the wet sand and sobbed.

When I returned home that night, my mother was sat by the fire knitting as usual and she looked up and smiled as I entered the room. "I'm glad you're home!", she said.

I didn't reply, my heart still doing flip flops in my chest and

I sat down, or more precisely collapsed into a chair beside her.

She didn't ask what was wrong, putting down her knitting and taking my hand in hers. She kissed it softly as only a mother can. What a way to spend Christmas Eve, I thought.

Thankfully, the next morning was the usual chaotic Christmas cacophony that it always was, with my sisters screaming and laughing while the boys squabbled over some trifling incident. I had, without realising it, become outside this bubble of family life and I looked on it in a different way that year. I was growing up and after being out there in a world that was millions of miles away from home, I was never going to settle back into my old life again.

We did have a good day though, playing silly games and singing songs with my father and mother, entertaining ourselves and not stuck in front of a TV set as subsequent generations were destined to do. It was the last Christmas I would spend with the whole family around me and if I could go back, I would give each of them a hug, even Seamus, the bane of my life, because whatever else they were, there were primarily MY family and we had grown up together under the same roof.

Time may have mellowed my memory a lot and no doubt the rough edges have been worn away by circumstance and the passage of time, but I remember that Christmas with only love.

St Stephen's Day (Boxing Day) was nearly over and I decided to go for a walk along the beach, but as I left the house, I saw my sister Shelagh looking upset. I asked her what the problem was, only for her to put a finger to her lips in an attempt to silence me. She took my hand and we walked out of the garden and down towards the beach without a word being said. Sitting on the seawall, listening to the tide conversing with the sand, was always relaxing, but that day it had no effect.

We sat there for a while in silence, her hand clinging to mine. Every now and again she gave a small sob and her grip tightened. She was obviously traumatised by something, but I decided to wait for her to talk, rather than pressurise her any more than she already was.

She attempted to speak but immediately sank back into silence, a pattern continuing for at least thirty minutes, until she finally took a huge breath and blurted out, "I'm pregnant!"

It was a shock to hear the words, but it had passed my mind while I sat there with her, listening to the sea. What could I say? I didn't have any experience of this sort of thing and I was desperate not to make the situation worse. I knew her boyfriend Tommy McBain so I asked her the obvious question. "Is Tommy the father?"

Tommy was in my class at school and was always the brightest one in the class. How could he be so stupid?

Shelagh nodded her head and sobbed again.

"Does he know?"

"No!", she sighed.

"I think we'd better tell him, don't you?"

Again, the nod. We walked slowly away from the beach and up the lane to Tommy's house, pausing several times while she collapsed against me, sobbing and sobbing, muttering all the time to herself "What am I going to do?"

My personal boyhood trials seemed piffling compared to my poor sister's predicament and I had no idea how we would solve it, but she needed my help and I had to step up.

Leaving her on the corner I went up to Tommy's house and knocked the door, luckily Tommy answered. I clumsily asked him to go for a walk, which met with a puzzled look that increased when my head started to jerk, as I tried to indicate where I needed him to go. Still he looked perplexed, so I whispered, "Shelagh!" and nodded again. He took the hint at last, shouting to his parents that he was going out.

I said nothing to him as we walked quickly towards the corner where Shelagh was waiting, despite him asking me what was going on.

She was in a dreadful state by the time we got to her and Tommy immediately put his arms around her, trying to console her the best he could. There was no getting her to talk, she was completely unable to summon up the words, so I said them for her. "She's pregnant!"

Now I had two people who were in tears and without their power of speech. They clung to each other in the vain hope everything would be ok, while I stood there trying to support them.

"What are we going to do?", she finally uttered in desperation.

I took a deep breath before answering, being in uncharted territory and realising my position as older brother.

"We should tell Tommy's parents and ask their advice first", I offered.

The look in Tommy's eyes was one of terror! His parents adored their only son, but I could see he was not happy with my suggestion.

"Then we tell our parents!", which elicited an even more horrified response.

"Only one option left then … Father Michael".

The lack of response to this utterance meant it was the one plan we had left, so I guided the reluctant couple towards the little cottage that stood in the Church grounds.

To avoid any potential disastrous meetings with anyone else I approached the cottage alone and gave the big brass knocker a good thump! Father Michael was known to be a heavy sleeper and although it was still early it paid to make sure he heard it.

After a short while, the good Father appeared in the doorway, peering over the top of his glasses at me.

"I thought that knock was made by somebody strong, Niall. What can I do for you?"

"It's not so much me but my sister Shelagh and her boyfriend Tommy. Can we come in?"

"Of course, you can, my boy!"

We sat in that little parlour, each nursing a cup of Father Michael's tea and talking about nothing important for a few minutes until he quietly asked. "What can I help you young people with?"

Relating the problem seemed to be a repeating job for me and having despatched the news we all waited for his sage words.

He sat there for a few moments deep in thought and said quietly.

"You are not the first you know and I am sure you will not be the last. That may not be any comfort at the moment but this can be dealt with. Tommy, do you love Shelagh?"

"Yes Father!", came the immediate emphatic reply.

"Shelagh. Do you love Tommy?"

"Yes Father" softer but just as definite.

"That is the main thing. As long as you love one another, you'll get through this. It's not going to be easy and not without tears but you will get through it".

The Father's words were delivered with such authority and yet tender tones, that I could see a weightlifting from my sister and her boyfriend. Even a small exchange of glances between them that spoke volumes.

"You stay here while I fetch your parents. Please help yourself to more tea." Then he pulled on his coat and left us to worry in anticipation of what was to come. The recriminations! The anger of both fathers! Both mother's tears! The shame! We were Catholic so we knew all about shame! Tension mounting its dragon, scorching the room, leaving us bereft of clothing, naked and humiliated before the world.

The sound of the door opening was as the executioner's axe scything through the air. Shelagh started to cry again, head in her hands and on the point of collapse. Suddenly there were two sets of arms around her, our mother's and Tommy's mother. They gently helped her out of her seat and slowly walked her into the adjoining room.

"You can go Niall!", said my father in a short abrupt manner.

"I'd rather stay Dad … If that's ok with you", paying due deference to him. He nodded and I sat back down.

Tommy's father, kneeling in front of his mortified son, took his hands in his, in a manner I had never seen before, saying, "Tommy. I'm not going to shout at you. It's a bit late for that. I know you love Shelagh and you have to face up to your responsibilities. Do you agree?"

"Yes Dad!"

"You know what you have to do. As long as it is ok with Mr O'Sullivan", he said, looking across the room at my father for approval. A nod was all that was needed.

"Then go into the next room and ask her if she wants to marry you. We'll wait here!" There was a slight pause, then, "And smile when you ask her! You don't want her to say no!" he smiled again at his son.

Tommy did go into the next room and the mothers came out and left them alone.

"Anyone like tea?", Father Michael enquired and without missing a breath, "And something to celebrate for the gentlemen".

We sat there drinking tea and whatever he gave to the fathers, while all seemed quiet in the next room. Conversation was a bit stilted but Father Michael was well used to it and filled in the gaps.

Eventually the door opened and Tommy and Shelagh entered, red eyed, but happy things were resolved. Both mothers hugged their children and then their new in-law child, whispering words of reassurance.

Shelagh looked at my father who surprisingly held out his arms to her and she ran across the room to him, crying on his chest as he embraced her. Tommy's dad hugged his son and then Shelagh. Dad shook Tommy's hand, saying, "Look after my girl!", in a very firm voice.

Father Michael stood back and watched the drama slowly defuse. We were his family and there was a glow about him that I had never seen before. He had known exactly what to do and did it. A model for my future? I doubt I could ever come close to that incredible man standing quietly in the corner, but he did give me a target to pursue.

My sister sidled up to me as we walked back home, whispering, "Thank you, Niall! I would have been lost without you!" Then she kissed my cheek, even though she had to stand on tiptoes to reach. I felt very grownup. Even though Father Michael had done all the hard work, I did feel a sense of achievement. Shelagh and I were always close! That she confided in me before anyone else was a testament to our relationship. I have never forgotten that.

Shelagh and Tommy's wedding day was a simple one. We all attended Church and then "The Shipmaker's Arms", for a party that went on well past closing time. The happy couple moved into Tommy's parents' house for a while and are still happily married, despite the traumatic events of that evening.

On New Year's Eve, I was walking down to the beach again, still feeling introspective, when I met Tim, an old school friend of mine. We chatted for a while and I told him I was looking for a job locally, until I went back to sea. By luck, Tim had only left his last job at Christmas and he knew the vacancy hadn't been filled. He told me they were great people to work for and that my previous greenhouse experience would be just what they were looking for.

It sounded good to me so I said I'd ring them in the New Year, but Tim was having none of that.

"No time like the present!", he said, as he led me by the arm to the phone box on the coast road, even dialling the number for me and talking to my prospective employer on my behalf.

Mike Finlay, the man on the phone asked if I used to work for Terry Swarbrick and I said yes. He said he had heard Terry singing my praises in the past and when could I start.

Before I could say anything, he said, "How about 2nd January?"

I asked if he wanted to see me first but he said he already knew enough about me and to report for work at 8.00am.

Tim and I had a celebration drink and I walked home to tell my mother I had a local job. She was as pleased as I had ever seen her and she gave me a big hug, the tears making another motherly appearance.

Working for Mike turned out to be just what I needed and I soon picked up where I had left off. He had some huge greenhouses just like Terry's and my previous experience came in very handy and to be fair to Mike, he paid me more than Terry did.

I fitted in immediately and worked hard to prove to him that I was as good as my reputation! It was wonderful to be doing horticultural work again! I hadn't realised how much I had missed it! The days passed quickly, as I kept my head down and concentrated on work.

After the episode with Caroline, I was reluctant to go out with the lads. Seeing her with someone else was unbelievably difficult to live with! I did think for a while, I would never get over it and maybe I didn't! Like a lot of other things in life, the pain had a wall, without doors, built around it.

Working for Mike was very much like working with Terry. He let me get on with it, trusting me to do a good job. Memories of my old employer got me to thinking of the boiler providing heat to his greenhouses.

I asked Mike what he thought about doing the same with his. Mike being the entrepreneur that he was, went out and came back with a ship's boiler in perfect working order. We built a concrete base for it and then constructed a boiler house around it that looked really professional. All that was left to do was pipe the hot water around the greenhouses, which I did myself, cutting and threading them, fitting couplings and connecting to the main header pipe.

The coal fired boiler was soon pumping hot water merrily around the greenhouses and making a massive difference to their internal temperatures, meaning a much better and longer growing season.

Most of you will have seen films of stokers shovelling coal in the boiler rooms of ships and know it is a hard slog keeping the boiler going.

In the end, several years later, Mike got fed up with having to get up several times every night to shovel coal and had it converted to gas. That first year was a roaring success and I was immensely proud of my contribution to the expansion of the company. I was learning that I had a flair for innovation and it would serve me well in the years ahead and I was never afraid to put forward ideas even if they occasionally got shot down in flames.

Mind you sometimes your good ideas come back to bite you in the arse.

One of the big problems with boilers is they get clogged

with lime scale and once a year they need to be emptied of water. Then, while the boiler is still hot, one brave, slim soul, has to climb in and chip off the lime scale with a hammer and chisel.

I have never worried about being out in the hot sun and I have visited many scorching hot countries around the world, without complaining about the heat, but inside that bloody boiler it was unbearable. The temperature was over 100 degrees and I would work in fifteen-minute shifts, the reason being, I could only just fit through the hole. I found that if I stayed in any longer it was difficult to get back out. My body seemingly expanding with the heat. Now that may not be true but it at least saved me from fainting with heat stroke.

Mike was on hand outside the boiler, ready to hose me down when I staggered out. I had a quick drink and went back in. This ridiculous looking routine went on for two days until all the lime scale was removed, by which time I had lost about a stone in weight. So, if any of you good readers would like to lose a stone in weight in two days, ask someone if you can descale their boiler for them. I can recommend it. Not!

Mike let me borrow the tractor from time to time and I would use it to harrow and drill our large garden so all my father had to do was plant the vegetables and potatoes that kept the brood fed most of the year.

All in all, I was content working for Mike and I was happy for a while.

Caroline left a huge hole in my heart and it took me a while to get over it or at least start thinking about other girls. There were a number of pretty ones in the area and by now I was about six foot three and muscle bound, so I wasn't bad to look at for a country boy. It was 1961 and the world was changing rapidly. A new age was burgeoning and I was along for the ride.

Every Friday and Saturday would be spent at the local dance hall, after the obligatory few pints of Guinness. Before I went out, my mum used to have to tell me to stop hogging the mirror combing my hair, as my sisters were also trying to get ready to go out.

We worked hard all week and when the weekend came, we were ready to party and so we did. There are some advantages to having sisters in that they have female friends you can get to know. Having one girlfriend was now out of the question as I played the field, kissing and running as they called it or having fun as I referred to it.

Every now and then I would see Caroline and whoever she was dating at the time, but she rarely spoke to me and was moving in a circle I had little time for. More money than sense was a way my father described them and who was I to disagree.

There was one girl who intrigued me, green eyes, blonde hair, with an hour-glass figure and dressed to kill. She didn't seem interested in me, until one night the band was playing a slow song and she made a bee line for me.

I didn't know at the time but she was trying to make someone else jealous and to be fair it wouldn't have worried me.

She moved in real close! So close, I had an automatic reaction that could not be missed at that range.

Her eyes lit up and she came in even closer, knowing full well the effect she was having on me, a smile gently breaking on that gorgeous mouth.

It was then that I felt a rough hand on my shoulder and a guy, tall but a few inches shorter than me, looking as if he wanted to kill me. There were a lot of shrieks as he threw his first punch, catching me off guard, but even more when I followed up with a pile driver that left him in a heap on the floor. That was it, one punch and it was over. I turned to the girl and we went back to dancing.

The guy didn't bother me again and neither did any of his mates. Lucky punch I guess, but all those years working on the land had made me strong and no one was going to mess with me.

The girl's name was Julie, but everybody called her Jules.

She was everything a young man could desire and we had quite a time for a while but she was no Caroline and it fizzled out when she moved on to an older guy of twenty-one. I was not hurt or miffed that she had left me, rather, grateful that she had taught me a lot in a short time and for that alone I'll never forget her.

The one thing I did realise though was, beauty isn't everything and I could never settle down with someone without a good brain and honest opinions.

It's funny how some random memories come trickling back when you are trying to write a book like this. We used to go drinking in the local pubs in Ballytreeny as I said earlier and at one of them there was always a donkey and cart tied up out front, usually to a telegraph pole. Everybody knew who the donkey belonged to and no one ever took any notice, it was just part of everyday life in those parts. I don't remember the old fellow's name but I know he lived on a farm about two miles out of town.

Every evening at closing time, the landlord would ask for volunteers to carry the old fellow out to his cart and carefully lay him in the back. They would then untie the donkey, who without any prompting would trot off, towing the aforesaid cart behind him, back home to the farm.

Couldn't make it up, could you? Just a random memory as I said but worth relating. Couldn't happen now, the poor guy would be arrested for driving a donkey while pissed or something. Or the donkey would be arrested for providing an unlicensed taxi service.

Wander lust was still wriggling in my brain, whispering to my inner self to leave the safety of the greenhouses and strike out into the world again.

Life has a funny way of getting in the way of plans, hopes and schemes pushing you in a direction you had never even considered.

I was walking down to the local pub for a quick drink when I bumped into Tim, again, walking in the same direction.

"Coming in for a quick one Tim?", I asked him.

"On my way to work, Niall."

It turned out that the ever-mobile Tim had changed jobs again and was now working at the Sandy Island Holiday Camp as a barman. He said he loved it and made more money in tips than in wages and the bonus was in meeting lots of attractive young ladies who only stayed around for a week or two.

Just like before he offered to get me a job interview and to my surprise I said, "Why not?"

So, a few days later, I found myself at the main gate about to attend a meeting with the manager.

"Hello Niall!", said a familiar voice at the gate.

I had to look twice because the person had a uniform and a hat pulled down to his eyebrows.

"Charlie?", I asked. "Well I'm buggered! How did you get a job on security you rogue?"

"Shhh! don't tell everyone our secrets!", he laughed.

We were a right pair when we were kids, me and Charlie.

I explained that I was there for an interview and letting me in, he pointed me towards the Manager's office in Reception.

Walking across the large grassed area, leading up to the main block, I was amazed at the floral displays in various perfectly tended flower beds and thought to myself. "Even my father would be proud of those!" Little did I know how prophetic that notion was.

I approached the reception desk and told them why I was there and they told me to take a seat until Mr McMasters was ready.

Billy McMasters was not from Ballytreeny but he was well known in the village, always immaculately dressed, clean shaven except for a handlebar moustache that telegraphed he had been in the R.A.F. during the war. A very upright gait made him stand out in a crowd as an ex-serviceman, who had never quite left that life behind him. He was known as a no-nonsense, stickler for the rules, sort of guy and one not to be crossed, if you wanted to keep your job. His office door opened and out he marched, hand outstretched to greet me.

"Come in Niall!", he ordered.

His office, as was expected, was neat to a point of OCD and every surface spotlessly clean, so much so, I wasn't sure whether to sit on the offered seat or give it a polish, but I chose the former.

"Now I hear you're looking for a job, young man.", opening the conversation.

"Yes sir!"

"I gather you have had a fair amount of work experience with plants and the like".

"Yes sir!"

"Jolly good show! We are in need of another gardener as our Head Gardener Frank is about to retire and our Assistant Head Gardner Alf is going to take his place, creating a gardener position for someone with green fingers."

"Sounds perfect sir".

"I've asked Alf to meet us and show you around. It'll be Alf's decision about whether or not we take you on, as you will be working for him".

"I understand sir".

"Good! Good! You're a big lad Niall".

"Yes sir. Six foot five and still growing".

"You should fit in well here, but I must warn you there are strict rules on fraternising with the guests. A young, good looking lad like you, will attract a lot of attention from some of our young ladies and that is strictly forbidden! It is a sackable offence and we don't want that, do we? Right ... enough lecturing, let's go and find Alf".

Of we went with me attempting to keep time with his metronomic military steps.

Alf was knee deep in a flower bed when we approached him and I recognised him straight away.

"This is young Niall I was telling you about Alf. Over to you now!", then with a quick nod he was off marching back to his office.

Alf stood there for a moment looking me up and down with just a slight look of disbelief on his face.

"Christ you've grown a bit since I last saw you Niall!", wiping his hands as he extracted himself from the flower bed.

I was astounded that I knew him! Alf was my father's assistant groundskeeper at the Lodge, where I used to go all those years ago and he was always good to me.

"If you're half as good as your dad, you'll be an asset to this place. Not hard toil but continuously making repairs to keep everything up to the standards that McMasters demands. Kids climb over plants to retrieve footballs and hats and God knows what else, treading down all our good work, so we have to be constantly checking for damage and repairing it.

The money's ok, not a fortune and we don't get tips like the others but it's not bad by Ballytreeny rates and the hours are good. As long as the place is spick and span, no one chases us, so it's a good life. So, what do you think? Do you want the job?"

"Of course I do! Sounds right up my street. When can I start?"

"Better give a weeks' notice at your job and we'll see you at 8.00 am on Monday, if that's ok?"

"Perfect!", I said, as Alf took me on a tour of the grounds and the potting shed that passed as our headquarters.

"What's the chance of getting accommodation here Alf", I inquired.

"It's much sought after, but Frank has accommodation and he will be vacating when he retires next month.

We may be able to wangle it for you. I'll talk to Frank; he still has a lot of pull around here. You'd better come and meet him; he knows your dad well and that can only help."

Meeting Frank was a wonderful experience, the man obviously had a passion for his job and had worked there since he was a lad, building the flower beds from scratch and creating the beauty that surrounded us. He was genuinely distraught at retiring and leaving his life's work, but he couldn't kneel in the flower beds or dig because he had severe arthritis in multiple places, probably caused by constant exposure to damp soil and repetitive crouching in awkward positions.

My father was a topic that revealed some details I had no idea about. Apparently, my father had worked here as a young man and only left because I was on the way and he needed to earn more money, taking on two jobs at local farms, working long days. Frank respected him for putting his family first and told him he could come back to his job at any time. Of course, he never did, but they kept in touch. So, to Frank, having me working there was a little bit like my dad returning after all those years and he felt the place would be safer for me being there.

He also said he would put in a word about me taking on his accommodation but couldn't guarantee it.

We nattered for quite a while until an emergency call to a flower bed where a rather oversized lady had bent over to smell the flowers and physics took over when her centre of gravity shifted. Squashed plants were the least of their worries as we, rushed to assist her. Yes, I volunteered to help, as we, as properly as possible removed the lady from her rather compromising position and then applied tender loving care to the squished flowers.

Walking back home that day I realised my life was about to shift on its axis once again and it was a very pleasant feeling, one of discovery and new opportunities.

Telling Mike that I was leaving was not easy. We had become awfully close in the last couple of years and he was genuinely upset, but he wished me luck and even gave me an extra week's pay when I left. Showing what a thoughtful man, he was and one of the best bosses I ever had, even if he did put me inside a boiler to almost sweat to death.

Cycling away from the place was quite a wrench and I did have some misgivings, but as usual in my life, I sucked it up, put my head down and kept going.

I soon settled into my work at Sandy Island and it gave me

a great deal of pleasure knowing I was carrying Frank's legacy forward and also following in my father's footsteps. My father too was very happy at my taking up his old position at Sandy's. He came over a few times after work to see how the place looked. We didn't always see eye to eye, but I could tell he was proud of me. Mind you, he talked more to Frank, about the old days, than to me.

The day of Frank's retirement he approached me with a set of keys. "Here you are my boy, look after the place for me, it's yours now." I could see he was quite emotional and I didn't really know what to say. I believed he sensed that and took me by the arm, nudging me in the direction of the staff accommodation.

To my delight my new home was on the end of the block, with a little enclosed rose garden on one side, complete with a wooden bench and a beautiful weeping willow that offered shade in the summer.

My heart was in my mouth as Frank showed me his pride and joy. This was my responsibility now and I was expected to look after it.

A sad footnote to this memory is that Frank died in his sleep a few weeks after he retired. I went to the funeral and his sister, who he had gone to live with, said that he had spoken about me and how I was the future. She cried a lot as I remember, mind you, so did I!

We were never allowed to enter the main ballroom where the guests spent their evenings, having to use a small staff bar instead. The advantage, however, was that the cost of beer was a lot cheaper for us, probably as an incentive not to gate crash the ballroom bar. Equally, guests were not allowed in the staff bar.

I had joined fairly early in the main season and by the time I had been there a few weeks the place was bursting at the seams with all ages, from kids to grannies. It was a riotous time and Alf and I spent hours repairing and relaying plants and bushes and turf.

It was hot work out there in the sun and although I was never allowed to take my shirt off, it was sometimes so wet with sweat, that it stuck to me! Wolf whistles were often directed at me by some of the younger female guests. As instructed, I stayed well clear, although it was quite a strain not following my natural instincts.

So far, I haven't mentioned the one set of staff that were allowed into the ballroom and that is the entertainers or "Blazers" as they were called. Young men and women from eighteen to mid-twenties would dance and sing on their small stage, organise games, dance with the guests and whip up the atmosphere, all led by the "Blazer Captain" Ernie Bowers.

Now Ernie, like Mr McMasters was ex-military but not in

any way stuffy. The guests idolised him and he was at the centre of every entertainment activity, whether it was bowls on the green, archery, billiards, knobbly knee competitions or the like.

Ernie had the accommodation next to mine and asked me if he could sit in the rose garden on his afternoon off, telling me Frank used to let him and only him, visit the inner sanctum. It didn't bother me so I said yes and we became quite friendly. In truth, he wasn't what you might call a ladies' man, preferring to stay well clear of them on his time off. We used to sit outside of an evening, having a quick bottle of beer, before he launched himself into the ballroom activities.

Before you start laughing at the next recovered memory, please remember I was young and knew nothing about Ballroom activities apart from the name.

We were sitting, relaxing in the Rose Garden when Ernie had a visit from one of his Blazer girls, in quite a panic. It seemed one of the Blazer boys had tripped on some steps and broken his arm quite badly and had been taken off to hospital. It was another Blazer boy's day off and he was nowhere to be found (what did we do without mobile phones in the sixties?)

To cut a long story short, Maria, the Blazer girl, was left without a male Blazer and there were going to be plenty of older ladies who wanted to dance and didn't have a male partner, relying on the Blazer boys to accommodate.

Before I knew what I was doing, I volunteered to become a Blazer boy for the night, as long as I got free beer. If only I had known what I was letting myself in for!

I was quickly fitted out with a uniform, but being six foot five and growing, as I have said before, I didn't fit well into normal sized clothes. There was nothing for it but to try not to burst the seams on the jacket and more importantly the trousers that exposed my short socks and a fair amount of hairy leg. The Blazer girls who kindly help dress me, thought it hilarious and were in fits of laughter as they guided me like a lamb to the slaughter, into the packed ballroom.

I heard one of the girls laughingly say, "The old dears are going to love him".

It was so old fashioned; I had a dance card that ladies could sign up to and I would dance with them in turn.

So far so bad, but it was soon going to get worse! You see I forgot to mention to Ernie that I had no idea how to dance, at least not in the fashion I was expected to.

A waltz? A quickstep? Was there a difference? I had no

idea. God forbid I had to do a 'Cha Cha', darling!

My first lady was as old as my gran but to be fair she was very mobile, taking my hand like a young girl at her first dance, all smiles and giggles. I trod on her toes in seconds! I had no idea what I was doing! She stopped for a moment and asked me if I knew how to do the foxtrot and I said, "Is that what this is?" and she laughed and said, "Plainly not!"

She was an angel and talked me through the dance, guiding me instead of the other way round and we moved around the dance floor, occasionally stopping as she posed me in front of her jealous friends. When the music stopped there was a minor stampede as old dears fought each other to put their name on my dance card or at least that's how I remember it.

Do you remember the free beer stipulation? Well, it never happened! I was marooned on that dance floor going round and round, continuously changing partners and dances until I was absolutely knackered!

When the band finally finished for the night, I was surrounded by my evening's partners, thanking me for dancing with them and asking me if I would dance with them the following night, which I promised to do knowing I was there for one night only.

I collapsed in the Blazer changing room, while others were

disrobing at the end of the evening and by others, I mean the girls! It was not something I had anticipated and their complete lack of self-consciousness was a real eye opener in more ways than one.

Ernie eventually came into the room carrying a beer and handed it to me. "You earned this my boy!" and I drank it in one. Followed by a massive belch that got me a round of applause from the young ladies and Ernie.

"I'll make sure you get paid overtime for tonight, Niall; you saved the evening for the old dears and we're very grateful aren't we girls?" Another loud cheer rang out.

"You certainly have to work a lot harder than I thought you did", I told Ernie.

"Tell the management!", he agreed. "They think it's easy".

Walking back to my accommodation that evening, I was tired but happy, realising I had a great time, probably only breaking toes on three or four ladies, which wasn't bad for a novice.

I slept well that night and was still a bit bleary when I went to breakfast in the staff canteen, where the news of my dancing prowess or lack of it was circulating like wildfire.

During the day I would normally be able to go about my

business without a crowd gathering but that day, people came over to talk to me and I couldn't ignore them and I wondered if Mr McMasters would approve, so I was sweating a bit when he came striding over with Alf in his wake.

Jumping to my feet I said, "Good morning, sir".

"Good morning, Niall, I have just been hearing about your rescue mission in the ballroom last night and I have to congratulate you on your initiative. I have never had so many comment cards filled in as last night and they were all positive, which again is a bit of a rarity. You will of course be paid overtime for your extra work and I wanted to tell you myself how pleased I am, that a member of my staff would step up at a time of crisis. Well done!" And with that he strode off in his typical military fashion back to his barracks, I mean office.

Alf was stood there looking at me and muttering something about blue eyes and then grinned like a patient showing off to his dentist, gaps and all.

"I hope you know what you've started!", he announced. "You realise the Blazer boy can't work with his broken arm, so they'll be after you to burn up the dance floor again tonight and for another couple of weeks probably! Just a quick warning. Be wary of the Blazer girls they'll eat you alive!", he chuckled, before leaving me to mingle amongst the flowers and the guests.

True to Alf's prediction, Ernie came knocking at my door, pleading for me to help him out again, just the one night more.

I knew he meant longer but there was no turning back now and anyway to be honest I enjoyed it. What I didn't appreciate at the time was the opportunities it would afford me. I would soon find out!

My dance card was full before I arrived in the ballroom that night, apparently a queue formed after dinner and stayed there until one of the Blazer girls came on duty. At least I wouldn't be the only Blazer boy tonight so it couldn't be too bad, could it?

Before the evening started, Avril, one of the Blazer girls gave some pointers on how to stand, how to hold and how to move, something I did on the fly the night before. I couldn't help noticing the curve of her waist as I put my arm around her. A completely different feeling to the ones I had with my earlier partners. She was beautiful and a first-class dancer, with perfect hair and makeup and a body to go with it. The pleasure was all mine.

Armed with my newfound expertise I launched myself into my new occupation, dancing gigolo and was soon accompanying ladies of a certain age around the dancefloor.

To my surprise my fourth dance partner was probably in her early thirties and incredibly attractive in a curvy way. She was the first of many to push the old dears off my list and onto the other Blazer boy's.

She put her hand on my waist and we waltzed effortlessly around, mingling with the crowd and then coming to a slight stop as we hit congestion. It was at that point I felt her arm slip quietly from my waist and down to the cheeks of my bum, where it lingered for a moment before giving it a quick but firm squeeze.

I was shocked for a moment, but it had the usual bodily effect easily provoked in a young man and she noticed. Oh boy she noticed, smiling a wicked smile, then whispered. "I'm in chalet 236." I desperately tried to remember the number as my flustered heart went bonkers! I had never been propositioned before and anyway it was strictly forbidden. Mr McMasters said it was a sacking offence, but I was a young man and young men do stupid things, so I quickly wrote down the number on my dance card and stowed it safely in my pocket.

There were other advances that evening but none quite as forward and none relished by me as much, so they were easily ignored, although gallantly of course.

I did manage to down a few beers this time, usually bought for me by my lady dancers, so I didn't even have to put my hand in my pocket and that was quite pleasant. All in all, I was beginning to warm to this Blazer lark. Little did I know how close I was to the edge!

There was a lull for me in the proceedings that night, as there was to be Cabaret! I had no idea what Cabaret was, but I was soon to find out!

There was a small stage and a reasonable size to work on, but Ernie announced that the Cabaret would be performing on the dancefloor and that no-one was allowed to be on there unless invited. He then positioned the Blazer girls and boys, including me, on chairs, at strategic places, to perform crowd control.

This was great for me, as I had a ringside seat to whatever was about to happen!

Ernie cracked a few gags that had the audience rolling and then asked for a drum roll!

"Ladies and Gentlemen, boys and girls! Tonight, we present, at great expense! All the way from California! U … S … A. The petrifyingly, pointed, piercing protagonists, perpetrating a proper people pleaser with probably perforating impalement! Please … lets have a thunderous reception for … The Pacific Pioneers!"

The audience went wild with excitement after Ernie's great introduction, with the band adding to the atmosphere with a song I had never heard before called "Ring of fire!"

Two figures walked out in the lights trained on the dance floor, bowing to the audience. The male dressed like Buffalo Bill and his assistant in Native American attire. In his hands he held two huge knives, which he wielded around, much to the audience's amazement!

There were oows and aahs a plenty as he made to approach the audience but always staying just far enough away to be safe.

His assistant wheeled a large upright disc onto the floor and stood in front of it! There were a large quantity of obviously spectacular blood stains decorating the battered prop.

I was taken completely by surprise, when the man grabbed me by the arm and bade me assist him in tying the young lady to the disc.

The music became more intense, with what passed for an Indian drum beat.

He had me stand by the side of the disc and asked me to rotate it. The assistant was soon upside down and then the right way up, then upside down. You get the gist! He then asked me to stand well clear.

I could not believe it when he threw the first knife! It buried itself into the spinning disc and inches from the assistant. A massive round of applause followed. He then asked me to spin it faster! Which I did! There was no way he was going to throw a knife now, surely! But he did! There was a thud as it entered the disc, this time on the other side of her body! I'm sure a few patrons fainted! I certainly felt like it! Thunder would not have sounded any louder than the applause!

We untied the girl and she took a bow, the smile never leaving her face.

Another bloodstained target was brought on to replace the disc and what followed was nothing but miraculous! He threw cleavers, hatchets, carving knives, even a spear, all landing within inches of his assistant's body! And still she smiled! She must have really trusted him!

Then came the twist I was not expecting!

He announced to the audience that he needed a volunteer! In truth, he said 'victim' and then quickly changed it to 'volunteer'.

Of course, no one dared!

Then he said it! Words that chilled me!

"I see we have a volunteer!"

The audience cheered! All looked around to see who the volunteer was!

The knife thrower was looking in my general direction, so I turned to look at the volunteer behind me. Just to see what the fool looked like. I couldn't see anyone!

When I turned back his assistant was next to me, offering her hand to assist me to stand.

"What a brave young man!" the knife thrower said!

I should obviously have said, "NO!", but somehow or other I was on my way to the target area.

"He is a very big target and I hope I don't hit him! It would be a shame to mutilate such a handsome young fella!"

What the audience were doing at this time, escapes me, as I was crapping myself.

Within moments I was tied to the target! He said it was for my safety, to stop me moving, but I think it was just to stop me running away!

There was a drum roll and he prepared to throw a hatchet at me! I closed my eyes! The drum roll stopped! The knife thrower walked over to me and asked me if I was religious?

I told him I was and he said, "It might be a good time to say a quick prayer!"

Now I was panicking!

Drumroll again! Hatchet being tossed around in his hands ... only for him to drop it! The drummer copying the sound by clattering all of his drums at random! It sounded like the drum kit had fallen downstairs!

"Sorry about that, young man! I don't drop the hatchets very often. My hands are a bit sweaty!" As he took a towel and wiped his hands.

Drumroll again! Hatchet about to be thrown! My eyes closed!

Drumroll stopped! So, I opened my eyes!

He was approaching me again, this time with his assistant beside him.

You keep shutting your eyes, so it's best if you wear a blind fold.

A blood-stained cloth was tied around my head!

"Help! Help!", I thought.

A softer drumroll started and then the audience went very quiet!

I heard ... "One ... Two ... Three ... then a short silence before I heard the hatchet dig into the target board inches from my head!

How I didn't shit myself, I have no idea!

The audience cheered and shouted!

Drumroll again! I could feel the atmosphere in the ballroom!

Again, I heard the countdown and then the thud! This time near to my other ear!

The audience cheered and shouted again!

The blindfold was whipped off! The hatchets were so close to my head I could have fainted! An inch or so out on his throw would have meant my ears would have been on the floor!

It didn't help when he said, "Oh! There's a little blood! I must have nicked your ear! Sorry! Sorry!" As he carefully wiped my ear with a clean handkerchief, only for him to show it back to me with a large red stain on it! As I was still tied, I couldn't put my hands up to feel my ear! Why didn't it hurt! Had he severed a nerve!

His assistant finally untied me from the target! She whispered, "Don't put your hand up to your ear! If the audience see blood on your hands, we could get sacked!" So, I meekly kept my hands down! I was then made to take several bows to the audience, who clapped and shouted my name. Then I returned to my seat to watch the rest of the act. People kept patting me on the back, saying well done!

I was trembling! He could have killed me! Or … or … I didn't dare to think of what else he could have potentially done to me!

The act was a roaring success and the audience loved them, giving them a standing ovation as they left the ballroom!

There was no time for me to go to the toilets and be sick, which was what I wanted to do! Ladies once again descended on me to dance with them, so I was stuck there until the end of the evening!

In the dressing room, after the festivities had finished, I sat, pint in hand. I could hear the 'Californian' act chatting! By their accents I could tell they were from Belfast! Americans my arse! They were no more American than I was!

One of the Blazer girls sat down beside me. "You were very

good tonight to go along with the joke! You were very convincing! The punters would never have known!"

"What the hell was she talking about?"

"When those hatchets were dug into the board by the assistant stood by you, I swear you acted like it was real! You should take up the stage! You obviously have a talent!", she remarked, leaving me to extrapolate those details into a workable theory.

It turns out, when I was blindfolded, the audience were given signs by the knife thrower to be silent! He didn't throw the hatchets! His assistant stood next to me and just dug them into the target! It was all a joke on me!

For a few minutes I was very angry that no one tipped me off about the ruse, but eventually I saw the funny side of it and laughed!

One or two of you readers, may have fallen for the same trick! If you have, then you know how I feel!

Anyway, the night was finally over! Ernie kept away from me! He knew I was unaware of the joke being played on me and wasn't too sure how I would react!

I had to find a release for all the tension in my body. At least that was the excuse I made to myself, as I dug the dance card out of my pocket. Now, what was that chalet number?

Sneaking around the chalets in the half light of some dim bulbs, under a moon that kept disappearing behind the clouds, was new to me but as usual I quickly adapted! I soon had the stealth of Tonto (or if you are much younger, a ninja warrior), or so I imagined.

It was difficult to make out the numbers, so I wandered about, half afraid I might get pulled into the wrong chalet or worse, caught sneaking around by Mr McMasters. I knew it was a sackable offence to be fraternising with guests! What if somebody thought I was a peeping Tom! I'd be run out of Ballytreeny! Never to return!

Chalet 236! There it was, with a light burning in the window! Surely a welcome invite to me! But what if I was wrong and her husband opened the door! What would I say?

I stood there for a moment, thinking of likely excuses to give, when the door opened a fraction and a whisper said, "Don't just stand there, come on in before someone sees you".

That was all the invitation I needed! Lateness excuses were not necessary! My inhibitions vaporised at the sight of a woman, a real woman, with next to nothing on, enticing me into her bedroom and everything that promised.

Here's where we do a cutaway to the ocean waves, cascading onto a lonely beach showered in moonlight. I think that's only fair, just in case we have any readers of a tender disposition and anyway reader I'm sure you have a good enough imagination.

It must have been about one o'clock in the morning that I opened the door to reluctantly leave my satiated lover.

She now had even less clothes on than before, wrapped in a sheet, on the squeaky old bed that had been put through its paces. I checked left and then right and then left again! Slowly, very slowly and on tip toes, I slid out of the doorway, closing the door behind me with a muffled click.

I was now out in the open, the moon hiding behind a cloud and the dim lights, from earlier, turned off. It was darker than the bilge of the ship, although not so smelly.

Edging along the chalet block, I was horrified to hear a door, just in front of me, open and a shadowy figure slipping out into my path.

Before I could stop myself, I was face to face with another guy, obviously up to the same things as me! He was also trying to be cautious, probably, like me, not wanting to face the wrath of Mr McMasters.

To my horror, the moon peaked out quietly from its temporary hiding place and lit both our faces. Rumbled!

Sacked in the morning!

Then it dawned on me who it was. It was Mr Mc Bloody Masters himself, the dirty bastard! The hypocrite! Hair askew. Tie nowhere to be seen. Moustache drooping and in need of wax. All these things ran through my mind in a fraction of a second.

"Evening Niall!", he remarked. "Out for a stroll?"

"Yes sir", I replied. "Couldn't sleep!"

"Me neither! … Goodnight".

Standing there in complete shock I realised I was ok! He couldn't sack me without dropping himself in it.

I suddenly noticed I was holding my breath! After releasing it in a relieved sigh, I went back onto tip toes and made my way as silently as possible back to my chalet and I never heard a word more about it.

I soon found myself in constant demand doing the chalet shimmer and I learnt more in that short time, than the previous twenty years, but when broken arm boy was well enough to resume his duties, I reluctantly retired, intensifying my work on the other type of beds.

Unknown to me I was being observed by a gentleman who was a frequent guest. He kept himself to himself and didn't seem to join in the frivolities, observing proceedings and occasionally writing in a journal. He carried it in a small black satchel, slung around his neck.

One carefree afternoon, when the workload was light, I sat on the grass with a glass of water, looking at my handiwork on the flower beds, metaphorically patting myself on the back for the splendid display.

"Good afternoon young man! Admiring the profits of your labour?", he queried.

"Yes sir! Beautiful, aren't they?"

"They certainly are! But it would seem to the casual observer, like me, that you are capable of far more than being a humble gardener. I was fortunate enough to watch your transition into Blazer boy and how you dealt with everything that was thrown at you with aplomb. Then, when the situation was reversed, you simply adapted again, without fuss or acrimony. Your newfound status diminishing overnight! You took it all in your stride and concentrated on doing a superb job in your original calling. That, young man, is a sign of a fine mind and temperament. I have a feeling you will go far in life."

"Thank you, sir. That's very good of you to say. I've always been taught to do the best you can, at any job you are given, no matter how low or how high the task."

"Very laudable!"

"Sir! Hope I'm not intruding, but I see you writing in your journal at every opportunity. Are you writing a book?"

"In a way I always am. I write down my observations of people and how they interact with each other and everyday situations. I may use those jottings later, in a book or a play. Not necessarily about this place, but in plots that spring to mind when my psyche is at its darkest. My name is Brendan!"

"Nice to meet you, Brendan. Never met a writer before. Does it pay well?"

"At times I suppose it does! But that's not why I write. It's more the passion of storytelling that drives me, not the money. To describe in words, a picture that can live in the imagination, conjuring up scenes of frantic love or utter devastation, is a moment of ecstasy not experienced by many. I can make you either love or hate a character, when that role is merely fiction. That is an awesome power and writers live off the energy!"

"Wow! It sounds like your passion".

"It is. What's your passion Niall?"

"Not really sure sir! Travelling, I suppose, oh and photography".

"And women from what I've heard. I'm with you there!"

"Isn't that every man's passion?"

"Not every man, Niall, but I take your point. You, young man, need to get some focus in your life. Don't drift from job to job! Set yourself some targets, be they in travelling or photography or even women come to that! But you must set them! Life has a way of passing us by if we're not careful and you have talents you shouldn't ignore".

"My school report said I was good at lifting things. Says a lot about me".

"My school report said I was a stupid boy who always had his head in the clouds. I had my head in the stratosphere, but I was not stupid! The remark about you being good at lifting may be correct, but it doesn't mean it is the only thing you are good at! You just have to find out what they are! I can see a host of qualities in you, needing to be given air to breathe. Take a chance! Get out in the world and experience its magnificence, its primal beauty, you're on the threshold of your life! How you live it is up to you and no one else".

That meeting was a turning point in my life and gave me a resolve to leave Ballytreeny for good and go wherever fate would take me. Brendan was an amazing man who lived far too short a life, touching many souls with his writing.

There were still many good days in front of me at Sandy

Island, but I slowly formulated a plan to leave at the end of the summer when all the flowers were safely in bloom, hoping Alf wouldn't feel too badly of me. What I couldn't know, however, was that fate had its own ideas for me.

Those warm summer nights, tip toeing along the chalet line will never dim in my memory and I suppose, after reading this, my wife may want to hear some more details and name a few names. Now what were they?

I can remember some of the bodies but the names have faded, so you can rest easy, ladies! Those heady days of exponential learning are part of who I am today and modern-day folk may think them crass and fool hardy, but to me they are part of my life story and I can't go back and rewrite them even if I wanted to.

Layer upon layer of experiences, good and bad create the fabric of our personality and the cloth we consist of. I'd like to think mine is gentle and kind, robust and supportive and above all loving.

We were lucky at Sandy Island to have a brilliant Show Band performing there. It consisted of Ballytreeny' boys, most of whom I knew from school and they were called 'The Ballyband'. They played all sorts of music, from the latest pop songs to old standards, plus lots of Irish tunes. The dancefloor was always packed when they played and they knew how to whip up an audience.

I should tell you that I was given permission to go into the ballroom, even without a Blazer on, as a lot of the guests would ask for me. Ringing loud in my ear, were the instructions! Behave yourself and not get drunk!

Let's put it this way, despite being a bit of a lad, I was never thrown out.

Among the many themes at the Ballroom, one of the favourites was the 'Talent Night', where the guests would do their party-piece.

They would usually sing a song, but sometimes they tried tap dancing, playing the spoons and other 'talents' they had long kept hidden.

It has to be said, there were some exceptionally talented guests as well who were good enough to be professional! Equally, there were some dreadful ones that it was hard not to laugh at. One comes to mind that we did laugh at, because he was impossibly bad, the audience were in stitches and I don't think the guy even noticed.

He was a trumpet player, but it appears he was tone deaf! The tune he was supposed to be playing was barely recognisable, despite the title having been announced.

At first the audience sat there open mouthed at the sonic abomination pounding their ears, but then one loose note was so badly out of tune it was funny and everyone laughed and clapped!

The guy, thinking he was going well, tried even harder, which resulted in even more misplaced notes and consequential hilarity exploding through the audience, who thought he was doing it on purpose.

It's difficult to remember anyone else ever receiving a standing ovation that nearly lifted the roof off, but this one certainly did! He finished with a beaming smile that won over even more fans.

"Give us another!", was the shout coming from the audience and remarkably he spoke to the band and then launched into yet another parody, but this time without telling the audience the title. You could see people asking each other what the tune was?

The poor band, almost doubled up with laughter, had to keep their backing going, whilst avoiding eye contact with the trumpeter.

Ernie was crying when he jumped on the stage to thank the guest, who was taking several bows. Ernie was hardly able to talk and waved his arms around, demonstrably, trying to get the audience to stand up and applaud. The ballroom saw loads of special moments, but that was a classic!

There used to be a noticeboard just inside the ballroom entrance, giving notice of what was happening there throughout the day and evening and any special guests appearing.

One day I saw a bunch of young women and girls, teeming around it in a frenzied manner and went to find out what was going down. Imagine my surprise when I saw the star guest that evening was the famous Irish singer Duncan Mulberry.

Now, if you have been paying attention you will remember that when I was thirteen, I caddied for him in a golf competition that he went on to win, for which he was truly grateful. It intrigued me whether he would remember me! After all it was seven years earlier and I was now more than a foot taller.

I persuaded Ernie to let me be a Blazer boy for the evening and when Duncan arrived, I met him and carried his bags to his guest room.

"Band call is at 3.00pm if that's ok Mr Mulberry" I offered.

"Sounds good to me. I'll be in the ballroom at about 2.45pm".

"I'll tell the bandleader".

"Before you go. What's your name?"

"Niall, sir!"

"Niall, ok. Ah Niall ... Have we met before? You look familiar but I can't place where?"

"We've met before Mr Mulberry, but it was a long time ago".

"Well, you have to tell me now!", he said sitting down. "You've intrigued me".

"Do you remember playing in a golf match at Ballytreeny when your father-in-law introduced you to the club?"

"Yes of course I do. Amazing day! And I won if I remember rightly. Brilliant young caddy named ... what was his name?" he reflected.

"Niall, Mr Mulberry!" I replied.

"Good lord! Was it you?"

"Yes sir!"

"Of course, you were only a child then, now look at the size of you. You're at least six inches taller than me!"

"How long have you worn the Blazer?"

I went on to explain why I was wearing it and we nattered about that and golf for quite a while, until I left him to get ready".

"Niall ... please call me Duncan".

"Yes sir … I mean … Duncan".

The band call went very well and it was my job to keep nosey guests out of the ballroom while Duncan was running through his set, after which I escorted him to his room via the back door of the stage, keeping autograph hunters fooled until the evening performance.

To be honest I had never seen a star performer before and it was a real eye opener for me. I was used to the high standard of the local bands but this was another level. Duncan had a command of his stage craft and audience control I had never experienced and it was mesmerising. When he sang everyone was quiet unless he encouraged them to join in, which he did quite a bit and when he sang his final song "Climb every mountain" the place went wild. Some of the younger women rushed up to the stage and I found myself as a human shield, preventing him being overwhelmed.

His appearance was a massive success and he spent a long-time, signing autographs and just chatting to fans, while I kept order around him. People knew me and were very polite in waiting their turn with the star.

Sitting quietly in his dressing room after the event he chatted to me about the evening and how well it had gone and told me he had thanked Ernie for providing such a good bodyguard for the day. I was a bit embarrassed by the praise but I have to admit it felt good to be appreciated, something else for my life lessons.

Always tell those people who work hard for you that you appreciate their diligence and dedication, it goes a long way.

There was a small knock at the door and I was surprised to find two of the Blazer girls outside, asking to see Duncan. I was about to say he was changing, when he said, "Let them in Niall." I thought at first, he was just being nice to them, but I could soon see he was revelling in the spotlight and openly flirting with them.

I was a bit shocked as I knew he was married, but all this was different to me, so I kept my mouth shut. Something I would learn to do in earnest over the next few years.

"I'll … eh … wait for you out front, Duncan!", I said as I slipped quietly out the door. Just about noticing the quick wink he gave me as I closed it. I would see that wink a lot in the future.

It wasn't clear at the time but that day was another of those major turning points in my life. You don't notice them at the time, only when you look back.

If I had not met Tim that day when he was walking to work, I would never have come to Sandy Island Holiday Centre. If that Blazer boy had not broken his arm, I would not have started work in the Ballroom. If I had not been such a good caddy when I was thirteen and so it goes on.

How our lives pivot on seemingly mundane happenings and we don't even notice until much later, if ever.

Ernie found me standing guard and asked if Duncan was ready and I coughed. Then I said quietly that he was a little busy at that moment, with the emphasis on busy.

Our Ernie had been in the business for a long time and only in later years settled down in Sandy Island, so he understood my emphasis and immediately sat down beside me to chat.

"You were exceptionally good tonight, Niall. Better than you think you were. You didn't panic when they rushed the stage, you managed it and the same with the autograph hunters. Well done! You are a natural figure of authority and not just because of your stature, it's something in your nature. I have a feeling you may be asked to do more of this sort of work and it could be good for you!"

"You mean here at Sandy Island?"

"I was thinking more about the wider world out there waiting for a young man like you to experience. Time for you to settle down when you're older, not now when you are full of life and energy. I suspect that Duncan may try and poach you for himself. He needs someone to keep the punters at bay and without upsetting them. Someone calm and commanding, just like you"

"But what about my flower beds? And Alf? He'll be upset".

"Alf will get over it. Tending flower beds in a quiet corner of Ireland is safe but not overly exciting. It depends if you are content to stay and follow in your father's footsteps or create your own path and your own footsteps.

If it doesn't work, you can always take up gardening again, but I suspect you will do much more in life.

There's something about you that makes me feel you will never be content to stay in Ballytreeny or even Ireland come to that. You're a wanderer by nature, a dreamer, it won't come to you Niall.

If you want it, you'll have to get it yourself. Don't look back on your life and say, 'What if?' Get out there and make it happen or at the very least do the best you can."

Ernie had never spoken to me like this before and I could see a depth in him that I had completely overlooked. I saw him in a whole new light, someone with a mass of experience who was trying to guide me, not push me, onto a path up and out of an everyday life and I have a lot to be grateful to him for.

Duncan and the girls eventually bundled out of the dressing room and Ernie suggested we all go to the bar. It was normally closed at this hour but had been reopened for us and a few more people who wanted to meet Duncan privately.

As we approached the bar Duncan said, "Thanks for understanding back there" and winked again, as I said previously, something I would see a lot in the future, but let's not get too far ahead of the story. We met the others in the bar and settled down with drinks being brought by a waitress. I remember thinking, "I could get used to this!", as I sat drinking my free pint of Guinness.

Duncan was brilliant with his admirers, taking time to respond to each of them as if they were long lost friends. Yes, it was fake in its way but I honestly believe the man meant it. He thoroughly enjoyed meeting people, not just because they fell at his feet but because they were kindred spirits, eager to share in his life.

What time did we fall out of that bar you may ask? I would have to say, "I haven't a clue!"

Because of my days as a dancing Blazer boy, most people knew me and were keen to talk to me as well and I had no problem profiting from reflected glory. The Guinness flowed and we laughed and joked, ribald stories were swapped and Duncan sang a song, completely unaccompanied and wowed us all. The man was obviously incredibly talented and secure in his abilities.

Even I related some of the antics I had perpetrated during my young life and Duncan sang my praises as an ace caddy.

Mr McMasters, who rarely moved out of his military persona, gave us a monologue that was more than a little risqué, probably a relic of his service days that had us all in stitches. He surprised me when he offered to take me to the Ballytreeny Golf Club as his guest to play a round of golf. Imagine me, walking in through the front door as a guest and playing golf, with one of the local lads as my caddy. Who would have believed it? Certainly not me at thirteen!

So, if any of you are that tender age and have dragged yourself away from your pet computer to read this book, although, thinking of it, you may be reading this on said computer. You can make something of your life! It may take time and you will certainly need a lot of luck, but your life and what you do with it is in your hands! Maybe not completely at thirteen, but it's a good place to start.

We eventually vacated the bar and made a rather slow and meandering journey to Duncan's chalet, where I poured him through the door, a tired but happy star. As I was about to leave, he said, "Thank you for looking after me today, Niall. Come and meet me for breakfast at about nine o'clock and we can have a chat. You may have to knock quite hard!" At which point, he collapsed backwards onto the bed. I took his shoes off his feet and covered him with a spare blanket and left him to his dreams.

Sleep should have come quickly for me that night, after my Guinness intake but I lay awake, thinking about the events of the evening, about all that Ernie had said and the possible reasons that Duncan would have for us having a chat, as he put it.

Round and round in my head, ideas and possibilities swam in many differing directions, colliding and dividing into fantasies that were undoubtedly fuelled by alcohol, until sleep crept up and caught me unaware.

The next morning, I woke to a terrible banging, I remember thinking "Who's making that terrible racket, they'll wake all the guests" until I finally realised it was inside my head. I checked my watch and saw it was past eight, so I reluctantly climbed out of bed and got ready to meet Duncan for breakfast.

I thought I was bad, but poor Duncan was worse! Still out for the count, he had no chance of hearing me, as my knocking on his door didn't seem to wake him. So, I went to housekeeping and borrowed a spare key to let myself in.

Duncan was still on the bed, fully clothed apart from his shoes, the blanket I had placed over him still in the same place undisturbed. He had plainly had a good night's sleep. It took a while to rouse him! I shook him gently and to my surprise, he sat bolt upright on his bed! Bright as a lark! He didn't seem to have any aftereffects.

I left him to get ready and went to the canteen to talk to the head waiter as we were likely to miss breakfast.

Would you believe it, Mr McMasters was just leaving the canteen, looking every inch the military man, moustache bristling, shoulders back. "Morning Niall"

"Morning sir. Just come to arrange for a late breakfast for our star guest, sir".

"Jolly good!", he said and walked with me to talk to the head waiter.

Breakfast was soon arranged and I walked back to Duncan's chalet where he was dressed and ready to meet his public once again.

We shared a table for breakfast in the now deserted canteen. I had never eaten in the main canteen before, always eating in the staff canteen. I was pleasantly surprised to find that the food was no different in quality or quantity to that served to the workers! Really well cooked and fresh, the only real difference was the decor of the room and the waiter/waitress service. Duncan and I tucked into the nosh provided and then shared a pot of tea.

"Do you want to stay here as a gardener, Niall?"

"It's a good life and the money is not bad. Good accommodation and I have a lot of fun".

"You didn't answer my question, did you?"

I supposed I hadn't but to be honest I was a little anxious about the prospect of leaving this comfortable life.

Taking a long breath, I took my time to think before I replied.

"I'm just about to be 21 and I have always had a wanderlust that's led me into situations I haven't always enjoyed at the time, but ... it's still there, niggling at me all the time. So ... yes, I do want to stay here, but on the other hand, I know there is more to life and it's not here tending flowers like my father".

"Well ... if you're interested, I need a fulltime assistant, a bodyguard of sorts. My life is changing all the time and I need someone to smooth the way and look out for me. Does that sound like something you'd fancy doing?"

It didn't take me long to say I was more than interested and by the time we had finished our second cup of tea, I had agreed to take the job, although I would have to talk to Alf about it too.

Duncan gave me a telephone number that I was to ring, to let him know when I could start. He said if it was possible, could it be the following Wednesday as he had a charity function to attend and he could do with my help. So, I left him after he was chauffeured away and went to find Alf.

It's not a nice feeling having to tell someone you like and respect, that you are moving on, but it had to be done. To be fair to Alf, he made it easy for me, telling me not to be afraid to step out into the world and take chances. He also told me I would make mistakes but when I did, I should acknowledge them and learn from them. I know he was upset at the thought of me leaving, but bless him, he only wanted the best for me. I had to promise to come back and visit him next time I was in Ballytreeny or 'home', as he referred to it. I asked him whether I should tell Mr McMasters personally, but he offered to do it and I was glad to accept.

Now all I had to do was tell my parents! My father would probably accept it without much comment, but my mother was likely to cry again. She liked the fact I lived nearby and she knew I was safe, had a good job and somewhere to live. All she could ask for really. She did not take it well at first but I was not going to sea, which was a relief and I was still going to be in Ireland, at least that's what I thought at the time. Good job I had no idea where I would be off to next.

Ballytreeny Boy

8. DUNCAN, MOUNTAINS, SANDCASTLES & VEGAS

Calling the telephone number Duncan had given, my heart was in my mouth. "What if he had changed his mind about employing me?" As the telephone rang, I wondered whether I should put down the receiver, but too late there was a female voice at the end of the line.

"Hello!"

"I'm calling to talk to Duncan?"

"Who's calling please?"

"My name is Niall".

"Hi Niall!", she said in a very friendly manner "Duncan told me that he met up with you again after all this time. I'll get him for you".

What a lovely lady. I would get to know her well over the next few years and never changed my opinion of her.

Duncan spoke to me and was thrilled that I had decided to join him, he then went on to explain the charity event that he was doing and the details intrigued me.

It appears that his manager roped him into doing a charity

event that could help promote his new single, "Climb every mountain". It was from a new musical on Broadway called, "The sound of music". I had heard him sing the song and was stunned by it and undoubtedly, a big hit for him if publicised enough.

The problem was, his manager had been truly crafty not to tell him until the last minute, that the charity had planned a walk up to the top of Kippure Mountain. All 2,484 feet of it. A famous beauty spot, it was situated on the border between County Dublin and County Wicklow! But it was a long difficult walk up to the top!

Then he was expected to sing and there'd be cameras!

If I was his manager I'd be in hiding.

I drove down the R115 in a car I borrowed from Tim. What do you mean I never mentioned passing my driving test or taking driving lessons of any sort, well I thought that would be boring so I missed it out, completely!

Now I come to think of it, I should have told you about Paddy Motors and their School of Motoring. We Irish do have a reputation for being idiosyncratic but Paddy, the owner, was off the charts!

His garage used to specialise in carts and farm machinery, a long time before the motor car caught on in Ballytreeny.

He was also prone to organising donkey rides on the beach for the guests from Sandy Island. This naturally progressed into him setting up races for the kids that the parents could place bets on. Cutting the Blazer boys and girls in on the profits was his way of securing a captive audience and to be fair, they loved it and so did the kids.

All this used to rake him in a small fortune every year, but the betting came to a grinding halt, when one of the kids did a backward somersault over his donkey's hind section! It would have been ok but he managed to land on the sand, just as another donkey was about to overtake.

Now this donkey, doing the overtaking was known as Sterling Moss, because of the way he went through the pack, had been nobbled! Paddy had placed an overweight jockey on him. Everyone prior to the race wanting to bet on Sterling, not aware of the lump placed on the poor donkey's back!

Paddy had taken a sizeable sum on Sterling to win and when he produced the horizontally challenged jockey, there was uproar and cries of cheat.

He, as usual, smiled, counting his betting profits and ignored it.

Unfortunately for Paddy, when the child did his acrobatic somersault and dismount, the other parents ran and stopped the donkeys from running.

All except the parents of the child on Sterling Moss, who had no chance of catching him. Sterling was having none of it, his head was down and he was going for it, desperate to rid himself of the burden he was carrying and so he won! Completely unchallenged! Paddy tried to void the race, but the punters were out for blood and he had to pay out! Serves him right! I was there to witness this fiasco and must admit to having a shilling or two on Sterling to win.

What has this to do with my driving skills? Nothing at all, just came to mind when I mentioned driving. Funny the way things pop up in your mind when you least expect them.

As far as driving is concerned, I had a few lessons with Paddy's instructor and passed first time, so no big story there. Agreed?

Right, where were we? Oh yes, I was driving down the R115 from Dublin to meet up with the walkers at a path that runs up to the Sally Gap. The carpark is at 1,650 feet, which meant we only had to climb another ... well you do the maths! At least we didn't have to walk from the bottom.

Duncan hadn't arrived by the time I got there, but I was early, not wanting to be late on my first day.

I took the opportunity to tog up for the walk, including

some sturdy walking shoes, again borrowed, as my hobnailed boots would not be suitable for this terrain.

A crowd started to gather in the carpark and introductions were made.

I met the photographer and a camera man who was to shoot the moving pictures.

Now, today we are used to camera phones, but in those days, they were much bigger, like the Sekonic 8mm movie camera this guy was using, not huge, but still heavy enough when it had to be lugged, with accessories, to the summit.

I was starting to get worried about Duncan, when his car arrived and he spilled out all enthusiastic and ready to go. No special clothes or boots, or anything else come to that.

The organisers looked at each other in disbelief and one of them approached Duncan, so I made a beeline for him, ready to do my bodyguard bit. There were some jovial introductions and then it was gently put to him that he was not dressed for the occasion.

In Duncan's defence he had never heard of Kippure Mountain and he had no idea how far we were going to walk or the type of terrain. It was a beautiful day and he thought we were going for a gentle stroll in the sunlight. I couldn't loan him my boots as they were far too big for him, so we were in a quandary.

Then I had a brainwave! I called the cameraman over and asked him who was carrying his gear up the mountain as I didn't think the highly skilled cameraman was going to do it. I was right and he had a couple of guys to help him.

My suggestion was that if one of the guys gave his boots to Duncan and stayed behind at the carpark, I would carry his load to the top of the mountain and back. There was a bit of toing and froing, but it was eventually agreed and Duncan received, not only a pair of decent boots, but also a weatherproof Jacket, which was more than I had.

It was good to prove to Duncan that I could help in a crisis and I could tell he was pleased, by the familiar wink he gave me.

I was now carrying camera equipment plus food and drink, supplies that Duncan had brought for us, so I was laden.

Duncan being Duncan just carried himself, nipping from group to group and chatting up the females.

The walkers were all seasoned people, each being sponsored by local firms for a substantial amount of money for the charity, which for the life of me, the name I can't remember. Perhaps it will come back to me later, like the donkey derby story, but don't hold your breath.

There is something exhilarating about walking up the steep sides of a mountain, rapidly leaving the start off point and looking back after a half hour or so and see it the size of a fingernail far below us.

Because of the pace we were taking I noticed Duncan had stopped yapping and was instead concentrating on keeping up with the others. I did wonder how he would manage to sing when we eventually reached the top.

By the time we had climbed about 500 feet the view was amazing, looking right out over Dublin in the distance and we paused to have a drink and admire the scenery.

Duncan, who was obviously not used to this sort of activity collapsed onto a large boulder that easily doubled as a chair, his feet dangling over the side. I poured him some coffee and passed it to him.

"Nothing stronger?" he joked.

"Drunk it already!" was my reply.

"I wouldn't put it past you" he laughed. "Wouldn't like to volunteer to carry me the rest of the way?" he joked.

"No problem", I countered. "Just jump in the rucksack next to the camera! Just be careful where you put your feet".

I daresay the conversation would have continued but the rest of the party were readying themselves to restart. I packed away the remains of the coffee and we once again joined our band of brothers (and sisters).

The going was getting a little tougher and I noticed Duncan getting weary and I think the borrowed boots were giving him problems, so I sought out a stout stick for him to lean on as he walked. This helped him to keep up. He was obviously a city boy with little or no experience of what we were doing.

When we did reach the summit and unloaded our packs, we took a moment to catch our breath and then took in the panoramic view of Ireland that we were rewarded with. If you are ever in Ireland there are some beautiful walks, some not for the faint hearted but plenty with fairly easy ascents, so don't go home until you have sampled one.

The coffee and sandwiches went down well and we sat in a hollow out of the wind, relaxing in the sun in this beautiful location, far from the industrialised areas and not a house in sight.

Our peace and tranquillity were disturbed by the cameraman who had been scouting for locations to film Duncan.

"I've filmed quite a few cutaways (this is a section of the movie that is not the principal object), Dublin in the distance, the path we came up, that sort of thing. Now I need to find somewhere to shoot you and I wondered if you might like to come with me to choose it".

"Take my assistant Niall, he's an expert on film locations, aren't you Niall" and that wink, working again out of sight of the cameraman of course.

Smiling to myself, knowing absolutely nothing about film locations, I walked confidently along with the cameraman.

He would suggest a location and I would say, "I think we can do better" and surprisingly he agreed with me.

Finally, we both agreed on a perfect spot, which when viewed from one angle looked like we were in the wilderness and if panned around the vista opened out into a view over Dublin City that was spectacular.

"He knows his stuff, your Niall", the cameraman told Duncan and he replied, "I told you he did" and the wink followed again with a smile. "He's my right-hand man".

It was then I saw Duncan the performer take over! It's almost like he flicked a switch and a power surge of self-belief took over, walking differently, talking differently and holding himself like the star that he was.

I remember thinking "This is why he has been so successful".

Duncan took little or no notice of the location because that was not important to him, his performance was! I need not have worried about his voice, because he was singing along to a recording of himself, that would be dubbed over the film track later, when they returned to their studio.

With that in mind he sang like an angel. It mattered little to him that the vocal would never be used and sang as if he was on the stage of the London Palladium with a packed audience and I know that because I saw him do it myself.

He sang the song four times and they filmed from different angles each time, only finishing when the light started to go. There was a spontaneous round of applause from the other walkers, who had sat there mesmerised by the whole thing and he took an exaggerated bow as if to thousands.

Our walk back down was surprisingly difficult, one because the light was fading and also because walking downhill although easier in effort to walking uphill, there is a great deal more balance needed as you are leaning backwards and not forwards.

We did arrive safely at our base and after lots of congratulations all round and the obligatory autographs, the group split up. Duncan gave me an envelope with money in it and said "Stick that in your pocket and we'll sort out a proper wage for you during the week. I knew you'd be good for me and you proved me right. You know I like to be right" and the wink took over again.

Driving home I felt a sense of achievement that I rarely felt in any of my previous jobs and I knew I had made the right decision. I had counted the money and there was more in there than I normally earned in a month. I could scarcely believe it!

I could hardly wait for the next assignment. Let me tell you, it was very, very different.

Tim's car wasn't going to be available all the time so Duncan loaned me one of his. It was an Austin Princess Vanden Plas and was amazing! I felt as if I was driving a Rolls Royce and when I drove it through Ballytreeny, heads turned. It is still one of the best cars I have ever driven, despite its bulk and high petrol usage! Plus, the exterior and interior were both spectacular! Exactly the car that a star like Duncan should arrive in.

I was living with my parents again after leaving Sandy Island and things were not good, as my brothers had got used to having more room in the bedroom the four of us shared.

Driving back and fore was not going to work anyway, so I found temporary lodgings near to Duncan's house.

My mother, as you can imagine, would have preferred me to be close by, but at least I wasn't at sea.

So, I loaded all my things into the boot of the car, said my goodbyes, although I wasn't going that far and then did one more lap of Ballytreeny, for old time's sake.

Imagine my shock when driving along the beach road I saw Erin walking along pushing a pram. It couldn't be hers surely? I stopped and rolled down the window to talk to her.

"Nice car!", she said. "Where'd you steal it?", she laughed and I realised I had missed her.

Looking at the pram I said, "Something you want to tell me?"

She laughed again. "It's not mine if that's what you think. I'm not that sort of girl. It's my big sister Kate's little boy".

"Glad to hear that. Had me worried for a moment".

Then with a flourish of her hand she showed me an engagement ring, all sparkling and new. Why did I feel upset that she should get engaged to someone else when we hadn't seen each other in ages? There was a connection between us and once that happens it rarely goes away completely, even now after all these years. She married the following year, but I wasn't invited to the wedding, luckily, I wasn't in the country at the time. The last time I saw her she was in her early thirties with two strapping lads to look after. She looked incredible and really happy. So, I hope wherever you are Erin and you by chance are reading this book, that you still remember the Ballytreeny boy who wandered far from home.

My new lodgings were in Shankill. It's just the other side of Dublin from Ballytreeny and not too far from a wonderful golf club. Duncan was a member and we did manage to play a few rounds in our spare time. Beautiful but difficult links course made worse when the wind was blowing in from the sea. I could get used to playing places like this! Little did I know that we would soon be making a leap and playing in the desert. Where? I'm not going to tell you yet, let it be a surprise, because it was to me.

Right … back to telling you about this new assignment and the challenges it gave me.

The video of Duncan singing on the top of a mountain was shown on Irish National Television and his single promptly jumped into the Irish Top Ten. He was a famous face in Ireland already, but now he was current news and his profile increased even more.

When the gig was originally booked, Duncan was a star but not hot property, so the bookers were thrilled when they realised, they had a major coup on their hands and for a very reasonable fee.

If only the organisers had put a little thought into Duncan's presence at the event there might have been a different outcome, but alas they were so thrilled at the elevation of his status that they neglected to think it through.

Every year there is a Sandcastle Competition on Killiney Bay and this particular year it was the 25th anniversary of the first event, so the local traders got together and booked local pop star Duncan, to judge and add a little kudos to the proceedings.

The contestants had been beavering away since early morning and from the pictures taken during construction there were some magnificent structures being created out of sand and water.

Why am I referring to pictures during construction? Well-read on and all will become clear.

News of Duncan being present on the seafront was heavily publicised in the local papers and in posters around the area. They were all ordered prior to the TV coverage of his mountain top excursion! The crowd of a hundred or so, that was originally expected, was already at least five hundred, well before we arrived. Estimates as to how many were in attendance, at the peak, varied wildly depending on the counter's vantage point, but let's just say the crowd was enormous and leave it at that.

We arrived in the Austin Princess and there was already pandemonium! This felt like a nightmare, where the Beatles were arriving and I was the only one on guard duty.

There was no way we could drive through the crowd, until we were spotted by the local Garda! With their help, we inched closer to the beach competition, all the time being thronged by screaming fans.

I told Duncan that we shouldn't get out of the car and risk him getting mobbed, but he would have none of it. I took a deep breath and got out of the driver's side, making my way through the pressing crowd to the passenger side.

The Garda were brilliant in their handling of the throng around us and we eventually got to the edge of the beach, but nothing could be done about the hundreds who streamed out past us, onto what was already a crowded beach.

There was a mini crowd surge that grew steadily into an out-of-control stampede and people were running in all directions, forgetting about Duncan for the moment, more intent on saving their own lives and I don't blame them. It was super scary and I was a big bloke!

From other accounts, we learnt that the stampede spilled out onto the beach, straight over the masterpieces waiting to be judged!

Some were hurdled over, others suddenly resident to a herd of water buffalo, disguised as young women, stamping sandy architecture as if it were ... well ... sand.

'Panicking people pulverise Palaces', was the inevitable headline in the Press! They showed before and after pictures of the exhibits! The former looking like absolutely stunning sand creations and the latter looking like a well-worn beach.

Duncan was being swept along by the sheer weight of bodies, we had lost our Garda saviours who were desperately trying to stop the panic, so it was up to me to get him to safety. I grabbed his collar and yanked him almost off his feet, pushing him onto the beach and hard right to a small pocket of space in front of the seawall.

As the wave of humanity swept past us, I was reminded of days on the Ramona Wave and I wished we had a safety rope now. If the organisers were there, we didn't see them in the chaos If they had any sense they would have run to the water's edge as quickly as they could. It was a miracle that no-one was badly hurt, a few people shook up and in tears but no trampling casualties and no broken bones.

Eventually the surge stopped and there was just a general melee that swirled like a flock of sparrows until coming to rest on sandy perches.

We did then manage to find an Organiser or rather she found us, recognising Duncan and apologising profusely for the carnage. Duncan being Duncan took it all in his stride and we found a good vantage point, where he was safe and able to sign hundreds of autographs. To be fair to the crowd, everyone was good mannered and waited their turn to see the star for a kiss, or an autograph and sometimes both, depending on how much Duncan fancied them. Yes … the wink did appear again … several times.

Judging couldn't be done that day for obvious reasons and was consigned to a panel, including Duncan, viewing press pictures taken before everything went tits up. There was a presentation for the winners and losers but it was kept private except for the press, fearing a repeat of the beach fiasco. Both occasions found Duncan on the front page of the nationals and undoubtedly the first time a beach invasion had been mentioned since the war.

Maybe looking back on things, I can be calm about what happened but it so nearly became a major loss of life event, saved only by providence.

Driving Duncan back home, I remember him clearly saying, quite dryly, "Well that was different!" Too true my old friend. Too true!"

Gigs came thick and fast for a while, with Duncan becoming hot property and days merging one into the other, without a lot of time off! 1962 started well. The first couple of months flying by. We visited parts of Ireland I didn't know existed and even went over by Ferry, to appear in Liverpool.

It was great to be back in that vibrant city again! Unfortunately, I didn't have a lot of spare time! We arrived in the morning, rehearsed in the afternoon and then did two shows in the evening! Duncan was very tired, or so he said! He retired to his room around 11.00pm.

I was going to bed as well, but I figured I would grab a drink in the hotel bar. Imagine my surprise, when I saw Duncan walking out of the hotel, with a girl on his arm! Crafty sod! Lied to me about being tired, so he could sneak out! Anyone would think I kept a close eye on him!

It took just a moment to finish my drink, then I was out of that door, on his tail!

The concourse of the hotel was empty, except for a doorman.

I just spotted a car disappearing out through the ornate gates that opened onto the main road.

"Bugger!"

"Given you the slip, has he?"

"Absolutely! Crafty bastard!"

"Want to know where he's gone?"

"That would be amazing!"

The doorman just stood there without saying a word! Just looking at me! I suddenly realised he was expecting a tip!

I wasn't used to handing out money, but I was holding some of Duncan's stash for safe keeping. I decided it was a legitimate expense and handed over a pound note. He still stood there, until I made it three quid! A fortune to me!

"Thanks Guv! He's off to the 'Beatbreak'. It's a club in the city centre. If you're going, I'll call you a cab!"

"I'm going!"

It took a few minutes but eventually I was on my way. We wound through the crowded streets to the centre of town and the cabbie dropped me in front of a dingy looking place, with a large billboard outside.

On the door was a bouncer who was almost as wide as I was tall! A monster of a guy! I could see there was no way round him! "I'm here to meet up with Duncan Mulberry."

He just stared at me, much like the doorman at the hotel! What was there with this town!

This time it cost a fiver! A whole fiver! What was the world coming to?

Although the place looked dingy from outside, the interior was much better. At least in the low lights, the bits I could see were.

A band was playing rock and roll on the stage in the corner, loud enough to require you to shout, to make yourself heard.

There was quite a throng of young woman lining up in front of the band, jumping, screaming and generally having a good time!

I remember thinking, "I bet they are not working tomorrow!"

There was no sign of Duncan, so I went to the bar and ordered a pint of Guinness. At least it was easy to get in Liverpool!

I was aware of a pretty girl sat alone on a table nearby. Just because I was looking for Duncan, didn't mean I would miss out on someone like this.

"Anyone sitting here?" I said as I indicated an empty chair.

"Well, if they are, luv! It must be the invisible man!"

I took that to mean it was available.

"What do you think of the band?", she asked.

"Me brother's the lead guitarist!"

"Which one is that?"

"The one playing bleedin' lead guitar! Do you always ask daft questions?"

"Do you fancy a drink?"

"Why not! Port and Lemon!"

I bought the drink and carried it over to the table, only to find a bloke sat next to her.

He wasn't very big, so I put the drink on the table in front of her and sat down in the seat I had recently vacated.

"This is Brian. He's a talent scout."

"Oh! Really? Have they got talent then?"

She curled her lip and I thought she was going to hit me!

He cracked a wry smile, glancing at me, but saying nothing.

"They are going to be in the charts soon!" she said.

"Charts?" I had no idea what charts were.

"You Irish?"

"I am indeed!"

"Thought as much!"

I was sure it was an insult, but she was a girl, so I left it.

Before I could continue the stilted conversation, I saw Duncan in a dimly lit corner of the club, with his companion. He hadn't seen me, at least I don't think he did. My view was then blocked as a second female walked over to his table and sat down!

"Found someone else you like?" said the sarky girl at my table.

"I'm here with Duncan Mulberry. Just keeping an eye on him."

"Who's he?"

The talent scout replied for me. "He's a hugely talented singer from Ireland. I invited him here tonight to talk business! He's conversing with a couple of my 'associates'."

He said associates in a strange way, but I got the gist.

"Just make sure he gets back to the hotel safely! We have to catch the midday ferry back to Ireland."

He gave me a knowing nod, as I stood to leave.

"Liverpool, too much for you, chuck?" my female table companion asked.

"Tonight, I think you may be right. Goodnight!"

There was absolutely no way I could watch Duncan all night and maybe it was better if I didn't know what he was up to. That way I wouldn't have to lie to Sinéad.

It was still after one before I got to bed but I have no idea what time Duncan got back.

He was his usual self at breakfast, so they did manage to get him back safely.

"Glad I got that early night!" he said. Followed by the customary wink. I had no way of knowing whether the 'talent scout' had told him of my presence in the club and I wasn't about to ask.

It did teach me to let him get on with his life. I was not his keeper!

A few days later, I received the gig list for the coming week and saw the word 'Airport' in big red letters. Being a little selfish I thought I'd get some time off, while Duncan flew somewhere to perform. Wrong again! When I asked him, I was flabbergasted with his reply and I need a cup of coffee before I relate it to you, because the enormity of it still shocks me. Don't go away!

Right … I'm back! Coffee was good, instant, but it hit the spot. Where was I?

I sat opposite Duncan and his wife Sinéad in their large

kitchen, I say large because it was bigger, a lot bigger than the house I was born in and the bombshell was dropped.

Duncan was flying somewhere in a short while but, and this took me totally by surprise, he wanted me to go with him.

First of all, did I have a passport? I did because I needed it for the Merchant Navy. That was checked off the list.

Had I heard of Las Vegas?

"The place where the Rat Pack perform? Yes of course"

Then I knew who Frank Sinatra was?

"Of course!"

"We are flying to Las Vegas to meet Mr Sinatra! I have been invited to perform in a St Patrick's Day show, with a number of other Irish acts".

I sat there for a moment, stunned into silence, just processing the impossible information my mind had just been invaded by.

"Me? A boy from Ballytreeny? Off to America? Frank Sinatra?" Was I dreaming or had I just been offered the job of a lifetime?

Duncan and Sinéad sat and watched with delight as I struggled to deal with the situation, guessing I was thrilled and enjoying the spectacle of me nearly wetting myself. The way I was shuffling around on that seat, it's a wonder I didn't!

Sinéad insisted on taking me shopping for clothes I would need for the visit. With Duncan picking up the tab again. Had I landed on my feet or what? Shirts and trousers and a jacket that fitted me at last, oh … and posh shoes that had a real shine to them and a tie. I had never owned nor worn a tie in my life before and I had absolutely no idea how to tie one. Again, Sinéad, bless her, showed me how to do it and after some practise runs, I perfected it, to a certain degree.

I made time for a trip back home to tell my parents where I was going. My father did his usual bit and nodded, without comment and my mother choked a little and then gave me a hug. My sisters … well they just jumped up and down and screamed and screamed! My brothers took after my father! Then I went over to Sandy Island to see Ernie and Alf and tell them the good news. I thought Ernie was going to faint when I told him, his jaw hanging open as if he had lost all control of it. Alf just smiled and wished me luck. Typical Alf, a man of little words but the smile said it all.

Ernie insisted on gathering the Blazers and telling them of my impending adventure. Amidst the "Oh get me an autograph!" etc, their pleasure for me was plain to see and they obviously hadn't forgotten me.

I was tempted to visit Caroline's house and tell her, but at the last minute I drove past and never looked back.

There have rarely been times in my life when I have been more excited and believe me, I have done a hell of a lot, but this was a biggie at the time and I'm sure you'll forgive my youthful exuberance.

The night before the trip, I lay in bed, unable to sleep! I wanted adventure in my life and here it was in the making!

My heart was pounding so hard, I sat up and leaned against the wall. What state was I going to be in if I was introduced to the Rat Pack? These guys were living legends! Stars of film and TV! And of course! They played golf! Yippee! I pictured myself out on the golf course with them, as I demonstrated my skills, with a hole in one! It was never going to happen, but to someone of my age, everything was possible! Would I meet any other film stars? Or perhaps a real-life gangster!

My excitement level was off the chart and I eventually had to get out of bed and make a cup of tea! I fell asleep leaning on the table before I took a sip!

When I woke, some hours later, my neck felt like someone had tried to screw it off overnight! I could only look straight ahead! Now what would I do? I had to drive us to Shannon airport and that was a long way!

There was no need to panic, as my neck gradually improved, but for a while I thought I would miss the trip!

Driving the short distance to Duncan's house, I couldn't help shouting "I'm off to Vegas!" at anyone I spotted along the way! Milkmen! Postmen! They must have thought I was a right idiot!

Sinéad greeted me at the door and ushered me in. Duncan's cases were in the hall, so I carried them outside and packed them in the boot, alongside my solitary case!

"Is he ready yet?"

"You know Duncan! You'd think he was just off to Dublin for the day!"

"I'll go give him a kick!", I said with a smile.

"You do that! And ... give him one from me! Wait ... before you do! Please keep an eye on him in Vegas! He can be a little impulsive and I don't want him to get into any trouble! In Ireland he's a star, but over there he'll just be another Irish immigrant! Albeit a temporary one! And ... ", she leaned in and whispered! "Keep him away from the ladies!" Then, back to her normal voice, "Be careful yourself! Now ... Go give him that kick!"

Duncan was lazing back in his chair, reading a newspaper!

"Come on Dunc! Suitcases loaded! All I need now is a passenger! If you miss this flight, I'm going instead of you! And you know what my voice is like!"

He smiled, carefully folding the newspaper and tucking it under his arm, as he rose from his chair!

"Yes SIR! Right away, SIR!" he laughed.

I stepped outside, while he said goodbye to Sinéad. She shed a few tears as he eventually got in the car.

"Aren't you supposed to be wearing a chauffeur's hat?" he asked.

"Not bloody likely!"

Then we were off! I watched Sinéad in my rear-view mirror, slowly disappearing. From her remarks, she obviously knew, or at least suspected, that Duncan was playing the field.

It was a long old trip to Shannon, as I said previously, but we made good time. Duncan slept a lot of the way! I though, had never driven there before and loved the excitement of reaching the brow of a long hill, to experience a spectacular vista laid out before me.

If you ever get the chance to drive across Ireland, you should grab it with both hands. The roads are vastly different these days, but the surrounding countryside is still very beautiful and uniquely Irish!

We did stop, for a few minutes, a couple of times and Duncan was recognised immediately. The price you pay for being a star, I suppose!

We were due to fly from Shannon airport at 5.00 pm so we had left nice and early, arriving in plenty of time to have a leisurely lunch before we took off over the Atlantic.

Airports, in those days, were very different from today's modern behemoths.

There was a porter waiting to assist with the bags! I was not even expected to take them out of the boot! I did try! Spontaneously receiving a stare, informing me of my error! Oops! In this strange new world, even servants like me, apparently had servants!

Passport control was over with very quickly, Duncan receiving the red carpet treatment.

We were shown into a VIP lounge, where some of the other 'stars' were already tucking into free booze and nibbles!

Now, I felt a little out of my depth! I had become accustomed to Duncan treating me so well. I guess I thought all celebrities would be the same with me. Wrong! I thought for a minute I was back in Quebec and invisible again!

It wasn't Duncan's fault! He was just swept up in the moment.

A young man, almost as tall as me and maybe four or five years older, approached me.

"You with Duncan?"

"Yep! Off to Vegas!"

"Me too!"

"I'm here with Del. He's over there catching up with the others! Don't take it personally if they blank you! They don't do it on purpose, they are just in their own little world. You'll get used to it. My name is Mickey!"

"Niall!"

"Hi Niall! Fancy a drink? We might as well live it up, while we can!"

It was great to meet someone so cool as Mickey. We relaxed and a waiter brought us a drink and some nibbles. This was really the first time I had experienced food of this type. I didn't even recognise it as food.

Mickey tried talking me through what it was, but in the end, I just shoved it in my mouth and took a chance! It wasn't half bad!

Sinéad's words still rang in my ears, so I moderated my alcohol intake and tried to keep an eye on Duncan. The latter being almost impossible as he darted about being his usual gregarious self.

"He'll be ok! He's an old hand at this!"

Mickey had clocked me eyeballing Duncan!

"Under orders from his missus, to keep an eye on him!"

"Fat chance of that, Niall! There's a reason the bodyguards in America wear dark glasses! To block out most of what goes on!" he laughed. "You'll need a motorbike to keep up with him in Vegas!"

"Oh, bloody hell!"

"You won't be alone! There are a few of us around to help! If you need it! And, of course, we hope you would extend that courtesy to us! If required!"

"Of course, I will. Thanks!"

"Looks like they are ready to board us. I'll catch up with you later! On the flight!"

"Ok!"

I found Duncan, chatting to someone I sort of recognised,

but couldn't quite put a name to.

"Excuse me, Duncan. It looks like we are about to board!"

"Thanks, Niall!" Then to the person next to him, "Catch you on the flight, Del! Lovely to catch up."

Walking across the tarmac to the plane was like being in a film. It felt surreal! Almost like a dream!

I waited patiently, at the bottom of the steps leading up into the plane, until Duncan was ready to go up. He was deep in conversation with some pretty one thing!

There was the wink again and we were off up the steps and into the aircraft.

It seemed a lot smaller inside than I was expecting, probably because so may people were milling around.

We found our seats and Duncan offered me the window seat. He said he might be up and down a lot! I thought "might!".

I remember sitting back in the wide comfortable seats while Duncan did the rounds, talking to the other celebrities on board and passengers wanting an autograph. It was so comfortable that I nodded off to sleep.

There was a mighty roar as the engines started! That woke me up quickly! Was I still asleep and dreaming or was this actually happening?

The stewardess came around and checked we were all strapped in and then we sat back and waited to take off.

Duncan looked very uneasy! Was he afraid of flying? Sinéad didn't mention that!

To my surprise, we were driven around on the ground for quite a distance, until I could feel the bumps and rumbles increasing as the plane gathered speed. I knew then, I was wide awake and it really was happening. I was going to make the most of it, leaving my humble beginnings behind and stepping out into a future life where no one could hold me back.

That moment when the wheels leave the ground and you are airborne has always resonated with me! There is a change in sound as the plane disconnects with the ground. A sort of silence amongst the roar of the engines that signals you are now flying!

It was the first time I had heard it and it was marvellous, as it has been every single time since. Never ceases to amaze me!

Taking off from Shannon Airport and climbing up over the breaking waves piling in from the Atlantic, was a new thrill to add to my growing collection.

I gazed out the tiny window, incredulity firmly grasping my attention, with the fervour of a young child tugging at his mother's apron. Tiny ships like bath time toys, wended their ancient way across a mighty ocean far below, whilst we in a cosseted cabin stretched our legs and flew like modern gods across the sky.

Duncan, eyes still tightly clenched, sat in the aisle seat, where he had planned to socialise with his fellow stars, at least that was the plan, but at the moment, fear held him by the short and curlies.

We were flying Pan Am in a Boeing 707, the ultimate passenger transport at the time. Once we were at cruising height, it was like we were on the ground and the windows were television sets provided for our amusement. There was a hum from the engines but that was quite relaxing in its way and I had no sensation of being miles above the vast ocean below.

As if this wasn't enough to please a young Irishman, a beautiful young woman in a pale blue uniform was offering me a drink, leaning across dead-eyed Duncan and talking to me in a warm sultry voice that oozed charm. Quick as a flash, Duncan miraculously recovered his vision, eyes now wide open and almost in contact with the body leaning over him. I was waiting for the wink but thank goodness it was still only seconds since he, not the most religious man, was praying for his life and regretting his sins.

Our stewardess, noticing his miracle recovery, moved discreetly out of his reach and addressed her remarks to him as well. I knew we were high up but I didn't think we would be this close to heaven, comfortable seats, good food and free drinks. The only downside was … no Guinness!

A couple of drinks later the cabin was a hive of activity. Duncan's fellow stars were mingling with each other and telling and retelling various scenarios they had witnessed in their careers, from falling into the orchestra pit during rehearsals to forgetting to zip up their flies before walking on stage. Laughter was once again the dominant sound in my ears. For a moment I felt a twinge, remembering the Norman Wisdom film and Caroline.

Duncan was elsewhere in the cabin and a sultry young woman suddenly flopped down in his seat.

"You're a quiet one!", she remarked, drink in hand and ever so slightly slurring her words.

"I'm leaving it to the stars", I replied.

"I'm Siobhan", followed by a slight hiccup. "Oh, pardon me, I'm sorry", she giggled. "You travelling with Duncan?"

"Bodyguard and general factotum, at least that's what Sinéad, his wife calls me, whatever that means".

"Oh, I must get one of them, they sound good!", giggling again. "Talking about good, I'm going to get another one of these!", she said, holding her empty glass aloft. "You want one?"

"No thanks!"

We chatted like old friends for a while, until she decided to drift off to sleep midsentence.

I suppose that could have made a hole in my self-confidence, but when she shifted a bit in her seat and leaned her head on my shoulder, I settled for that. Life with Duncan was far from boring!

Inevitably, I dozed off as well, only to be woken by a flash going off. "That'll look good in the papers!", laughed Duncan, putting my camera to ill use, or so I thought at the time.

"Ireland's No1 Female singer found in compromising position with bodyguard. I can see the headlines".

Siobhan was still spark out and totally unaware of the joviality around her.

"You lucky bastard!" commented one of Duncan's star friends, a rather wrinkled individual with long white hair and a cravat.

Duncan in full flight now said I probably didn't even know

who she was and he was right, which everyone thought for some reason was hilarious.

Rather than disturb her Siobhan was left to sleep it off in Duncan's seat, not stirring for over an hour.

When she did finally wake, she squinted at me as if to say "How did I get here? Who are you?" until it finally came back to her where she was.

"I'm sorry … Niall isn't it? … Of course, it is. Must have dropped off. Too many courage bombs, I think. Never did like flying much".

Gradually her senses returned and I couldn't believe it when she ordered yet another drink. It was a lot more than anaesthetic for the flight, more like a way of life, but who am I to comment with my own love for the drink, as my mother used to call it.

I thought she might have wanted to go back to her celebrity friends but she called them "Boring old farts".

I could see what she meant. We were the youngest by far and I suppose we bonded over that single factor. Genuinely not knowing who she was, made me easy to talk to I assume and we talked about lots of different things but not about her career.

Under her makeup, I guessed, was a different person to the

one she showed to the world, having been isolated in the spotlight most of her young life. She knew the Beatles and I relayed the story of my short job as a roadie, which she found hilarious.

I told her about the Great Lakes and she told me about Lough Neagh the biggest lake in Ireland, where she used to visit her aunt and uncle. I told her about the toilet down the garden and having to carry water from the well across two fields.

She told me about tending to the cows and the pigs for her father. We talked for an awfully long time, until she thought it right to give Duncan his seat back.

As she stood to leave, she leaned over and very lightly kissed my cheek. I could see she had been herself for a while and was grateful.

There were the usual ribald remarks as she retook her seat, but she was well able to fend them off. Doing so with an edge that had quickly resurfaced.

Having crossed the Atlantic in a ship, the journey time to fly there was ridiculously fast, maybe not up to the current standards, but in those days, it was phenomenal.

We arrived at New York Airport to fanfares of … nothing! It appears that Irish stars have no traction in America and one or two were a bit miffed.

I would have loved to have stayed in New York City for a few days and seen the sights, but we had a connection to catch, so it was, grab the bags and onto Las Vegas.

The internal flight was long and tedious. We thought, we were in America, so it couldn't be too far to Vegas. Could it? Two and a half thousand miles! Bloody well was and no first class either! And my legs were cramped! Glad to get off in the end!

It was a very pleasant 72 degrees as we stepped off the plane and unlike New York, this time there was a welcoming party and a fleet of limos to whisk us away. Now, I'm a big guy, but some of the entourage were built like the side of a house. They had bulges in their jackets that were either large wallets or a packed lunch! I didn't make the mistake of asking. I might have been young, but I wasn't stupid, well not that stupid anyway.

Vegas in those days was not like the Vegas of today, all Neon and flash, it was a more elegant time and I use the word loosely. Our hotel was the Sandford and was just off the strip, considered an "upmarket joint" at least that's how it was described to us.

Our limo pulled up in the VIP area and we were immediately surrounded by doormen and porters, who took our luggage and opened doors.

I stood outside the foyer, in disbelief at the enormity of the building that loomed above us. The façade was stunning! Who ever designed it, had probably 'borrowed' features from classic buildings around the world and melded them into this unique structure!

Making myself a promise to capture the scene on my camera, I followed Duncan into the Hotel.

What a foyer! It was the VIP entrance, of course and no expense had been spared in its construction and décor.

We were invited to sit on one of the plush white leather sofas, that were strategically placed to give a measure of privacy. I sank into one and could easily have dropped off to sleep in its luxurious comfort.

"This is the life! Eh, Niall!"

Duncan was lapping it up, already casting his eye around the place for shapely ladies!

"Sure is! Maybe this is what heaven looks like!"

"If the right people are running it, you may very well be correct!"

A beautiful young man, immaculately dressed in hotel livery, approached us and introduced himself. Apparently, he was our personal contact throughout our visit! Day or Night! Sounded like he worked long hours!

We were already booked in and he politely asked if we would like to see our suite.

I didn't know what a suite was! I thought he meant a sweet! Luckily, I kept my mouth shut.

Duncan suggested that Danny, that was his name, show us the facilities first. Typical Duncan! Always on the lookout!

Danny led the way, pointing out bars and restaurants, of which there were several. All very grand! He also showed us where the VIP lounge was. I did wonder whether I would be allowed in there, but again I kept my mouth firmly shut.

The biggest shock off all was walking into the casino!

I had never been in such a large room before or seen so many gamblers under one roof. It looked like we could have fitted most of Dublin inside and had room for Ballytreeny in the corner.

To think this was one of the 'smaller hotels' was mind blowing. There were beautiful women everywhere, elegant and poised. By poised, I mean on the lookout for suckers! In the employ of the hotel, they would encourage men, usually older, to spend a fortune and reaffirm their virility.

All this and we hadn't even got to our room!

We were offered complimentary drinks and gladly

accepted! They had never heard of Guinness! Heathens! We settled for a Martini Bianco, whatever that was! Someone mentioned 'dry' and I was at a loss to understand! I thought all drinks were wet! Then I noticed there was fruit in my drink! As you gather, I had a lot to learn!

The trek to the room, via a hurtling elevator (lift, in our language!), was another new experience for me.

We entered a small room, big enough for probably ten people and the door slid closed. Danny touched a number at the pad on the wall and it felt like we were flying again! I was nonplussed! Why did no one warn me about these things! But I learnt quickly at that age, so it went into 'everyday event' category.

The door slid open and we stepped out into a long, long corridor. Danny pointed the way and we followed behind! I didn't want to get lost! I wasn't even sure how to get back to the foyer!

We stopped at a pair of ornate doors, with the number 1642 in gold leaf on it. I found out later, that it meant we were in room 42 on the 16th floor.

Danny unlocked the doors and bade us enter, then after indicating where everything was, he left us. With the entreaty that we call him if we needed any assistance.

Duncan and I were sharing a suite of rooms that had three bedrooms, three bathrooms, two balconies and a lounge that you could hold a convention in. All this for two guys? I couldn't quite believe it.

To compound my shock Duncan picked up the telephone and ordered room service, but not before opening a door to reveal a bar stocked with all sorts of booze.

I picked up a bottle of beer, went into my bedroom, kicked off my shoes and launched myself onto the king-size bed dominating the room and promptly fell asleep, booze untouched.

Duncan woke me to let me know he was going to a meeting with Frank and he'd be back in a few hours. Shoving a considerable amount of dollars in my hand he said, "Go enjoy yourself, but be careful, this isn't Ballytreeny".

I hid most of the money, unaware at the time there was a safe in the room and wandered down to the foyer and out onto the forecourt. I say wandered down, but to be honest, I went up in the lift, when I wanted to go down. Got off twice at the wrong floor and generally acted like a confused tourist! Which I was!

Outside in the sunshine, I stood back to observe, thinking of how Brendan would have noted all the toing and froing in his journal. I just discreetly used my camera, having been warned by Danny, not to take pictures of guests.

Large cars were constantly pulling up and spewing out mainly lavishly dressed, overweight male gamblers.

A fabulous limo stopped and the rush to open doors had to be seen to be believed! It must be a very important customer.

An elegant, older woman was assisted out of the vehicle, accompanied by a trio of what looked like bodyguards. She was approaching the area near where I was standing and suddenly caught her shoe in her dress. She was diving headfirst into the concrete when I instinctively reached out and caught her in mid-flight.

It was all over in seconds and the trio quickly took hold of her, brushing me aside in the process. So, I just walked on! But only for a second or two! My shoulder was suddenly grasped by a mechanical clamp! At least that is what it felt like! I turned to remonstrate, only reining it in when I saw the guy was acting under orders from the woman!

She was beckoning me over, thanking me loudly for saving her life. A bit dramatic! But sincere in her praise of me. Her hand disappeared into her bag and she took out a wad of money and offered it to me. I was taken aback, but I quietly refused telling her that I didn't expect a reward for being a gentleman.

"At least come and have a drink with me!", she offered and judging by the trio I didn't feel I had much of an option.

So, back into the lobby I went, only to see the staff running around and treating the lady like royalty. I remember thinking, incorrectly as I found out. "The courtesy to customers in this place is off the charts".

We were shown into the main casino and then into a roped off area with a private bar.

The trio took up guard duty, leaving me and the lady to sit down on some wonderfully comfortable chairs.

As if by magic an attendant appeared with a bottle of wine that he first showed to the lady to gain her approval and then two glasses. I gathered the trio were on duty tonight.

"I hope you like the wine. It's a Rothschild and I love it", she said with an openness that belied her appearance.

She was extremely easy to talk to and seemed genuinely interested in how I grew up in Ireland. But first of all, where was Ireland? Was it anywhere near New York? I was very careful not to laugh and carefully explained where Ireland was, which intrigued her no end. It seems she was from humble beginnings in Chicago, her parents being immigrants from Italy.

I thought of course that she was there on holiday, but I was completely wrong. Her husband owned the hotel! She had no airs and graces about her wealth, knowing the value of money and what it was to be without it.

We had a common denominator in being from a similar background and we bonded very quickly.

The trio came to attention as a well-dressed man approached, the rope being moved as soon as he was spotted.

I had a feeling of being x-rayed by a chilling pair of deep-set dark eyes.

Maria, that was her name, introduced us and told him of my supposed gallantry, refusing to take a reward. It turned out he had already received word of our encounter and he had his staff check me out.

Luigi or Lou as he introduced himself, took a seat and joined us in a glass of wine. He proved himself to be a real contradiction by belying his appearance, talking fondly to his wife and genuinely appreciating my intervention.

Maria told him about Ireland, where it was and my humble beginnings there. He knew about Ireland and he could empathise with how I was brought up and the hardship the family had faced.

"He still sends money home to his mama, Louie. Just like a good boy", and she patted my hand.

"You're here for the St Patrick's show aren't you?"

"I am I'm …" I didn't finish as a gunshot rang out somewhere in the casino. Lou immediately protected Maria as naturally as someone in love would. The trio formed a shield as the turmoil continued, although out of our sight. Then as quickly as it started, it was over. Someone came to talk to Lou, which he did at a discreet distance from us. When he returned, he dismissed the event as a disgruntled gambler who had now been dealt with. I didn't ask how!

"Would you like to join us for dinner, Niall?", Lou asked and I gratefully accepted the invitation from this powerful but loving guy. People are very rarely one dimensional and Lou was a perfect example.

We ate in a private dining room, just the three of us and it was an absolute delight, just swapping stories and making each other laugh. It didn't quite seem possible we had only met a short time before.

As we were getting towards the end of the meal, the same man who spoke to Lou earlier, came in, apologised to Maria and asked Lou if he wouldn't mind stepping out for a moment.

Maria was obviously used to this sort of interruption and we carried on chatting, drinking some delicious coffee until Lou returned, unflustered as if he had been to a board meeting.

He poured himself a coffee and was about to take a seat, when I noticed blood on the shirt cuff that was protruding from his jacket sleeve. Without Maria noticing, I caught his eye and brought his attention to the bright red stain. Without breaking a stride, he apologized to Maria and said he had forgotten something and he'd be back in a moment. Which, true to his word he was.

Sitting down once again with us, he smiled and carried on as if nothing had happened, a fresh white shirt testifying to his ability to switch roles.

We parted at the end of what was a delightful time and Maria gave me a kiss on the cheek and so did Lou, plus a card with his telephone number with his remark, "Just in case you need me".

Walking back to my room, which incidentally is one hell of a long way from where we were dining, I saw Duncan running towards me in a dreadful state. He was incoherent, babbling something about Siobhan, whilst half dragging me down the hall towards our room.

The scene was not pleasant! A partially clothed Siobhan,

pale as the bedsheets, face contorted so much I hardly recognised her, lay rigid on the king size bed. I knew truly little about first aid and stood anchored in that desolate harbour, listening to a distraught Duncan, screaming for me to do something. Grasping her by the shoulders I shook her, gently at first and then gradually, as panic set in, as vigorously as I could. With hindsight of course, that was not the safest thing to do, but it was all done by instinct and nobody was more surprised than me, when she spluttered a few times and opened her eyes the smallest amount.

Laying her head down gently onto a pillow, I picked up the bedside telephone and rang the number on the card Lou had just given me. A polite female voice answered the phone and asked my name then asked where I was calling from. She politely requested I replace the receiver and I would be contacted.

It was a tense couple of minutes before the phone rang. I picked it up and said "Lou?"

"Didn't expect you to ring this quick kid!"

"Sorry Lou, but one of the stars of the show is laying on the bed and looking terribly ill. I don't know if it's alcohol or drugs or both or something else. Do you have a discreet doctor who can help us?"

"Put the phone down kid! I'll have someone there straight

away".

That next fifteen minutes or so were torture. I tried my revival methods again but there was no response although I could see she was still alive, even patting her cheeks and talking loudly.

I know it sounds ridiculous but I was completely out of my depth and Duncan was not helping, crying, moaning and talking to himself. It did pass through my mind about what had been going on between them, but only for a fleeting moment amidst the chaos.

The doctor and two nurses arrived and immediately took over Siobhan's treatment, asking us if we knew what she had taken or drunk. I had no idea and Duncan was a total mess! We were ushered out of the bedroom! The professionals then used proper medical practises rather than knee jerk reactions to treat her.

Lou arrived, leaving his companions to guard the door. I had never seen someone so calm in a crisis, almost as if this was a daily occurrence and maybe it was to him! To me this was life spiralling out of control and my heart was pounding in my chest, more than it was during that storm at sea.

Duncan slumped in a chair with his head in his hands, still trying to come to terms with what had happened.

Mumbling again, this time about Sinéad and how she'd never forgive him.

It seemed strange when Lou asked me who Duncan was, but of course this was America and not Ireland, where Duncan was famous. I explained who he was and who Siobhan was and he made a few remarks, which I won't repeat as I don't want to offend you, my tender readers. Suffice it to say performers were not high on his list of likes.

When the doctor emerged from the bedroom, he looked nervous when he saw Lou and addressed him as Mr Bianco, Siobhan was alive and doing ok, but they were moving her to a private hospital, where they would be very discreet.

Lou made a phone call to the hospital and spoke to someone in charge, repeating the need for absolute discretion and telling them he would be monitoring the case. I suspect that would have put them on their mettle.

I thanked Lou for his help and he said it was payback for helping his wife. So, there we have it, a favour for a favour, that's how this crazy town kept revolving and no one, I repeat, no one lost count of who owes who. Lou and I were even and I knew I shouldn't expect to ring him again, unless I wanted to be in his debt, which was something I had the common sense to avoid at all costs.

No one in Siobhan's condition could be transported out of

the hotel via the crowded lobby. Many years of experience had provided anonymous exits, away from prying eyes, guarded by trusted personnel who knew how to keep their mouths shut or risk having them shut permanently.

My job now was to bring Duncan back to some sort of normality, which was easier said than done! He persisted in folding into a ball, attempting to block out the outside world and the consequences of his dalliance with Siobhan. It took me well over an hour to cajole him back to some semblance of calm, all the time assuring him that Sinéad need never know. Siobhan would recover in time for the concert the next day. Gradually I could see him regaining his composure, room service helping with coffee and food, that at first, he refused, but eventually consumed with relish.

Looking at this fragile man semi collapsed and fighting his demons, I realised that life is a complex and bewildering experience even for those who are elevated from the herd and boosted by their superficial world. Maybe more so, as we mere mortals stumble and fall in private, rather than in a blaze of publicity.

I really liked Sinéad and couldn't understand how Duncan could deceive her, with so many women, when he had her to go home to. Falling in love with someone else and consequently destroying a current relationship is horrible, but fathomable.

Playing the field just because you can, is a primitive impulse that I found hard to reconcile, although there was no way I could make him aware of my feelings. He insisted I call the hospital and I did, although I was sure Siobhan would probably only just have arrived. That fact was confirmed by a charming female voice, who went through a few guarded questions before giving me any answers. I was told to ask for her by name the next time I rang and assured that if there was any adverse change, she would call me. Incidentally, she told me all the costs were being covered by the hotel, which I wondered if that meant I was now in Lou's debt.

The rest of that evening and most of that night I sat with Duncan, carefully trying to repair his fragile mind, constantly repeating that we could fix everything and there was nothing to worry about until I felt like I was on a permanent loop. Perhaps that's where the term "driving me loopy" comes from, because it is certainly how I felt. My older self would probably have handled it better, but I was winging it the way I generally approached life and it seemed to be having a gradual effect on his demeanour.

When I woke the next morning, I was still in the main living room and sprawled on the couch, aching and wondering if I had dreamt it all, especially when I saw Duncan sitting in the dining area, drinking coffee and reading the paper.

Collecting my thoughts from the depths of the couch, I sat

up and rubbed my eyes, carefully opening them to see if Duncan was still there. He was! Happily munching away on a piece of toast. The telephone rang and I instinctively picked it up, it was the hospital with an update on Siobhan. She was conscious, responding well to treatment and likely to be released that morning. They would provide transport to bring her back to the hotel, if someone (me), would meet them at the private entrance. I said of course I would and asked what time I should be there, realising I didn't have a clue as to where the private entrance was, but I assumed I'd soon find out.

Relaying the situation to Duncan should have really got his attention, but he seemed to have wiped yesterday's trauma from his mind. He accepted what I said with an air of total disinterest, something I had a hard time believing. I could now see how he could cheat on Sinéad and go home to her without a guilty conscience. It seemed to evaporate after 24 hours or less.

"She'll be back for rehearsals then?", he said almost rhetorically.

"I guess!", was about all I could muster and I could see myself distancing from this shallow man, star or no star!

It was difficult to carry on a conversation with him at that moment and I helped myself to whatever breakfast was left over, determined that I was not set out for this life of being a sycophant and factotum.

The funny thing is, the older I get, the more I see people as they really are! I find it difficult to relate to them, because the truth is, we are all flawed! Once you accept that, you also accept that you yourself are equally flawed and that is a sobering thought that rarely occurs to the young.

Excusing myself from Duncan's half attention was easy and I made my way down to the lobby area. I thought I would be able to spot the guy that kept reporting to Lou the previous day. Almost immediately, I saw him sitting anonymously in the corner, coffee in hand and eyes on a swivel.

As I approached, a guy who was almost as tall as me and much wider stepped into my path. If I had learnt anything about this place it was to assume an air of authority and so I simply nodded at where I wanted to go. No fuss or histrionics just a simple gesture. He held out an arm, palm first towards me and turned his neck to look at his boss, who merely blinked an ok and then my roadblock removed himself quietly and vanished back into the throng.

"Good morning, Mr O'Sullivan", was his opening, rather polite remark. "How can I be of service?"

"Good morning!", I returned. "I have been asked to meet our mutual guest at the private entrance and of course I have no idea where that is".

He was very gracious in his reply, radiating the manner of someone who was used to dealing with outsiders, as I certainly was, whilst retaining an air of authority that you would not want to question.

The minion was recalled and told to assist me in any way he could, for which I was incredibly grateful and after thanking the floor boss we walked quietly away, with minion leading.

Was I glad I asked for directions? There was a multitude of security along the way, that you would not want to argue with. They were all armed but looking like they would rather give you a good beating, than shoot you.

There was a small lounge at the private entrance and I assumed VIPs and their guests would arrive here, far away from prying eyes. I could envisage Presidents and their floozies, laughing and playing in the knowledge they would not be seen by the public, whilst the in-house security quietly photographed and filmed them without their knowledge. High rolling gamblers bent on reaping rich rewards, usually dipping into their trust funds, would feel so special being escorted to the private gambling area that was in close proximity! Almost a business within a business.

This was thrilling for me to observe! A slice of life I doubted I would ever see again and I was right! Although I have been to Las Vegas a few times since, this was the one and only time I was invited to this private area.

When Siobhan finally arrived, she looked pale and walked with a bit of a wobble, but at least she was alive! Which I thought she wasn't, for a moment the night before. Her smile when she saw me was a genuine reaction to seeing someone she knew, even though we hadn't known each other long.

Escorted by the minion, we walked slowly back to Siobhan's room, where he promptly left, having performed his allotted task.

She found it a little difficult to look me in the eye and for a moment I thought she was going to cry, but it passed. She didn't ask about Duncan, which was significant. I think she felt very guilty about her association with him, especially as she knew Sinéad. Deep down, she was a good Catholic girl and did not enjoy breaking the rules, unlike me.

I stayed with her until she was ready for rehearsals and then escorted her there. A limo was waiting outside the foyer to whisk us to the world famous "Golden Beach" hotel. I couldn't help marvelling at the way she bundled all that hurt and distress up into a ball and kicked it into the ocean. Letting it flow out on the tide, without being aware that the tide might turn and deposit all her baggage at her feet one sorry day.

Standing in the wings with my security badge displayed on my jacket I was amazed to watch these star performers going through their party pieces, all chosen as Irish favourites known by ex-pats and 3rd and 4th generation immigrants still identifying as Irish. It all seemed to come so easily to them as they strutted their stuff in front of the house orchestra, looking every inch the stars they were. Siobhan and Duncan were outstanding, giving a polished and professional masterclass in their art form, belying their recent traumas. This was the first time I really realised that performers of this calibre pull on a cloak of invincibility as they walk on stage, a persona that radiates charm and confidence, endearing them to their audience.

There would be many times in my later life that I would be associated with major stars, who were household names and they all had this aura about them. Something that set them aside from ordinary folk. It never slipped my mind, that the person behind that masquerade may have been quietly screaming, as no doubt Duncan and Siobhan were all those years ago.

That night we arrived at the stage door, where a large crowd of autograph hunters had already gathered! "Better use the 'quiet door', Andy!", our bodyguard said to the driver.

It was as easy as that to bypass the throng! The quiet door was inside a fenced compound and hidden from prying eyes. Privacy was a must when designing this venue.

Security was expecting us and we were all issued with backstage passes. I was personally briefed, not to approach any of the stars, unless summoned. It was said in a way that made it very clear what the result would be if I ignored the advice.

They needn't have worried! I was in awe of the names of the people on the show and would not have known what to say to them!

I made sure Duncan was safely deposited in his dressing room. Checked he had everything he required! No, I didn't respond to his remark, to go find a pretty girl for him! Despite the wink he gave!

I wished him luck and said I would be side stage if he needed me.

There was a room for us 'assistants' to chill in, so I grabbed a coffee and sat down in the corner. No sooner had I reclined than Mickey entered, looking frustrated! I watched him pour a coffee and look around the room. He clocked me straight away!

"What's up Mickey? You look harassed!"

"Bloody right, I'm harassed! That twat Del has been playing 'I am God' again! I'm quitting once we get back! He is insufferable."

"What's he done now?"

"I already ferry him everywhere! Pick up his clothes when he drops them on the floor, in the dressing room! Wipe up the umpteenth drink he has knocked over! Put him to bed when he is pissed! Now he wants me to get him a girl! Any pretty one with big tits will do! I ask you! He's well over sixty and not in good shape. What sort of girl would be interested in him? Only a hooker and I'm not getting one of those for him! His wife deserves better."

"Just tell him you will, then don't! If he asks, say they are a thousand dollars a night in Vegas! That'll shut him up!"

"Nice thought, but it won't! He'll expect it to be put on the room expenses that someone else will pay. And he's probably right!"

"Try telling him that you were keeping it from him, but you have found out, his wife has paid a private investigator to follow him in Vegas. She suspects he is playing around and wants evidence for a divorce. She thinks she'll get a better settlement if she does! That should shut him up!"

"Brilliant! I'll do that! If only to see the look of shock on his face!"

"Make sure you advise him not to confront his missus, as there would be an almighty row! Oh ... and she's got a gun!"

"That's an amazing idea! Where are you getting this stuff from?"

"Just comes naturally! Guess I grew up making lots of excuses for the mess I got in."

"You should write a book!"

Well Mickey, it took me a bloody long time, but I'm doing it now!

"The show's about to start in a few minutes. I met the stage manager and he said I could sit on the prompt side with him. You can join us. I'm sure it will be ok!", Mickey offered.

Off we trotted to watch a show that the customers were paying a fortune for!

When we got to side stage, there were Secret Service people everywhere! We were frisked before they would let us through.

We did indeed join the stage manager and quite a lot of other people. Most were standing on tiptoes, desperate for a view of the stage! Luckily, being a foot taller than a lot of them, I had a perfect view!

There was a massive cheer and applause as someone came on stage. At first, I didn't realise who it was and then I saw it was Frank. He stood there bathing in the adulation for a few minutes and then said, "Thank you Ladies and Gentlemen, especially all those Irish Americans in tonight!"

Cue a massive roar!

"We have a very special St Patrick's Day Concert for you, with Irish Star acts, all the way from the Emerald Isle!"

Cue another massive roar!

"Before we start the show. There is someone in the wings whose ancestors came from over there. I know that ... because of all the blarney he keeps giving me!"

Cue laughter.

"You will, I'm sure, give a wonderful Vegas welcome to the great man himself ... Ladies and Gentlemen. The President of the United States of America ... John F Kennedy!"

If we thought the roar before was massive, this one went off the scale. People were screaming! There was a wall of sound coming from the auditorium! And he hadn't yet walked on stage!

He was a man who knew exactly how to milk an audience! Frank stepped off, just in time, as the man himself slowly walked on stage.

I had never heard a crowd like it before! I have never heard a crowd like it since! This man was lauded as the ultimate leader!

He stood there, arms aloft, playing the crowd like a master puppeteer! He had still not uttered one word!

In my ear I heard a female voice say, "He's wonderful, isn't he?" I wasn't really listening, but then she said, "I'm going to stand on a chair to get a better view. Will you hold my waist for me! I don't want to fall off in this dress. It's that tight, I won't be able to get back again!"

This comment intrigued me, so I turned to see the most beautiful woman I have ever seen, standing right next to me.

She said, "Hi. I'm Marilyn." As if I didn't know! The most famous woman in the world was talking to me.

I didn't really know what to say, so I just took her hand and helped her up on to the chair. Everyone around us was now looking at her! And me!

I put my big Irish hands around her waist to stabilise her and they almost went all the way around her.

She smiled, the most genuine smile, at me. There was a vulnerability in her eyes that made me want to protect her from the crowd. So many have talked about her over the years and I doubt any of them understood her. I joined the ranks of admirers who fell at her feet!

Then she started jumping up and down on the chair and I had to hold her really tightly or she would surely have fallen off. She also started shouting with the rest, except she called him Jack!

Then a hush descended over proceedings as the President was preparing to talk.

"My fellow Irishmen!", he started.

That ovation again!

"America and Vegas salute you!"

And again!

"Like a lot of you, my family came to this great country with only the clothes on their back! They worked hard to build a land of opportunity!"

Cheers again!

"They never forgot where they came from! The hardships that forced them to leave a place they loved, to brave the ocean! Sickness! Starvation! All to seek a new life in a new world! One where the only limitations were their dreams! It was hard at times. But they kept going forward! Creating the world they desired! Thank you, Ireland, for sending us your best! Tonight … we salute you!"

Then came the crescendo to end all crescendos! The band played "When Irish eyes are smiling!" The audience belted it out, especially when Frank joined the President on stage as they both sang along. Although, totally drowned out by the audience.

Marilyn was singing along, having a whale of a time. Her hand was on my shoulder for stability and my hands around her waist. Not in my wildest dreams could I have imagined what was happening to me at that moment!

I have rarely recounted it to others as they would never believe me. But it's true!

Yes, I did help her down and then she was gone to be with the President, I assumed. But … not before she kissed me full on the lips! Giggling as she walked away with the Secret Service guys, she turned and blew another kiss before she disappeared

That evening was the single most amazing night of my life! Perhaps I should close my story at this point! There is no way for me to top it!

The rest of the evening was special, as well. It was marvellous to see the one and only Frank Sinatra, in his prime, wooing an audience with a sense of style and musicianship that was nothing short of miraculous.

The orchestra was sensational, swinging the music like I have never experienced anywhere since and I've heard a few!

When the Irish acts did their thing, the audience took them to their hearts. Many of the so called 'Irish' in the auditorium were probably 3rd or 4th generation, but they still identified as Irish or Irish/American.

Duncan sang 'Climb every mountain', after recounting the climb we made to the top of Kippure. He exaggerated the pain in his feet and had them all laughing as he hammed it up! It all led to a standing ovation for him.

Siobhan sang her heart out and no one would have guessed she almost died a short while ago.

I wasn't aware they were going to perform it, but Duncan and Siobhan sang a duet of 'Danny boy'. It was as sweet and pure as the streams running off Kippure Mountain. There were tears in most people's eyes, as they swayed in their seats. That was what they were working out in the room that night! Apparently, Siobhan was getting tired, so she took something, one of the other acts gave her to keep going!

All in all, the night was a resounding success!

There was a massive after party, where we all ate and drank far too much. I tried to keep my eye on Duncan but he insisted I have the night off and enjoy myself. Most of that was a ruse to keep me from cramping his style.

Mickey was open mouthed when I caught up with him.

"Did I really see you and Marilyn, together!"

"You did!"

"You jammy bugger! If I hadn't asked you, I would have been the one!"

"Sorry, Mickey! And I got a kiss!"

"What!"

"On … the … lips!"

"Oh … you … sod!"

Then we both collapsed laughing!

Somehow, I didn't want that night to end. It was magical! The stuff dreams are littered with, but reality, rarely ever experiences. This boy from Ballytreeny who would never amount to anything, just did! So there!

We were packing to leave the hotel when there was a knock at the door. I answered and there was a delightful young lady with a beautiful smile waiting in the corridor. "Niall?" she asked and when I answered, she produced a large bottle of red wine with a bow on it and a card. It was from Lou and Maria, hoping that I had enjoyed my stay and wishing me a good flight back to Ireland. What a lovely thought. Thankfully, it came with a proper box to carry it in safely, otherwise I would probably have broken it on the journey.

I did keep it safe and shared it with my family on my return. It wasn't until sometime after that I showed someone the bottle, I had retained, only to be told the worth of the wine. To say I was stunned would be trivialising my reaction and I did say a few words I would not say in front of Father Michael, because the value was astronomical, but I shared it with my family telling them of my meeting with Maria and Lou and leaving out any sordid details and that was worth it.

Our journey back was a little less boisterous than our arrival but I was now accepted as one of the group. Some rather tasty stories were confided in me, maybe to get me to talk about Siobhan going missing and my role in it, but they learnt nothing from me.

In a quiet moment just before our descent into Shannon Siobhan dropped into the seat next to me and kissed me on the cheek!

"What was that for?" I asked.

"For being a real gentleman and a life saver!"

"That's two things!" I joked. "I only got one kiss!"

She laughed and kissed my cheek a second time!

"Maybe we'll meet up some day on the road to goodness knows where! I sing there quite a lot!"

"I'll look forward to it"

She became a really big star with several top ten hits and out paths never did cross again! I hear she is still singing. She made the transfer to Nashville many years ago and is well thought of the country scene there. She's not the star she was in Ireland But, I think, from what I hear, she is much happier.

Duncan finally took up his seat, just before we were due to start descending.

"What did you think of that, Niall? Quite an experience, eh?"

He was right, it had been a wonderful experience that I would never forget!

Duncan and I would not part company for a number of

years, fate would entwine us even further, pursuing a route that would see us travel far and wide and share adventures of epic proportions, but that must wait for the moment. My mind reels from the extraction of long buried memories and I need a break. Time is catching up with me and I need to spend a little time in the here and now, leaving the past to tend to itself for a while. To quote a famous line "I'll be back".

Sitting in my luxury seat on that fabulous aircraft, I knew it was only the start. The thought uppermost in my mind was, "Where to next for a Ballytreeny boy?"

ABOUT THE AUTHOR

Paul Kaye Jones has been professionally writing scripts for musicals, pantomimes, children's shows and lyrics for songs, for many years. As a professional singer as well, Paul's spare time was very limited, only just about squeezing in golf matches on odd occasions. When the Virus Lockdown came along, Paul like many others suddenly found himself out of work and with enough time to write his first novel, Ballytreeny Boy. Since then, he has written three other novels and a children's book.

Now living in Wales, the land of his birth, Paul is revelling in his new occupation, "Novelist".

If you are interested in Paul's Lyrics, check out Matthew Lee's Album "Rock'n'Love" with seven written by him.

https://www.welshwriter.co.uk

Printed in Great Britain
by Amazon